MOVING IS MURDER

SERIES BY NELLIE H. STEELE

Cate Kensie Mysteries

Shadow Slayers Stories

Lily & Cassie by the Sea Mysteries

Pearl Party Mysteries

Middle Age is Murder Cozy Mysteries

Duchess of Blackmoore Mysteries

Maggie Edwards Adventures

Clif & Ri on the Sea Adventures

Shelving Magic

MOVING IS MURDER

A SALEM FALLS B&B PARANORMAL COZY MYSTERY

MIDDLE AGE IS MURDER COZY MYSTERIES
BOOK ONE

NELLIE H. STEELE

A Novel Idea Publishing

For Jacob

CHAPTER 1

This? This was what he left her to deal with?

A sigh escaped Ellie's lips as she slogged up the rowhouse steps. The building's bricks towered above her, limned against a blue sky marred by dark rain clouds.

This place may as well be a prison rather than a home. How did her life become this? And how could she ever fix it?

Ellie slid the key into the lock and turned. Nothing. She jiggled it, grimacing as she twisted it. The metal edge dug into her fingers. She snapped them back, and shook her hand to relieve the discomfort throbbing through it.

"Come on," she muttered with a tense jaw as she wiggled the key again.

"Hey, Ellie!" a woman's voice called to her. "Trouble with the lock again?"

The voice startled her and she lost her grip on the mail she'd stuffed under her left arm as she'd struggled up the few steps to the door, lugging two bags of groceries, her purse, and her messenger bag. The mail pieces clattered to the ground below, slipping down a few steps.

"Oh, hi, Mrs. Billings," Ellie said with a wave and a fake

smile on her lips. "Yeah, trouble with the lock. I'm going to get it changed one of these days." Ellie gave her an awkward laugh as she fought against the lock, keeping a smile plastered on her face.

"Uh-huh," the woman answered. "Toby used to say if you pull toward you, it'll work."

"Oh, did he?" Ellie asked as she gave the key another turn, frowning with effort. She bristled at the mention of Toby's name. Her absent husband, gone for six months now after running off with a local waitress, still managed to raise her ire.

"Pull toward you," the older woman said again, motioning for Ellie to tug it toward her.

"I've got it, thanks," Ellie assured her.

With a shrug, the woman disappeared into her house. Ellie turned her full attention to the lock. She cursed it under her breath as she begrudgingly yanked the door toward her. The key spun easily and the lock released. Despite the success, Ellie found herself annoyed.

Not only had Toby's suggestion worked, but she still resented the idea that the neighbors didn't seem to mind his cheating ways. "What a nice man he was," Mrs. Billings lamented when Ellie had admitted the source of Toby's absence. Ellie had stood in stunned silence at her reaction.

"Who?" another neighbor, Tina, had asked. "Toby? I can't believe that! What'd you do?" She tugged at a strand of her honey-blonde pixie cut as she made the tongue-in-cheek accusation. When Ellie'd reacted badly, griping about her statement, the woman had turned defense. "It was only a joke. No wonder he left you."

The sainting of Toby Larson irked her to no end. She sighed for the umpteenth time over the situation as she swung the door open to the narrow foyer. She tossed in her grocery bags and peeled her messenger bag off, throwing it in, too. With her purse still dangling over her forearm, she began collecting her scattered mail.

With everything shoved in one hand, Ellie climbed the stairs again and disappeared into the safety of her house. She slammed the door shut behind her, twisting the lock to shut out the world.

Ellie slumped against the door as she blew out a long breath. She searched the dim light in her tiny entryway for the grocery bags. As her eyes adjusted, she snagged her fingers around the two blue plastic bags. A step forward sent her stumbling as she tripped over her messenger bag.

"Shoot!" she cursed under her breath before she kicked it aside and continued down the hall to the tiny eat-in kitchen.

A small table and chairs stood in the middle of the windowless, square space. White laminate countertops with a central sink topped worn cabinetry. A backdoor with a frosted window provided the only source of natural light in the room. Dim beams of sunlight struggled to shine through onto round wooden table and chairs.

Ellie dumped the bags on the well-worn chestnut wood along with the mail. She pulled the few items from the bags, stowing the milk in the refrigerator, the bananas on her fruit tree, and a few boxed items in her otherwise bare cupboards.

She retrieved a bowl from one cupboard and a spoon from the drawer. Kernels of marshmallowy cereal tinkled into the bowl. A few spilled out onto the counter. Ellie retrieved them, tossing them into the bowl before adding a splash of milk and carrying her meal to the small table.

She filled her spoon and slid it into her mouth, slurping the milk and crunching on the sugary cereal. She glanced over at the pile of mail, spotting an envelope with a large red stamp across it.

With a sigh, she turned it over and retrieved her phone to

3

scroll through her social media feed while she finished her meager meal.

After washing and drying her utensils, Ellie sank into a chair at the table. She stared at the pile of mail, giving it a disgusted sigh. She pulled it over toward her and began sorting through it. After tossing the junk, she stared at what was left. Several envelopes were from various billing departments. Large blood-red lettering marked the front of each, announcing they were overdue.

Ellie tore open the envelopes, staring at the numbers on each statement. With a hard swallow, she stacked them in a pile and toggled on her cell phone's calculator. A quick addition of the bills showed a number higher than her bank account had seen in months.

She shook her head, again cursing her absent husband, who'd cleaned out their joint bank account before packing his things and leaving. She'd arrived home to find his closet empty, his suitcase gone, and a zero balance in her bank account along with a note stating his intentions.

"Thanks a ton, Toby," she groaned as she felt the familiar thumping at her temples. The bills placed her seconds away from another stress headache as she struggled to determine how she could manage to keep up with their small home's expenses on her current income. With the current trend, she'd likely need to sell the place and move. The sooner, the better, too, by the looks of the stack and the total showing on her phone.

A credit card statement announced she could no longer shift balances to that account since she'd reached her limit. She shook her head, sinking it into her hands and letting her fingers dig into her brunette hair.

With a lick of her lips, she pulled the last two large envelopes over to her. She pursed her lips as she sliced into one addressed to Eleanor Larson. A set of scales preceded the return address of one law firm named Donaldson & Donaldson.

"Great," Ellie murmured. "Probably suing me for the overdue bills."

She slid the papers out of the large envelope. Her name appeared above the line marked Defendant. Toby's name appeared as the Plaintiff. Underneath the declaration of the parties involved in large bold letters, the papers read DECREE OF DIVORCE.

Tears stung her eyes as she read those three words. She blinked them away as she continued to read through the document. On top of the divorce declaration, Toby sought payment for one-half of the house, stating Ellie could keep it if she bought him out.

Sadness turned to anger as she read the demanding words. It wasn't enough that he'd left her destitute but now he had the gall to demand more.

She couldn't pay him. They'd have to sell the house and split the money, she assumed. Where she'd go on what little was left, she didn't know.

With a shaky hand, she dialed a number on her phone and listened to the line trill. She quickly wiped at any tears that had escaped to her cheeks and sniffled.

A female voice answered on the other end. "Hey, Mia, it's me," Ellie said with another sniff.

"Hey, El, you okay? You sound awful."

"Yeah," she answered. "I'm okay. Toby filed for divorce."

"Oh, that stinks," Mia answered her. "Sorry, El."

"It's fine. I don't want him back or anything, but…"

"But you do?" Mia asked.

Ellie sighed and pressed a palm to her forehead. "No. No, it's just… this isn't what I thought fifty was going to look like. And he's suing me for half of the house." A whimper escaped her lips and she winced as she attempted to collect herself without breaking down.

"Oh, you're kidding," Mia groaned. "That... well, never mind. He's unbelievable."

"I can't pay him, Mia," Ellie cried. "I'm behind on my bills. I can barely afford food. I can't pay him. What am I going to do?"

"We'll think of something. Look, I have a friend who's a realtor, maybe she can help you out if you decide to sell."

"Decide to sell? I don't think I have a choice. I can't afford to pay him."

"Have you talked to an attorney yet?"

"No. I can't afford an attorney. I'm going to have to just call his lawyer in the morning and tell him I plan to sell the house and see what he says."

"You shouldn't go in there unrepresented, Ellie," Mia told her.

"I'm not sure I have another choice."

"I have a friend... he's... it was a long, long time ago, but he owes me a favor."

"No," Ellie said, waving her hand in front of her. "No, I don't want you to do that."

"Too late. I'm doing it. I already sent him a message."

"No, you didn't," Ellie countered.

"I did. I just sent him a text. When he answers, I'm giving him your number. Answer your phone when he calls. I'll send you his contact card so you can't complain you didn't know his number."

With a sigh, Ellie offered Mia a tired "thanks." They spent a few minutes chatting about Mia's life and the latest developments with her job before hanging up. Mia told her to get some rest before clicking off the line.

Ellie sat for a few more minutes, biting her thumbnail as she stared into space. She collected her phone, leaving the stack of bills and divorce papers behind, and headed for the couch to zone out with some television.

Her ringing phone startled her awake. On-screen, two detectives discussed a crime scene as Ellie struggled to orient herself. The phone rang again, buzzing across the cushion next to her. She glanced at the display, not recognizing the number. She was about to toss the phone down when Mia's words rang through her mind. "Answer your phone when he calls."

With a frown, Ellie swiped to answer the call.

"Uh, is this Ellie?" a male voice inquired.

"Yes, who is this?"

"Luke Danvers," the man said. "I'm Mia's friend." He phrased the last part like a question.

"Oh, right. Yes, the attorney."

"Yes. She explained your situation and I can definitely help."

"Listen, Mr. Danvers—"

"Call me, Luke," he interrupted.

A smile crossed her face. "Luke, I appreciate the offer but I can't pay you…"

"Don't worry about that," Luke said, interrupting her statement. "I owe Mia a favor."

"I couldn't do that…" Ellie tried again.

"Listen, to make this official, you will have to pay me. One dollar should do it, but above that, nothing else is needed."

The statement stunned her into silence for a moment. She considered her response.

"I won't take no for an answer."

She chuckled. "All right, then, I guess I'll hire you."

"Great. Can we meet tomorrow for a coffee so I can go over the paperwork you received?"

"Uh, I work tomorrow at eleven, but I can do any time before then."

"Great, let's meet at eight if that's all right? Coffee Bean on the corner of Walnut and First Street?"

"Ah, sure, yes, I'll see you then."

Ellie jabbed at the red button to end the call. As always, her best friend, Mia, had come through in the clutch for her, finding an attorney willing to work for free. What that would do to help her afford her bills or stave off the sale of her home, she didn't know. She supposed she should be grateful to be going into the meeting with some representation. But she didn't believe it would do any good. With both their names on the house, she was likely fighting a losing battle. She was likely doomed.

CHAPTER 2

*screaming sound shrieked through the air overhead as Ellie stood in a nightmarish version of her current home. Potential buyers milled around, nitpicking about paint colors or a too-worn rug. Her realtor shook her head at Ellie and dragged a finger across her throat in a kill sign.

Ellie winced as she realized she'd have to sell for peanuts and give half the money to Toby. Her head pounded as the shrieking continued. "What is that?" she murmured before her world began to slip away.

Her eyes slowly opened, and she groaned at the screaming alarm on her nightstand. With bleary eyes, Ellie sat up and stumbled to the shower. She pulled on clothes for the day as the sun rose higher in the sky. With a yawn, she stuffed her phone into her purse, grabbed her keys, and headed out the door. "Dang it!" she hissed as she caught the door just before she swung it shut.

She glanced at the clock ticking on the living room wall as she hurried toward the kitchen. Her forgetfulness would likely cause her to be late again. She reached the kitchen and dove through the door, scooping the divorce paperwork off the kitchen table. The other papers fluttered around, some landing on the floor.

Without a second look, she dashed to the front door and hurried out to the sidewalk.

Out of breath, Ellie rushed into the Coffee Bean Cafe and scanned the tables. She glanced at her cell phone. It read 8:07. "Shoot," she breathed.

She spun to search again, assuming she missed her appointment. "Ellie?" a voice said from behind her. She twisted, spotting a well-dressed man about five years younger than her. His neatly trimmed blonde hair was side-parted and combed into a traditional style. He carried a well-polished briefcase in his right hand. "Are you Ellie Larson?"

"Yes," Ellie said, smoothing her hair back and thrusting her hand out. "Yes, I'm Ellie."

"Hi. Luke Danvers," he said as he pumped her hand up and down, a broad grin on his face. "Should we grab a table?"

"Sure," she said. "Can I get you a coffee or anything?"

"No, I've got one ordered. I grabbed a mocha latte for you. I texted Mia for your usual."

A barista shouted Luke's name and they collected their coffees and slid into seats around a table near the window.

"I brought the papers," Ellie said, sliding them over. "Thanks, by the way. I can't thank you enough for this. I'm just... I'm totally broke. Toby cleaned out our account when he left and now this. I'm barely making ends meet."

Luke held up his hand to stop her speech. "First of all, don't worry about it. But I will need a dollar at some point to make this legal."

"Right!" Ellie said, digging in her purse. She grimaced at her wallet and dug around before she slid two quarters, three dimes, three nickels, and five pennies across the table. She offered him a weak smile.

"Thanks," he said, sliding the coins off the table and dumping them into his pocket. "Now that I'm on retainer, let me get this straight." His brow furrowed as he shuffled through the divorce paperwork. "Your soon-to-be ex-husband cheated on you, cleaned out your joint bank account, and willingly left your home?"

"That's the long and short of it, yes," Ellie said with a nod.

"And how long ago was this?"

"Six months."

He nodded. "Do you know how much was in the bank account before he cleared it?"

"We had about fifteen thousand dollars in there. We were saving for a bigger place." Ellie bit her lower lip as the statement slipped from between her lips. It sounded ridiculous at this point.

"Okay, so he willingly left the house and he took fifteen thousand dollars. You didn't ask him to leave or tell him to get out?"

"No," Ellie said. "I didn't know he was leaving until I came home from work. I found a note, his clothes gone, and got a zero balance alert on my phone."

"This guy sounds like a real piece of work. How long were you married?"

"Fifteen years."

"And was he the primary breadwinner in the house, or you?"

"He made more than I do. I'm just a clerk at a boutique."

"And Toby?"

"Toby's a sales manager at a car dealership."

"Kids?"

"None."

Luke bounced his head around, giving her a mouth shrug as if he was weighing all the information. "Okay."

"Is there anything I can do? I can't afford to pay him half of the house. I can barely afford the house as it is."

"The fact that he left already gives us some fodder to suggest that request is inappropriate. The fact that he's helped himself to money in your account is another thing on our side. He didn't do anything illegal, but it casts him in a negative light.

"I'd recommend we ask for you to get the house solely as part of the settlement. He provided you with a lifestyle and now he's left you with nothing. That's not fair."

"Do you think we'll get it?" Ellie asked, hope filling her. If she could hang onto the house, she could work to dig herself out of debt. She could work two jobs if she had to. Or three.

"We'll see. But I think there's a good chance we can get a better settlement than this and get you set up in the best position possible as you move into your new life."

For the first time in six months, a slight smile turned up the edges of Ellie's lips. "Okay," she said with a nod and a deep exhale. "Okay."

* * *

Ellie stalked through the door of her row house. Exhausted after her earlier-than-usual morning, she shambled into the kitchen and tossed her messenger bag onto one of the chairs. She stared at the mess. In her mad dash to grab the divorce papers this morning, she'd knocked over most of the other mail she'd left lying on the table the night before.

With a groan, she bent over and scooped one of the papers off the floor. Her overdue gas bill had landed on the seat of her chair. She added it to the pile as her foot slipped on a large envelope. She wriggled it from under her shoe and stared at it. The envelope, now with a large footprint stamped onto its back, felt thick.

Ellie turned it over and stared at the address. Eleanor Byrne. Her brow wrinkled. Her maiden name, she questioned? Why would someone send this to her maiden name? She glanced at the return address. It read Law Firm of MacArthur Doyle.

"Now what?" Ellie muttered aloud. "Is he suing me twice?"

She stared at the brown envelope for another moment, not sure she wanted to open it. With puckered lips, she decided she'd better. She slid her finger under the flap and tore it open. Several papers slid out as she turned the envelope over and shook it.

She studied the top letter. She screwed up her face as she read it.

Dear Ms. Byrne -

I represent the estate of the late Susan Byrne. First, please let me express my condolences for your loss.

Ellie paused. "Aunt Susie?" She hadn't seen her father's sister in years. She hadn't even realized she'd passed away. She continued reading.

My primary purpose for correspondence is as your aunt's executor. As you have been named in her will, I would like to set up an appointment at your convenience to discuss the details. I am able to travel to you. Please contact my office using the phone number below to schedule.

. . .

Thank you for your attention in this matter.

The letter was signed by MacArther Doyle in a rather hurried scrawl. Ellie studied the letterhead. The address indicated the offices were located in the town of Salem Falls, a picturesque small town about five hours across the state. Ellie recalled visiting it once as a child with her parents.

Ellie keyed the number into her phone. She glanced at the time as she pressed the send button. Already after 6 p.m., she figured she'd have to leave a message. As the line trilled, she wondered how this might impact her divorce, if at all.

After several rings, the familiar "I'm not here right now" message Ellie expected to hear played. She prepared her statement in her mind as the man droned on about his usual business hours and to leave a message after the tone.

A beep sounded and Ellie launched into her spiel. "Hello, uh, hi," she stammered around. "This is Ellie, uh, Eleanor Larson. Eleanor Byrne. Byrne was my maiden name."

Ellie shook her head at herself as she babbled incoherently about her name. "I received a letter from you about my Aunt Susie's estate. Uh, that's Susan Byrne…"

A ruckus sounded on the other end of the line and a voice offered an emphatic, "Hello!"

"Oh, uh," Ellie stuttered.

"Hello, Ms. Byrne?"

"Yes, Ellie Byrne. Well, I used to be Ellie Byrne. Now I'm Ellie Larson. I'll probably be Byrne again soon, anyway, yes, that's me."

"Oh, I'm so glad to get a hold of you," the man said. "I'm MacArthur Doyle. You can call me Mac. I was legal counsel for your late aunt. I'm so sorry for your loss."

"Thank you. I didn't even realize she'd passed."

"It was over a week ago. It took me a few days to find you.

Anyway, I needed to speak with you about your aunt's estate."

"Oh, okay," Ellie said as she eased onto her kitchen chair. "Are there personal effects I need to deal with? And her funeral?"

"Uh, well," Mac said, "yes and no."

"What does that mean?"

She heard the shuffling of papers on the other end of the line. "In the absence of other family members, yes, you'll need to claim the body and make whatever arrangements you see fit. But also, your aunt named you as the sole heir in her will, outside of a few odds and ends donated to friends."

"Sole heir?" Ellie repeated.

"Yes," Mac confirmed. "She's left the bulk of her assets to you. We'll need to discuss the terms and provisions, and…"

"I'm sorry, Mr. Doyle."

"Oh, Mac, please," Mac said, interrupting her.

"Mac," Ellie said as she rested her chin in her palm. "What assets are we talking about? Her collection of romance novels or her cat?"

"Technically, yes, her cat is included. Along with her home, Salem Falls Manor, her dog, and all of her monetary assets."

Ellie sat in stunned silence for a moment. She's inherited her aunt's home, pets and some cash? She barely remembered the house from her childhood visit. All she could recall was a large Victorian sitting on a few acres with a wooden swing hanging from a large oak tree. Perhaps this could help her out of the hole she was in. Perhaps this was the break she needed.

"So, am I supposed to handle the house's sale?"

"Oh, no, no, quite the opposite! Your aunt wanted you to keep the house. She also hoped you'd keep the animals in their home. The property is zoned for commercial use. It was once a Bed and Breakfast. It very well could be again."

Ellie's mind churned as he spoke. Could she run a B&B? Could she live in Salem Falls? Would Toby be able to get his hands on half of Salem Falls Manor? She could sell this house and leave. Leave her bills, her troubles, and her bad memories behind.

"Oh, please forgive me, I'm getting ahead of myself."

Ellie guffawed. "Yes," she said with a chuckle. "I think we both are." Reality landed hard as she realized if she couldn't make a go of things in this house, she likely couldn't afford a month at her aunt's house. She had no funds to get a B&B up and running, nor to keep up a large house like that.

"Sure," Mac said, his voice sounding soothing. "I understand this might come as a shock and there certainly are many things to discuss. As I mentioned in my letter, I can come to you, or if you'd like to head up to Salem Falls, we can arrange that, too."

Ellie rubbed her forehead with her fingers. "The thing is, Mac, I'm pretty certain I can't keep a house like Salem Falls Manor. Financially, I'm not in the best place. I…"

"Oh, no, no, no," Mac interrupted. "Your aunt provided well for you to be able to keep the Manor."

"What?" Ellie questioned, her brow wrinkling at the statement.

"The monetary assets your aunt left are not only diverse but also very, very large."

Ellie blinked her eyes once and stared at the worn wooden table. "I'm sorry, what?"

"I'm saying your aunt left you enough money to live comfortably for the rest of your life without even opening the Manor as a B&B."

* * *

Ellie sat with a bowl of popcorn as a movie played on her television. She munched on a kernel as her mind ran over the details of her conversation with MacArthur Doyle. According to him, her aunt had left her quite a large sum of money. Enough that she could be self-sufficient for the rest of her lifetime. The caveat was she needed to take over Salem Falls Manor.

It would mean she had to move. But what did she have keeping her here? A mountain of bills and a runaway husband were the only things she had left in this area.

Her phone chimed, pulling her from her thoughts. She glanced at her phone's screen. It was from Luke. Following her conversation with Mr. Doyle, she had texted him about the new information. Her main concern was how the divorce would impact her inheritance.

She eagerly read the response from him: *It won't. In this state, inheritances are not considered marital property. He can't touch it.*

Ellie smiled at the words on the screen. She still needed to meet with MacArthur, a meeting she'd put off until after her divorce settlement meeting in three days, but her aunt's inheritance may just be the answer to her prayers.

CHAPTER 3

"What I'd like to discuss is Mrs. Larson's dishonesty in these discussions."

Ellie squeezed her eyes shut with annoyance at the comment from her husband's attorney. The buxom woman with her impeccably coiffed blonde hair and a beautifully tailored suit tapped her pen against the desk. An annoying rapping noise filled the air. Ellie tilted her head at the woman, pondering how her soon-to-be ex-husband afforded this attorney.

"I don't know what you're referring to," Luke said as he shifted in his chair with an annoyed groan.

"I'm referring to this, Mr. Danvers."

The attorney slid a black and white copy of something across the table to Luke. He intercepted it and scanned it before tossing it back.

"Your client is in legal proceedings to receive an inheritance. A fact she's concealed."

"A fact that is immaterial in these proceedings."

"I find it very material given that it could fundamentally change Mrs. Larson's life."

Luke shrugged, unaffected by the posturing from the opposite side. "The fact of the matter is: Mrs. Larson's inheritance, whatever it may be, is not subject to dispersal to a spouse under state law."

"But it can…"

Luke waved his hands in the air and leaned forward. "Look, Ms. Paxton, you can hem and haw all you'd like, but Mrs. Larson's potential inheritance has little to nothing to do with the matter at hand. Now, unless you'd like to discuss actual terms, we'll adjourn for the day so you can quit wasting my client's time. Our final proposal is here. It's fair. You have forty-eight hours before it comes off the table and we submit a proposal asking Mr. Larson, who has abandoned his marital home willingly after admitting to infidelity and left my client with no money for which to provide for herself, to return half the money to their joint account and pay her for half of the house. Choice is yours." He straightened his tie and stood, snapping his briefcase shut and hefting it from the table. He jiggled his head, motioning for Ellie to collect her things and follow him.

She swallowed hard, grabbing her purse and pushing away from the table. The cumbersome chair stuck on the cheap carpet and nearly toppled as she struggled to stand and squeeze past it. After two awkward bumps into the table with her hip, she managed to free herself, took two stumbling steps, and continued on toward the door, following Luke.

They stepped into the hallway and proceeded outside into the sunshine. Ellie slid on her sunglasses and shoved a hand into the back pocket of her jeans.

"You're sure he can't touch the inheritance?" Ellie questioned as they walked away from the building.

"Positive," Luke said.

"I'm sorry to keep asking. I must sound really greedy but

this may be my chance at a fresh start. I'm so afraid he's going to ruin it."

"He can't ruin it. And if I read his overpriced lawyer correctly, he'll take this deal and leave you alone."

"Really? How do you know?"

"She has no case and she knows it. That's the reason she continues to pick on your inheritance. It's a scare tactic. I'd guess before you leave for your weekend trip to Salem Falls we'll have this mostly wrapped up."

Ellie stopped walking, an expression of surprise on her face. "From your lips," she said.

Luke smiled at her before he stepped to the corner. "I'm heading this way. Don't sweat it, Ellie. We'll get this settled."

"I'm going straight. Thanks, Luke, really, thank you."

"Of course."

Ellie continued another two blocks before hanging a right onto another street and entering the business district. She approached The Frock Shop and pushed through the door and into the shop's interior.

"Hey, Skye, I'm here!" she called into the back.

Ellie hurried to the register and stowed her purse in the cubby below the counter. She shoved her long hair behind her ears as she bobbed her head above the counter. Skye sauntered into the store from the backroom. Her auburn hair was flipped out in a retro style, complimenting her vintage 1960s minidress and go-go boots.

"Sorry, I'm late," Ellie continued. "The meeting went longer than I thought. Toby's attorney is a real... witch and she just kept going on and on about my aunt's death and..."

"Ellie, we need to talk," Skye said.

"Oh, okay," Ellie said, surprise filling her voice as Skye cut her off.

Skye winced as she tapped her pink nails on the counter-top. "I don't know how to say this," she began.

Ellie shook her head, shoving her hair behind her ears again. "Whatever it is, just say it," she encouraged.

Skye pursed her lips and nodded. "I have to let you go."

"What?" Ellie said.

"I'm sorry, Ellie. It's nothing personal. I just can't afford to have you here anymore."

"But I need this job!" Ellie said.

"I'm really sorry," Skye said. "Look I'll pay you through the end of the week, but I'm sorry, today will be your last day."

Ellie let out a stunned breath. She blinked a few times as she processed the information. After a lick of her lips, she glanced around. "Is there a point to me staying for the day?"

Skye gave her a tight-lipped smile. "You don't have to stay."

"Fine," Ellie said, annoyance creeping into her voice. She grabbed her purse and yanked it from the cubby, tossing it over her shoulder and storming toward the door.

"Ellie," Skye called from the register, "please don't be mad. Like I said, it's nothing personal, but I can't afford to pay you."

"Yeah, sure," Ellie said as she pushed through the door.

Ellie dug in her purse for her sunglasses. She whipped them open and attempted to slide them on her face. The arm cracked and the sunglasses dangled from one ear before clattering to the sidewalk below.

"Of course," Ellie said as she snatched the broken pieces from the sidewalk. She jammed them into the first trash can she happened upon as she continued on her way to her house.

Squinting against the bright sun, Ellie shielded her eyes as she stomped down the sidewalk. "Watch it!" she shouted, flailing her arms as she stepped into the crosswalk and a speeding car swerved around her, continuing down the street.

"This day is just going wonderfully," she moaned to herself. She wound through the streets to her row house. After another fight with the front door lock, she pushed into her tiny foyer and closed out the world behind her.

She slumped against the door. Inside her purse, her phone chimed. Ellie dug through her hobo bag and found the chirping device. A message showed up on the preview screen.

Luke's message glowed on the screen. *Didn't have to wait until the weekend. They took the deal. Divorce will be final as soon as we file signed paperwork.*

Ellie's head banged into the door behind her as she breathed a sigh of relief. At least one thing had gone right today, she thought, as she sent a return text to her attorney.

She wandered to the kitchen as she finished the last few words of the text and clicked send. She tossed her phone on the counter and pulled a canister of coffee from her cupboard. As she popped the top, she caught sight of the paperwork from MacArthur Doyle.

Ellie stared at it for a moment before she tossed the scoop back into the coffee can. She returned the canister to the cupboard and picked up her phone. She scrolled through her contact list and pressed the call icon next to Mac's name.

After the third ring, the older man's voice answered.

"Hey, it's Ellie. Uh, Ellie Byrne."

"Oh, Ellie, hi!" the man said, his voice rising with excitement. "What can I do for you?"

"My schedule cleared and it looks like I can head up to Salem Falls sooner than I expected. Would you be able to fit me in before the weekend?"

She heard a rustling on the other end of the line. "Oh,

absolutely! That's great! I'd really rather tackle this sooner than later. Are you leaving today?"

"I was planning on throwing a few things into my suitcase and getting a start on the drive in about an hour or so."

"Tell you what, why don't you come straight to my office when you get here. I've got your aunt's keys for the house, you can stay there tonight. We don't have to go over all the details of the estate today, but I'll take you to dinner and we can discuss some preliminaries."

"Ah," Ellie said as her mind parsed through the situation, "sure. I'll come straight to you. It's about a five-hour drive. With a lunch stop, I should be there around six?"

"That sounds perfect. See you when you get here, Ellie."

She ended the call and bit her lower lip as she rested her chin on the top of her cell phone. With a deep inhale, Ellie pulled her mind from rambling forward to the future to focusing on the present. She shoved her phone into her back pocket and strode from the kitchen. After climbing the steep narrow staircase, she headed for her bedroom and tossed several things into a small suitcase, grabbed the necessary toiletries, and zipped the suitcase shut.

She shoved a cell phone charger into her purse along with a few other necessities. After grabbing a water bottle for the road from her fridge, she climbed into her car and fired the engine. Her GPS unit showed a five-hour and seven-minute drive ahead of her.

With a deep breath, she slid on a pair of sunglasses and eased her car onto the road, heading toward Salem Falls.

* * *

As the sun hung low in the sky, Ellie exited the highway and approached the small town of Salem Falls. Quaint buildings sat behind sidewalks along the tree-lined streets. A shopping district of independently owned storefronts made up Main Street.

Ellie smiled at a family sitting outside an ice cream shop enjoying cones in the day's waning warmth. She pulled off the main road and onto another as she wound through the town on her way to MacArthur's law office.

A fifties-style diner sat to her left. The neon sign boasted the name *Cookin' With Gas Diner* and an "Always Open" message.

"Cute," Ellie murmured as she ducked to check out the building, designed with glass block and chrome details.

She continued, making another turn before she found a white single-story building set on a wooded lot. A white sign with black letters announced the Law Office of MacArthur Doyle was housed inside.

Ellie eased her car next to the curb and climbed out. She stretched after the long drive, taking another swig from her almost empty water bottle. She inhaled a long breath before she strode up the sidewalk and rang the bell. A screen door separated her from the inside, but the main door stood ajar, allowing her a view of the entrance. A small desk sat unmanned, the chair pushed in neatly.

"Come in!" a loud voice hollered.

Ellie pulled open the screen door and entered the dim space. She glanced side-to-side before a tall, hefty older man appeared in an archway to her right. His sleeves were rolled to his elbows and a coffee stain graced the left side of his shirt. His dark gray hair remained thick despite his advanced years. Ellie pegged him to be around seventy or a few years older. Though despite his older age, he didn't wear any glasses.

"Ellie?" he questioned, his bushy eyebrows wiggling at her.

Ellie slid a lock of hair behind her ear before she stuck her hand out. "Yes, I'm Ellie. Mac, I presume?"

"That's me!" the man said with a wide grin. He grasped her hand with both of his and gave it a hard shake that sent a tremor through her whole body. "It's a real pleasure to meet you. And I'm so glad you could make it up to Salem Falls sooner than you expected."

He stood with a broad grin, his hands shoved in his pockets. Ellie waited a few moments before she spoke again. "Well, the whole thing took me by surprise and I'm working through a few things at home, but..."

"Oh, I don't mean to pry," he said, waving his hands in front of him.

Ellie nodded and ceased her babbling. They stood staring at each other for another moment before Mac jumped, seeming almost startled. "Oh, what am I doing? I promised you dinner and I am standing here shooting the breeze. Where are my manners?"

"Oh, it's fine," Ellie said, waving her hand at him and wrinkling her nose.

"Well, unless you'd like to sit down, I'll grab your aunt's keys and we can head over to *Cookin' With Gas*."

"Oh, the little diner I passed?" Ellie asked, crooking her thumb out the door.

"Best food in town!" Mac called over his shoulder as he retreated into his office. He swiped several things off of his desk, shoving a wallet into his pocket, a set of keys, and a cell phone, and then stared at the desk for a moment before deciding he had everything.

With a nod, he spun to face Ellie. "Ready? I can drive if you'd like."

"Oh," Ellie said as she considered it. "I could follow you, that way I can go straight to my aunt's after."

"Good idea, Ellie. Your aunt said you were a smart cookie." He offered another smile and a wink. "Just follow me to the diner. I'll take you out to the manor after, show you around, and introduce you to the pets. Then I'll get out of your hair and let you relax."

With their plan set, Ellie exited into the warm night air. Mac followed behind her, locking his door and pointing to a car around the corner. "That's me there. I'll see you at the diner."

Ellie nodded and they parted ways. She slid in behind the wheel of her car. After completing a three-way turn, she pulled up behind the waiting Cadillac sedan and waved. Mac pulled away, leading her the short distance to the diner.

Mac climbed from the car and stretched as he waited for Ellie to swing in and park. She exited her car and slung her purse over her shoulder. "I saw this place on the way in. It's cute."

"And boy is the food good," Mac said with a grin. "After you." He waved for her to precede him as he held the door open.

Ellie entered the diner. A checkerboard floor paved the way to oversized shiny red booths lining the windows on either side of the door. A long white counter stood across from the entrance. Red stools were placed at regular intervals along it. A large jukebox glowed from across the room.

"Hey, Mac!" a waitress in a retro red uniform with black and white checked trim greeted them with a wave.

Mac motioned for Ellie to head to her left. "My favorite booth is open," he said as he guided her to the second booth from the end of the line.

Ellie slid onto the shiny red seat with her back facing the door while Mac shimmied in across from her. The waitress approached with a set of menus. She smiled as she studied Ellie before flitting her eyes to Mac.

Ellie flipped her menu open and perused the wide selection. "How are you, Val?" Mac said.

"Can't complain, how about you?"

"Doing fine. Doing fine. Can't keep up with all the criminals here in Salem Falls." The two shared a hearty laugh over the weak joke. Ellie eyed them before returning her gaze to the menu.

"Val, this is Ellie Byrne. Oh, ah Larson, sorry. Susie's niece. Ellie this is Valentina Montgomery, Val for short. She owns the diner."

"Oh, you're Susie's niece," Val said, nodding her head at Ellie.

"I am. Nice to meet you."

"Pleasure. Sorry it's under these circumstances. Terrible shame about your aunt." She clicked her tongue. "Would hate to go like that."

"Ah, let's not scare the poor girl off just yet," Mac said with a nervous chuckle.

Val pursed her lips and nodded again. "So what can I get you?"

"Ah," Ellie said, her eyes bulging as she studied the menu. She flipped it shut. "What d'you recommend?"

Val tapped her pencil against her chin. "Are you a meat eater?"

Ellie nodded at the question.

"I'd go for the burger, toasted sesame bun, lettuce, onion, pickle. Side of onion rings and a shake."

"They're famous for their shakes," Mac said, leaning forward and offering her a wink.

"I'll take it and make the shake chocolate."

"Make that two, but a…"

"Strawberry shake," Val and Mac said together.

"You got it, buddy," Val said as she collected the menus. "Coming right up."

Ellie glanced out the window at the small town outside. She rubbed her hands together between her knees as her eyes flitted back to Mac.

He offered a jolly smile, but before he could speak, another individual wandered to the table. About Ellie's age, she clutched at her worn purse straps with one hand, smoothing a lock of straight dirty blonde hair that had escaped her low ponytail behind her ear with the other.

"Oh, hi, Evelyn," Mac said. "Didn't expect to see you here."

She offered a fleeting smile. "Figured I'd stop in for one more shake. They are so good."

Mac smiled and nodded then jumped in his seat. "Oh, this is Susie's niece, Ellie. Ellie, Evelyn was Susie's home nurse. She checked on her every few days."

The woman turned round green eyes toward Ellie and offered a consoling smile. "I am so sorry for your loss."

"Oh, thank you. And thanks for taking care of my aunt."

"Oh, no problem. I loved Susie. She was such a lovely person. I'm glad I had the opportunity to know her."

Ellie nodded and smiled, unable to offer any additional words.

"Well, I'll let you two enjoy your meal. I just wanted to stop by and say hello since I probably won't be back in town after this."

"Thanks, Evelyn. You'll be sorely missed. And who says you can't stop back for a shake."

"They certainly are good enough to make a special trip for!" Evelyn exclaimed. "Take care now."

Mac offered a similar sentiment before the woman wandered away. Ellie eyed the man again, offering another smile.

Mac raised his eyebrows at her before speaking. "Ah, well I guess I should give you some information." He dug into his pocket and pulled a set of keys out, setting them on the table.

He slid them across to Ellie. "Keys to Salem Falls Manor for you."

"Oh, thanks. Umm," Ellie stared at the keys for a moment before she pulled her hands onto the table. Still clasped together, she used them to punctuate her words as she dropped them with each beat of her statement. "The thing is, Mac, I'm not certain I can stay."

Mac's brow furrowed. "Do you mean for the weekend?"

"No, I mean overall. I know you mentioned money, but…"

"Oh, yes," Mac said. "Sorry, I sometimes don't cut to the chase quickly enough. Yes, there's enough money for you to live on easily. Though if you reopen the B&B, you'd have a nice little business for yourself."

"I didn't realize my aunt was that well-off."

Mac nodded, his fingers tracing the edge of the paper placemat in front of him. "She did very well with her investments after she closed the B&B."

Val flitted over with a large tray. She set down two plates filled with food and two shakes in thick, curvy glasses. The delicious scent of grilled beef and fried food filled the air. Ellie's stomach rumbled as she eyed the juicy burger hidden under the leafy green lettuce. Crisp onion rings were scattered on the opposite side of the plate. Thick chocolate liquid filled the green-hued glass, topped off with a spiraling pile of whipped cream and a large red cherry.

"Thanks, Val," Mac said as he squeezed ketchup onto his burger. The waitress flitted away after a broad smile.

Ellie shook her head. "Do you know why she left everything to me?"

"She said you needed it."

"What?" Ellie said before she bit into her burger.

Mac shrugged, lining his burger up for a bite. "That's what she said."

"How could she know that? Did she keep up with my life? I haven't heard from her in years."

"I couldn't say," Mac said. "She never mentioned it. But when she got older, she drew up her will. She had no kids and when I asked her what she wanted to do with everything she'd accumulated, she said 'Give it all to Eleanor, she needs it.'"

"That's weird," Ellie said. "Though I'm not complaining. She was right."

"Oh?' Mac said, his eyebrows raised.

"I'm going through a rough time." She glanced up to find Mac's eyes on her. "My husband left me six months ago, cleaned out my bank account, and left me broke. And this morning, I lost my job."

"Ouch," Mac said. "Sounds like Susie was right."

Ellie nodded as she took another bite of her burger before sipping her shake.

"We can go over all the accounts tomorrow. But the house is yours, money's yours, oh and the pets are yours. Contingency on the will is the pets stay in the house."

"What's up with the pets?" Ellie asked, biting into an onion ring. The warm, fried food tasted like heaven.

"Lola and Cleo? They were the most important things to Susie. They were like her kids. She spoiled them something terrible." He held up a finger before wiping his hands and digging in his pocket. He retrieved his cell phone and swiped around on it before he turned it to face Ellie. "Lola's a miniature bulldog."

Large, round brown eyes stared up at the camera from a light brown face with a frown for a mouth.

"And this is Cleo, short for Cleopatra." Mac swiped to another picture showing a lithe, jet-black cat with green eyes lounging across the back of a couch.

Ellie nodded as she wiped her greasy hands on her napkin. "Cute."

"Do you have pets?"

"No, I don't. But I like animals!"

"Oh, good, that'll work out then."

"I'm sorry, I'm still getting used to the whole idea that my aunt left me all of this."

Mac flicked his gaze to her. "So you do plan to move here, right?"

"I feel like I'd be foolish not to," Ellie admitted.

Mac nodded and smiled at her. "That's great. I'll get started on all the paperwork. How soon do you plan to move?"

Ellie pictured the stacks of unpaid bills on her counter at home as she weighed her answer. "Right away. I'll call a listing agent tomorrow and get my house on the market as soon as I head home."

"That's great. I'm sure Lola and Cleo will be happy to have someone living with them again instead of me visiting them every so often."

"They're at the house alone?"

"They're pretty self-sufficient. And I stop in a few times a day."

"Oh, wow, you're a full-service attorney!"

"Susie was more than a client. She was a friend." His smile faltered for the first time and he swallowed hard.

"I'm sorry," Ellie said, offering a consoling smile.

He nodded, pulling his lips into a thin line. "May I ask how she died?" Ellie inquired as she took another bite of her burger.

"She drowned."

31

CHAPTER 4

"*W*hat?" Ellie asked, nearly choking on her burger. "Drowned?"

Mac nodded, a grim expression on his face. "In the stream that cuts through the property at the manor." He shook his head at the words. "Must have tripped and fallen in. Sheriff found her face down in the water. Her housekeeper called him when she couldn't find Susie. Poor Lola was inside the house barking her head off. Coroner's doing an autopsy to see if maybe she had a stroke or heart attack."

"I thought... I thought she died of old age or some ailment," Ellie said.

"No," Mac answered. "That's what Val meant by her comment earlier. Quite frankly, the whole town's still in shock over it."

Ellie sipped her milkshake as she pondered the latest revelation. "When will they have the results?"

"Should be any day now."

"What a shame. She made it to eighty-something and died like that."

"Would have been eighty-three next month. Yeah, it's a

real shame. Especially when she usually never went near the stream."

Ellie screwed up her face at the news. "Geez, what bad luck. The one time you venture down to the water, you fall in and drown."

Mac wiggled his eyebrows. "With any luck, this should be cleared up soon and you can have her buried. Things tend to move a little slow around here, so I wouldn't hold my breath though."

Ellie pursed her lips and bobbed her head. "At least you're honest."

Mac offered her a crooked smile. "I try, despite my profession." He chuckled at his own joke. Ellie smiled at him as she sucked up the last drops of her milkshake.

"Do we need to wait for official word from the police before we move forward with anything?"

Mac shook his head and turned his mouth into a puckered frown. "Nah," Mac said. "I can't imagine anything surprising coming from their report. Plus, unless she's alive, her will has to be executed."

"Sorry, that probably sounds suspicious, but I'm anxious to move. I just... I have nothing left in Winwick."

"I can't blame you. Sounds like your life there is over. A new life awaits you here in Salem Falls." He offered another wide smile as he pulled his wallet from his pocket.

"Oh, please," Ellie said, waving at his hand. "Let me pay for mine."

She dug in her purse in search of her wallet.

"I won't hear of it," Mac said as he slid a few bills from the brown trifold leather wallet.

"Please," Ellie said again, "I didn't expect you to treat me to a meal."

"You should have! That's how folks are around this town!

And of course, you're a client. Happy to do it. Consider it a welcome to Salem Falls!"

Ellie let her empty wallet drop back into her bag. Despite her insistence on paying, her wallet contained no cash. She could have tried to use one of her over-wrought credit cards, but she preferred to save what little balance she left for the items she may need for the move.

"Thank you, Mac. I really appreciate it."

"And I didn't mean to rush you, but I figured you'd want to settle in for the night."

"I do," Ellie said with a nod.

Mac smiled at her as she shimmied out of the booth and stood. He tossed the bills on the table and motioned for Ellie to precede him. He rapped his knuckles on the counter and wiggled his fingers at Val. "Be seeing you, Val!"

"You take care now, Mac!" Val responded as she brewed a fresh pot of coffee. "Nice meeting you, Ellie! Don't be a stranger while you're here, huh?"

Ellie gave her a wave and a tight-lipped smile as she pushed through the door and headed for her car.

"If you follow me," Mac hollered over his hood, "I'll lead you out to the Manor."

"Thanks! I haven't been there since I was a kid. I'm not sure I could find it again."

She slid behind the wheel and fired her engine before motioning she was ready to Mac. He backed from his spot and waited for her to pull behind him before easing onto the road.

Traffic was light in the small town and Ellie had no trouble following him as they wound through the streets before they veered off onto a road leading to the outskirts.

Salem Falls Manor sat on a large lot a mile from the edges of the town. Pine and deciduous trees closed in around them as they traveled along the winding, two-lane road. With the sun hanging low behind them, some areas were already dark, hidden under the shadow of the tall trees.

Mac's left turn signal blinked and he veered off the quiet road and onto a gravel driveway. Ellie eased off the road behind him, slowing as she ducked to take in the large house emerging from behind the mask of trees.

Mac swung his car around, parking perpendicular to the entrance. Ellie pulled next to him and climbed from the car, staring up at the impressive Victorian structure. Five concrete steps led to a wide, covered porch. White pillars held the roof overhead and a decorative white railing trimmed it. The porch continued to the right, wrapping around the side of the house.

Gray siding with red and white trim covered the sides of the house. Tall windows rose on both the first and second stories. A few windows peeked out from the gray roof and twin chimneys rose on the right.

"Wow," Ellie whispered.

"She's a beaut," Mac said with a grin. "Come on, I'll show you around. Can I grab your luggage?"

"Oh, don't worry about that. I'll grab it later."

They climbed the few short steps onto the porch and Ellie grabbed the keys Mac had given her earlier.

"Uh, the gold one's for the front door," Mac said as she sorted through the keys.

After a click of the lock, the front door swung in on creaky hinges. Dust motes floated in the setting sun's glare. Thick, dark woods decorated the foyer. A staircase rose against the right wall, disappearing around a corner to the next level. Doors opened on the left and right to other spaces. A darkly stained door past the staircase led to another room.

The tick-tick-ticking of animal claws clicked across the hardwood. A shin-height dog appeared from the room on the left. She stared up at Ellie and Mac, her tail causing her entire back-end to wag along with it.

"Hey, there big Lol!" Mac said, darting past Ellie and dropping to a knee to ruffle the dog's floppy ears. The dog balanced on her hind legs, resting her front paws on Mac's shoulders. She offered Ellie a quizzical glance before returning her excited energy to Mac.

Next to her, a black cat sashayed from the confines of the living room. With her tail standing straight in the air, she tilted her head and glanced at Ellie before she turned her attention to Mac, offering him a curt "meow" and rubbing against his leg.

"Hello, Cleo," Mac said as he ran his hand down the cat's back. He turned to Ellie, still standing in the doorway. "Well, come on in, don't be shy. This is your home now."

Ellie smiled as she took in the space again, stepping over the threshold and into Salem Falls Manor. The cat offered a sniff in her direction and Lola returned her gait to all fours to study Ellie.

"Hey, girls," Ellie said, squatting down to them. She held out her hand. Cleo gave it a tentative sniff before returning her attention to Mac. Lola ventured closer. Her tail wiggled tentatively.

"Hi, girl," Ellie said. "Hi, Lola." A smile spread across Ellie's face. The gesture eased the dog's nerves and she approached Ellie, offering her hand a sniff. Ellie tickled her chin. The dog stepped closer and collapsed to her haunches to allow Ellie to continue the petting.

"Making friends, eh, Lola? Good thing. She's going to be your new owner," Mac said as he rose to his feet. The dog cocked her head quizzically. "Come on, I'll show you around. We can feed them while we're in the kitchen. Then I'll let Lola out."

"Okay," Ellie said, rising to her feet.

With the dog and cat in tow, Ellie followed Mac through the various rooms on the first floor. A generously-sized living room led to an octagon-shaped breakfast nook with access to the porch and a covered patio.

A central kitchen opened to a spacious east-facing sunroom. Mac pulled open the tab on a can of cat food and emptied it into a dish marked CLEO on the outside. He instructed Ellie on Lola's feeding instructions. Ellie dumped the kibble into a pink bowl with LOLA printed on it and set it down for the dog.

They left both animals happily consuming their dinner and wandered into the spacious dining room. It attached to a large library and a screened-in porch.

As they rounded back to the foyer, Mac let a waiting Lola out the front door, then led Ellie up the main stairs. Double doors opened to the master suite at the top of the winding staircase. Ellie glanced inside.

"This was your aunt's bedroom. It has the ensuite and a large sitting room overlooking the front property."

Ellie nodded as she explored the other spaces upstairs.

"There are bathrooms attached to each bedroom," Mac explained as Ellie stuck her head into a generously sized bedroom across the hall and down from the master suite. "Which makes it nice for a B&B. No one likes a shared bathroom."

An octagonal-shaped bedroom stuck off the rear of the house. Ellie checked out the three other bedroom spaces on the second floor. Most of the furniture in them was now covered in white sheets. A third floor offered one additional bedroom, a reading room, and a small office.

"Each bedroom has a name and a theme," Mac said. "Your aunt kept notes somewhere around here. You know, in case you want to open up the B&B again. Of course, you can name them anything you'd like, but she's already got the decor there if you want to keep with her ideas."

Ellie smiled and nodded. "Well, everything still looks like it's in good shape, so why change it?"

"Good thinking, Ellie," Mac said with a grin.

"Well, anyway, I stocked the fridge with a few necessities earlier. Milk, bread, cheese, some lunch meat, oatmeal, cereal, some OJ, eggs..." Mac ticked the items off on his fingers.

"Wow," Ellie said. "That's perfect. That's more than enough to get me started."

"Oh, great," Mac said with a nod and a smile. "Well, I guess you're all set then. I'll let you settle in for your first night."

"Thanks," Ellie said as they descended the main stairs to the foyer. "I'll walk you out and grab my luggage."

"Okay," Mac said as he palmed his car keys and pushed through the wooden screen door onto the porch. Lola hurried into the foyer past him. "If you could stop by tomorrow, I'll get everything together to go over the particulars with you and collect a few signatures. No rush, I'll be there all day, so take your time. Have a leisurely morning."

"Okay, that's perfect. I'll see you tomorrow morning. Ah, probably later in the morning. I'm not much of an early bird."

"Sounds perfect, Ellie. Well, you take care. If you need anything, don't hesitate to call. Have a great night."

Ellie waved as his car disappeared down the driveway, a cloud of dust billowing behind him. With a light tap of the horn, he turned onto the road and disappeared toward town. Ellie blew out a long breath as she pulled her suitcase out of her trunk. She stared up at the house in front of her for a moment before she lugged the bag up the steps and into the foyer. A ticking grandfather clock was the only sound she heard as she stepped onto the hardwood floor and pushed the door shut behind her.

Two sets of eyes stared up at her. "Well," she said to them, tossing her arms out to the side, "should I take Aunt Susie's old room or is that too weird?"

Lola cocked her head at Ellie as though considering it. Cleo bobbed her head. Ellie raised her eyebrows at the cat. "Was that a yes, I should take the room or yes, it's weird?"

In response, Cleo spun and darted up the steps. She disappeared around the corner before looping back and staring at Ellie.

Ellie puckered her lips as she hefted her bag up and followed the cat up the stairs. Lola trailed behind Ellie. Cleo sauntered up the remaining steps and over to the door leading to the master suite.

She rubbed against the door frame and meowed.

"I guess that's Cleo's vote for me to take the master. I suppose it makes some sense. If I stay here and open the B&B, this is the best place for me."

Ellie entered the rose-colored room and tossed her suitcase on a floral barrel chair. With a sigh, she glanced around the room. Lola sat at her feet and Cleo lounged on the bed.

"Well," Ellie said to the two animals, "I guess I'll change and try to relax."

Ellie furrowed her brow, doing a double-take as Cleo appeared to nod her head in agreement. "You're kind of odd, Cleo."

The comment earned a scratching yowl from the cat. After a quick change of the sheets on the bed, Ellie unzipped her suitcase and found her pajamas. She wandered into the large ensuite and set out a few of her things on the large counter. A claw-footed tub sat against a wall, a glass-enclosed shower stood next to it.

Ellie frowned at the blue toothbrush in the porcelain

toothbrush holder. A brush sat on the counter, a few blonde hairs poking from it. A tube of hand cream stood on its end.

A wave of sadness swept over her as she stared at the things awaiting their owner's return. An owner who would never return to use them again. She hadn't been close to her aunt, but she still felt the loss as she stared at all the unfinished business.

Ellie tore her eyes away from the personal belongings and focused on changing into her pajamas.

Her aunt had left a lifetime of memories here. She'd need to sort through it all. Perhaps she could put off any decisions about reopening the B&B until she'd had the chance to settle in.

Her ringing phone interrupted her thoughts. She tugged her shirt over her head and hurried back into the other room, retrieving her phone from where she'd tossed it on the bed.

"Hello?" she said, out of breath from the room-to-room hustle.

"Hey!" Mia's voice answered. "Where have you been? I've been texting you and getting no answer. Are you that busy at work?"

"Hey, Mia," Ellie said, shouldering the phone as she strutted back to the bathroom to retrieve her discarded clothes and fold them. "Yeah, sorry, I've been tied up."

"You done at the store? Want to meet for dinner?"

"I can't," Ellie said. "Something's happened."

"Oh no," Mia groaned. "Now what? Is it that no-good louse of a soon-to-be-ex?"

"That situation seems to have resolved. Thanks for the connection to Luke. We reached a settlement this morning. Hopefully, soon that'll be behind me."

"That's great! So, are you busy signing paperwork or what?"

"No." Ellie tossed her clothes back into her suitcase and sank onto the bench at the foot of the bed. "I'm actually in Salem Falls."

"Where?"

"Salem Falls. Over near the Poconos."

"Never heard of it. What are you doing there?"

"My aunt passed away."

"Oh, Ellie, I'm sorry. Were you close?"

"No, we weren't. But she didn't have any other family."

"Oh, so you need to deal with her stuff, huh?"

"Sort of. She left me everything."

"What are you going to do? Clean out and sell? Do you need any help?"

Ellie drew in a deep breath. "No," she said. "I'm going to move here."

CHAPTER 5

"*W*HAT?" Mia practically screamed into the phone. "Ellie! Are you serious?"

Ellie scooted back onto the bed, her hand falling absent-mindedly to the black cat next to her. "Yeah," she said simply.

"But you can't leave Winwick!"

Ellie's head bobbed around as she considered Mia's latest statement. "Well, I can," she said. "Look, I have nothing there. Toby left me, I've got a mountain of bills in a house I can't afford, Skye let me go this morning. I have nothing in Winwick."

"You have me," Mia said. Ellie heard the pout in her voice.

"I didn't mean... You know what I mean, Mia."

"If you can't afford the place here, how will you afford your aunt's?"

"Apparently, she left me some money, too. But I've got to move here with her dog and cat."

"Seriously?" Mia questioned.

"You should see the house. It's a beautiful old Victorian. She had a B&B here that I can reopen if I want. This is a great opportunity for me. The perfect way to restart my life."

"At least say I can visit you," Mia said.

"You can visit me next weekend when I move my stuff," Ellie said.

"Deal," Mia answered. "Text me the deets and I'll clear my weekend."

"Okay. I'll be home Sunday. Let's get together Monday night."

Mia agreed to the meeting and, after a few last pleasantries, Ellie ended the call. She tossed the phone on the night table and leaned back into the pillows. "I'd be a fool not to move, right?" she said as she stroked the cat's fur. Her head bobbed again.

"What do you say we hit the hay early?" Ellie proposed. From her spot next to the bed, Lola's tail wagged. "Okay," Ellie groaned as she climbed from the bed. "Come on, let me let you outside one last time before bed."

The dog rose to her feet and padded after Ellie, leaving Cleo to sprawl on the bed. Ellie watched the dog from the porch as she nosed around the front yard. After finishing her business, Lola trotted back up the steps and followed Ellie into the house. She double-checked all the lights downstairs before she climbed up the L-shaped staircase.

Lola trailed behind her, only darting past her as she entered the bedroom. The dog took a running leap, landing on the bed and curling in a ball next to the cat.

"Uh, seriously?" Ellie inquired. "Did Aunt Susie let you sleep on the bed?" Lola laid her head down on the mattress.

Ellie glanced over to the dog bed and blanket on the floor. "Here, here, girl," she said in a high-pitched voice. She bent down and patted the bed with her palm. Lola picked up her head, a curious expression on her face. Her tail gave a slow wag.

"Come on, come on, Lola."

The dog let her head sink back down to the duvet. "I'm

fighting a losing battle," Ellie said, straightening. She held her hands up in defeat. "Okay, okay. You can sleep with me."

She crossed the room and climbed in, sliding between the sheets and switching off the light. "Well, at least move over a little," she said as she shimmied her hip against the animal wall. She felt the warm lumps shift away and she adjusted herself, sprawling her feet out. She glanced over in the darkened room. A pair of cat eyes glowed at her and a purring sound filled the room.

"Poor girls," Ellie murmured, shifting onto her side. "You probably miss your real mom." She reached out and stroked Lola's head. The dog shimmied a bit before sighing. She left her hand against the dog's side. Her other arm reached toward the cat. A small paw touched her palm. Cleo had stretched her front leg to lay her paw in Ellie's palm.

"At least you two are sweet," Ellie murmured as she drifted off to sleep.

* * *

Bright sunshine streamed in through the open entrance to the bedroom's sitting room the next morning. Ellie awoke on her back. A black cat sat on her chest, staring at her face.

"Ah!" she shouted with a wince. "Not cool, Cleo." Lola sat next to her, staring down, her wrinkled face a mask of concern.

Ellie lifted her chin. "I guess it's time to get up." She squinted against the bright light coming in through the many windows in the sitting room. "I'm going to have to get blinds."

The clock next to her read six-thirty. "This is way earlier than I intended to get up, you know," she confided to the two animals as she shuffled into the bathroom.

With her long hair tugged up into a ponytail, she donned

a bathrobe and a pair of slippers and clamored down the stairs, letting Lola out on her way to the kitchen.

Cleo waited on the counter, sitting next to her empty bowl. "Hungry, huh? Me too."

Ellie emptied a can labeled Salmon Dinner into Cleo's bowl and filled Lola's with kibble. Lola waited with her tail and behind wagging, at the mudroom door off the kitchen. Ellie let her in before pulling open the refrigerator to make herself breakfast.

With everyone in the household fed, Ellie grabbed a cup of coffee and headed for the screened-in porch. After a leisurely cup enjoyed in one of the room's rockers, she perused the house, pausing every so often to examine some of the items. The two animals followed her on her trek around the place.

Ellie climbed the stairs to the office on the third floor. She hoped to find more information on the bed and breakfast set-up to study over the weekend. The floorboards squeaked as she crossed the room to the tidy desk.

Plopping into the wheeled desk chair, she perused the drawers, finding nothing of interest. A file cabinet stood across the room. Ellie crossed to it and tugged it open. "Aha!" she exclaimed.

Several manila folders were placed in the hanging file folder system. One folder was marked "Current B&B." Ellie pulled it out and flipped through. It detailed the room setups, names, and more. She found a logbook of reservations. Shoving both under one arm, Ellie grabbed the folder called "Future B&B." A quick glance through it showed her aunt's ideas for running murder mystery parties.

"Hmm, interesting, girls. Aunt Susie wanted to run murder mystery weekends here. That sounds fun. We'll look at these later. I'd better get dressed to head into town."

After a quick shower, applying a little makeup, and

pulling on clothes, Ellie slid behind the wheel of her car and aimed for the town of Salem Falls. Within minutes, she was pulling along the curb outside of Mac Doyle's office.

Ellie hopped out of the car and hurried up the sidewalk, knocking on the screen door.

"Come in!" Mac's voice shouted.

"Hi!" Ellie called as she stepped into the empty foyer. "It's Ellie!"

"Come on in, Ellie," Mac called from his office. "I'm in here!"

Ellie stepped through the doorway Mac had appeared in last night. He sat at his large desk, placed in the middle of the room. Papers were spread across the desk in every direction.

"Have a seat," Mac said, motioning to a chair in front of the desk.

"Hope this is a good time."

"Yep," he said as he scrawled a note on a piece of paper. "I've got everything together here. We'll start with the basics." He shuffled through papers, stacking a few and straightening them by tapping them against the desk's top.

"Obviously," Mac said, "the house is yours along with the three acres surrounding it. Your aunt left specific instructions that you should keep the pets."

Ellie nodded as she sank into a seat across from him.

"We'll need to take care of some paperwork to put the deed into your name. That's what I was working on when you came in."

"Great. I found some information on the B&B. She had some notes on hosting murder mystery weekends. I didn't have a chance to get very far into her notes, but the idea sounded interesting, so I may just reopen the B&B."

"Murder mystery parties, huh? Well, Susie was very forward-thinking. Definitely, something to consider. And it would be great to see the old place open again."

Ellie's ponytail bobbed as she nodded and smiled. "And I'm hoping you can help me with any paperwork I need to get this up and running when the time comes. I'm sure there's a process through the town."

"I'd be happy to, Ellie. Before we do that, though, I'd like to go over the accounts and holdings. Then we can get the money and assets transferred over to you."

"Right. Yeah, I'm getting ahead of myself. I'm just very excited. That sounds terrible. My aunt is dead. But it feels like she's given me a second chance at life. And it couldn't have come at a better moment."

"I understand. And I think Susie would be extremely happy to see someone with this enthusiasm for Salem Falls Manor."

Mac pulled a thick folder from the floor next to the desk. He plopped it down on the desk and flipped it open. Papers stuck out at various angles.

"Okay," he said with a sigh, "we've obviously got the standard checking and savings accounts. I can issue checks from these accounts for you to pay for any funeral expenses while we wait for the paperwork to clear. Susie also had a healthy set of certificates of deposit with local and national banks. And she had a number of investments in the stock market."

Mac flashed the paperwork at Ellie. She scanned the account summary, her eyes bulging at the numbers.

"She also kept several business accounts open despite the B&B not being active for several years. They all have healthy balances and will allow you some startup funds for whatever you need."

Another set of paperwork came over to Ellie. She hadn't seen these types of values in bank accounts in her life, certainly not recently.

"Susie also had a number of other business interests both in town and beyond." Mac patted a large stack of papers. I made a summary list here for you." He passed another paper over.

Ellie scanned the list noting her aunt had owned interests in the town's ice cream shop, laundromat, grocery store, and even the *Cookin' With Gas Diner*.

"Wow! Aunt Susie was really quite the businesswoman!"

"That she was. She made smart business moves. As a result, a lot of people, both in town and out, asked her to invest in their businesses."

Ellie nodded as Mac's phone rang. "Oh, excuse me a moment," Mac said.

She gave him a silent nod and returned to studying the financial details. Mac wasn't kidding when he said she'd be set without needing to reopen the B&B. Still, she thought it sounded like a fun project. Ideas brewed in her head about updates and additions.

"You must be joking!" Mac shouted, drawing her attention with the tenor of his voice.

Ellie glanced up, spotting an expression of shock on his face. "No, no, I believe you, but... well, I just don't know what to say."

Ellie studied the papers again, wondering if she should step out.

"Yeah. Yeah, I've got her right here, actually."

The words piqued her interest. She glanced up at Mac. He held out a finger toward her. "I can do that. Yeah... sure, we'll be right over. Okay. Thanks a lot, Rick."

Mac ended the call and blew out a long breath as he stared at the desk. He shook his head after the moment and glanced up at Ellie. She straightened in her seat. "Everything okay?"

"Afraid not," Mac answered. "I've got some... bad news."

Ellie's heart sank. There must be a problem with the will.

She figured it was too good to be true that her problems would be ended by a miraculous inheritance.

"Gosh, Ellie, I don't know how to tell you this but..." The man looked ready to cry. Ellie felt sorry for him. He probably didn't know how to break it to her that she'd not be inheriting anything.

"It's okay," Ellie said. She collected the papers and slid them back across the desk to him. "I understand."

"You do?" he asked.

"Yeah," she said in a soft voice as she collected her purse. "Yeah, I get it. I was surprised when you said Aunt Susie left everything to me. I figured it must be a mistake."

"Oh, no," Mac said, waving his hands. "No, it has nothing to do with the inheritance. Well, very little."

Ellie cocked her head at him. "That was the sheriff on the phone. They just finished your aunt's autopsy."

"Oh," Ellie said, confusion apparent on her face. "Okay?"

"Ellie, your aunt didn't drown accidentally. She was murdered."

CHAPTER 6

*E*llie's jaw dropped open. "What? Murdered? How? How do they know this?"

"When the coroner examined her body, there was no water in her lungs which means..."

"She was dead before she hit the water," Ellie said.

Mac nodded. "Right. The sheriff has officially opened an investigation."

"How did she die?"

"Rick didn't say. He just asked if I'd been able to find you yet and asked us to come straight over."

"Oh, sure," Ellie said, shouldering her purse again. "We can head over whenever you're ready."

"We'll finish this paperwork later," Mac said. "I can drive."

They drove the short distance through the streets to the police station, housed in the town's municipal building along with meeting rooms and the library.

Mac led her inside through the special entrance and to a counter where he spoke with a curly-haired blonde. "Oh, hey, Mac," she said in a friendly, bubbly voice.

"Hey, Hazel," he said, leaning on the counter.

"Sheriff's in his office. He said to send you back as soon as you got here."

"Thanks, kiddo. By the way, this is Ellie... ah..." He paused as he motioned to Ellie.

"Ellie Byrne," Ellie said, extending her hand to the woman. "I'm Susan Byrne's niece."

"Oh," Hazel said, her eyebrows raising and sadness creeping into her voice. "I'm so sorry for your loss."

"Thank you."

Her eyes flitted back to Mac. "Sheriff said to go right back," she said with a nod.

"Thanks." Mac led Ellie past the counter and wound through a few desks, entering a doorway in the back. A few rooms jutted off the hall. Mac wandered past them and through an open door on their left.

A dark-haired man leaned over his desk. He glanced up as they entered the room. Piercing blue eyes shifted from Mac to Ellie before darting back to Mac. He stood and smiled at the man. "Mac, thanks for coming by," he said, with a slight Southern drawl to his speech.

"Sure thing, Rick. This is Ellie Byrne, Susie's niece. Ellie this is Rick Crawford, Salem Falls's sheriff. Rick is a transplant to the area from Georgia."

"Ah, that explains the accent," Ellie said as she extended her hand.

"Nice to meet you. I'm sorry it's under these circumstances."

"Thanks," Ellie said as she shook his hand.

"Have a seat," Rick said, motioning toward two chairs in front of his desk. He rounded the desk and plopped into his chair, wheeling it closer to the desk. "I assume you told her."

"I did. Rick, can you give us any details?"

The sheriff shuffled through a few papers and flicked open a folder. "Coroner expected to find water in Susie's lungs but when she didn't, she started to look for another COD, uh, that's cause of death," he said glancing at Ellie.

Ellie nodded as she clutched at the strap of her purse.

"Maddie, that's our coroner," he said with another glance to Ellie, "figured she died of a heart attack or stroke or something. But when she looked further, she found no evidence of either."

Ellie's eyebrows shot up. "So, what killed her?"

"Poison," Rick answered.

"Poison?" Ellie questioned.

"Sodium fluoroacetate was found in her bloodstream."

"I'm sorry, what?" Ellie questioned.

Rick waved his hand in the air as he explained. "It was a pesticide years ago used to kill coyotes, rodents, and the like. You'll sometimes hear it called 1080."

Ellie grimaced. "Like rat poison?"

"Sort of, yeah," the sheriff said with a nod. "It's colorless and basically tasteless. Easy to slip into someone's food or drink."

"So, you think she was murdered?"

"I doubt Susie poisoned herself," Rick answered.

Mac shook his head. "How quick moving is it?" he asked.

"Takes a couple of hours. Maddie puts the time of death around six to eight in the evening Monday night. Which means she could have ingested the poison anywhere from late morning to early afternoon."

"So, likely with her lunch," Mac said.

Rick nodded, jutting out his lower lip. "Yeah, I'd say that's a good bet."

"Do you know who she had lunch with?"

"Not at this time, but we'll be launching a full investigation," Rick answered.

"Will you keep me updated?" Ellie asked.

"Definitely," Rick said. He bit his lower lip as he spun a pen on his desk. "Ms. Byrne…"

"Ellie, please," Ellie said.

"Ellie," he said with a grin. He paused again. "I hate to ask you this but, do you have an alibi for Monday?"

"Now, wait just a minute, Rick. You can't be serious," Mac said.

"Just hold on, Mac, I'm not accusing her of anything. You don't need to get your lawyer voice out." He paused, his eyes shifting back and forth between them. "But we need to rule her out. She had the most to gain from this financially, so she's naturally a suspect."

"It's fine," Ellie said. "I was working Monday from nine until six."

"And someone can verify that?"

"Yes, my boss, well former boss, Skye Lawrence. She owns The Frock Shop in Winwick. I can get you the number." Ellie started digging in her purse.

Rick waved his hand at her. "Whenever you have a minute."

"You can't be serious, Rick," Mac complained.

Rick shrugged. "If I can rule her out right away, it just makes my job easier."

Ellie grabbed her phone and scrolled through her contact list. She passed along the number and Rick jotted it down on a sticky note. "Thanks," he said, waving his pen in the air. "I'll give her a call and verify this and then you'll be officially off the hook."

Mac slammed his fist on the chair's arm. "You shouldn't waste your time with someone who couldn't have done it and start tracking down whoever did this to Susie!"

Rick held out a hand toward Mac. "I'm just being thorough. The first place we look is family, especially when an estate of this size is involved."

"I understand," Ellie said. "And the faster to cross me off the list, the faster you can focus on finding my aunt's killer."

"Right. I'm glad you understand. I'm just doing my job." He shot a glance at Mac. "Anyway, that's all the information I have right now."

"Well, thank you, Sheriff," Ellie said.

"Rick, please."

"Rick," Ellie said with a smile.

He stood and Ellie and Mac followed his lead. "So, will you be moving into Salem Falls Manor?" he asked as he walked them toward the door.

"Yes," Ellie said. "I'm staying the weekend before I head home and list my house in Winwick."

"That's great, that's great. Any plans to reopen the B&B?"

"Actually, yes! I found some of my aunt's notes about her future plans and they sound really fun. After I settle in, I'm going to work on getting it up and running again."

"Wonderful. I'm really glad to hear it. The town will be happy to have that back in business."

"For the most part," Hazel chimed in as they stopped at the desk to finish their conversation.

"What d'you mean?" Ellie asked.

"Oh, nothing," Rick said, fluffing off the comment.

Ellie focused her gaze on Hazel, who gave her a shrug.

"Well, again, thanks for stopping by. And I'm sorry we had to meet this way, but welcome to Salem Falls."

"Thank you, Rick," Ellie said with a wide smile, shaking his hand again. "And nice meeting you Hazel."

She slid on her sunglasses as they stepped outside the building and walked toward Mac's car. Ellie sighed as she slid into the passenger's seat. "Wow," she murmured as Mac fired the engine. "I can't believe this."

"I'm really sorry, Ellie," Mac said. "In light of the news,

why don't you head home. I'll get the paperwork together and send it over for you to review and sign this weekend."

Ellie offered him a closed-mouth smile. "It's okay. I can sign everything before I head back to the manor," she said. "If it's all the same to you, I'd like to get everything moving."

"Sure thing. I just didn't want to push," Mac said. "I understand this must be quite a shock."

"It is, though I'm sure it is for you, too. After all, you were friends with her."

Mac eased the car into the driveway near his office. "I can't fathom who would kill Susie. And I don't mind finishing the paperwork. Then I'll have everything ready to file on Monday morning. Tell you what, I'll order us some lunch in and we'll tackle all this."

Ellie nodded as they climbed from the car and returned to Mac's office. She spent her early afternoon signing paperwork over a pepperoni pizza from a local pizzeria, Salem Slice. She stretched and shook out her hand as she finished the last one.

"That'll do it!" Mac said.

"Great," Ellie answered. "Wow, she did own a lot. I hope I can live up to her legacy."

"She always said you were smart, so I'm sure you will."

"Suddenly, the idea of murder mystery weekends seems a lot less appealing."

Mac puckered his lips and bobbled his head around. "Susie would be the first one to tell you to move ahead with that."

"It seems disrespectful."

"Nah. She was excited about that idea. If she was still around, she'd tell you a murder on the premises would only add to the draw."

Ellie snorted a laugh. "She sounded like an interesting lady. I wish I would have known her better."

"She was," Mac said with a nod. "Well, I have everything I need. So, you're free to go home and relax."

"Home," Ellie said as she lifted her shoulders. "It sounds really nice."

"I'm glad you feel that way. Oh, ah, when are you heading home home?"

"Sunday. I'll take care of a few loose ends there, pack up my stuff and be back by next weekend."

"Fast mover. Susie would like that. She wouldn't be happy with Lola and Cleo being alone long."

"Oh!" Ellie said. "Gosh, I never thought. I can…"

Mac chuckled and waved her concern away. "I can take care of them for the week, no problem. You do what you need to do."

"I won't be later than Friday," Ellie assured him.

They finished their conversation with a final few pleasantries before Ellie wandered out into the warm late afternoon air. Within minutes she was making the turn into Salem Falls Manor's driveway.

As she pushed through the door of the house, she found two furry faces staring up at her. "Sorry, I was longer than I expected. I got some bad news." After leaving Lola outside for a few moments, she led them to the kitchen for their dinner. "I can't believe Aunt Susie was murdered," she murmured as she emptied the beefy shreds of cat food into Cleo's bowl.

Cleo nearly toppled off the counter as she spoke. Lola whimpered at the words. "Yeah, that was my reaction, too. Who could have done this?"

The two animals stared at her. "I'm not sure either. But I'm going to get to the bottom of it."

Ellie blew out a long breath as she watched the two animals eat. With her late lunch, she wasn't very hungry. She wandered into the pantry, pulling the chain for the lightbulb dangling in the room's center.

With a loud pop, the light bulb burned out. "Oh, of course," Ellie groaned.

She recalled seeing a stepladder in the entryway's coat closet. She dragged it to the pantry and found a lightbulb. She unscrewed the burned-out bulb and replaced it with a fresh one.

As she pulled the string to test the light, the stepladder wobbled. With nothing to grasp, she flailed her arms in a bid to stay on her feet. She lost that battle and toppled backward, landing hard against the wooden floor. Her head smacked off the solid surface. Her vision closed to a pinpoint, and she lost consciousness.

CHAPTER 7

*V*oices floated in the blackness. Pain throbbed through Ellie's head as she squeezed her eyes shut. Everything hurt and breathing was painful.

"She's dead," a sassy female voice said. "That's just perfect! Another one bites the dust."

"She's not dead," another woman with a sweet voice answered.

Ellie felt someone poke her as she struggled to wake up. "Dead. She's dead. Done."

Ellie issued a groan.

"Ellie?" the sweet-voiced woman called. "Ellie?"

Ellie's eyelids fluttered open. The room still spun above her.

"Ellie?" the voice called again.

"Huh?" Ellie groaned. Her eyes scanned the room for the source.

"Are you okay?"

She scrunched up her face as she rubbed at the bump on the back of her head. Through the window outside, she saw night already beginning to fall. "How long have I been out?" she murmured as she pushed herself up to sit.

"About an hour," the sassy voice answered.

Ellie crinkled her brow and glanced around again. "Hello?" she called. She grasped hold of the edge of a shelf and used it to pull herself up to stand.

"Must have taken a heck of a hit," the sassy voice said. "She's totally confused."

"Poor Ellie," the other voice answered.

"Hello? Who's there."

"It's us, dummy."

Ellie's eyes went wide. "Who?"

"Cleo and Lola," the sassy voice answered.

Ellie blew out a long breath and steadied herself against the shelf as she bent forward and rubbed her temples. "I must have taken a harder hit than I thought," she said to herself.

The sweet voice said, "Are you okay? Are you in any pain? Maybe you should go to the hospital."

"She can't drive to the hospital, you dope, she hit her head! She's got to call an ambulance. Quick, get the phone."

"I'm hearing things. I probably have a head injury. Maybe I should sit down," Ellie reasoned aloud.

"Yeah, that's it, Ellie, sit down."

She stumbled from the pantry and into the kitchen, pulling out a chair and plopping onto it. Cleo jumped onto the table next to her and stared at her. Lola raced into the kitchen, Ellie's cell phone in her mouth. She nudged Ellie with her nose, then stood on her hind legs and dropped the phone on her lap.

"There you go," she said.

Ellie sank her head into her hands. "This can't be happening."

Cleo tapped her hand with her furry paw. She wrapped it

around her finger and tugged. "Ellie, maybe you should go lie down."

Ellie flicked her gaze to the cat. She shook her head. The cat's green eyes stared at her, filled with concern. "Ellie?"

"No," she said, shaking her head. "No, I must have really hit my head. I'm hearing things. I'd better go to the hospital."

Ellie nodded at her own statement, then stood on shaky legs and wandered from the room. She climbed the stairs and headed for her bedroom to retrieve a sweater. She ducked into the bathroom and checked her makeup and hair. After wiping away a smudge of mascara, she picked up her brush and began pulling it through her long hair.

The cat and dog followed her. "Ellie, you can't drive to the hospital, you know," Cleo said.

"Like heck I can't," Ellie answered. She shook her head. "What am I doing? I'm answering a cat."

"It would be rude if you didn't," Lola said.

"Yeah. Like the first night you were here. It was like you couldn't even hear us," Cleo added.

"I couldn't hear you! I can't hear you!" Ellie pressed her hands to her face and groaned. "Ohhhh."

"Are you in pain?" Lola questioned.

"No." She sighed and shook her head again. "Okay, I'm going to the hospital."

"You can't go to the hospital!" Cleo said as Ellie stalked across the bedroom.

"I think she should go to the hospital," Lola argued. "She may be hurt."

Cleo raced ahead and stood in the doorway. She arched her back, her tail standing straight up in the air. "And what are you going to tell them?"

"That I fell and hit my head. Why am I answering you?"

"And what else?" Cleo questioned.

Ellie's eyes flitted around the room.

"You can't tell them you're hearing voices," Cleo continued. "They'll think you're crazy."

Lola's brown head bobbed up and down. "Probably," she added.

"See? Even the dummy agrees," Cleo said.

"She's not dumb," Ellie answered as she sank onto the bed's edge.

"She's not as smart as me," Cleo said, stalking across the room and leaping onto the bed. She sat on her haunches next to Ellie and reached out with her paw.

"I can't believe I can hear animals talking. Maybe I'm having a nightmare."

"Why? Susie could hear us," Lola answered, sitting at Ellie's feet.

"Aunt Susie heard you?"

Lola nodded. "Yes. She talked to us all the time. We were her only friends. Outside of Mac."

"Why don't you have some dinner and then go to sleep. See you how feel in the morning?" Cleo asked.

Ellie bit her lower lip.

"Please, Ellie. You can't leave us now," Lola said. "We've already lost Susie. I was afraid we'd have to go to a shelter. If you leave and something happens like it did with Susie..." Lola's chin sunk to her chest.

"Fine, fine," Ellie said. "I'm just going to eat and go to bed. Maybe then this will clear up."

The animals followed her downstairs and watched as she poured cereal into a bowl, drizzled some milk over top, and sat down to eat.

She stared with narrowed eyes at Cleo, who perched on the counter. "What?" Cleo asked after a while.

Ellie returned to her cereal without a word. After washing her dishes, she climbed the stairs, changed into her pajamas, slipped between the sheets, and switched off the light, letting darkness settle around her. With a deep inhale, she squeezed her eyes shut.

They popped open a moment later as she heard hushed whispers behind her.

"I hope she's okay," Lola said.

"Shh, quiet. You'll wake her up. She's fine, she just needs a good night's sleep."

"Poor Ellie."

"Poor Ellie, my eye!" Cleo retorted. "She spent almost an entire day ignoring us."

"I don't think she could hear us."

"What? That's crazy."

"It's not. I think when she hit her head, she finally was able to hear us."

"Susie heard us and she didn't hit her head."

"Maybe she hit her head a long time before she got us."

The voices died down for a moment before Cleo said, "Either way, she can hear us now. And not a minute too soon. Did you hear what she said when she got home? She said Susie was murdered!"

"Yeah, I heard that! Why would someone do that?"

"That's what we've got to find out! And we're gonna need Ellie's help to do that."

"Poor Susie," Lola said before she sighed.

The conversation died down and Ellie closed her eyes again. With any luck, she'd wake up and be perfectly normal again.

* * *

"Pssst! Ellie! Hey, Ellie!" a voice called.

As Ellie started to awaken from her sleeping state, she felt pressure on her chest. What was happening, she wondered?

Was she having a heart attack? With a pained wince, Ellie snapped her eyes open.

A black cat hovered over her, waving her paw in her face.

"Hey! Wake up!" she shouted.

"Huh?" Ellie asked as she glanced around, a fog still hanging over her senses.

"I said wake up!"

As she became fully awake, Ellie's eyes darted around before she flung her arm over her eyes and groaned. "Oh, no," she whined, "I'm still hearing voices."

"You're not hearing voices, dummy. It's me, Cleo," the cat answered.

"And Lola," another voice added from beside her bed. "We were just checking on you."

"No," Cleo countered, "you have to get up."

"Why?" Ellie murmured, her eyes still trapped under her arm.

"I'm starving," Cleo answered. "You gotta get up and feed me."

"You have dry food down there," Ellie answered.

The cat made a retching noise. Ellie pulled her arm away, afraid the animal would vomit on her. "That got your attention," Cleo said, settling back into a sit on Ellie's chest.

"Are you sick?"

"No, I'm hungry. Can't you hear?"

"Go eat your dry food."

The cat gagged again. "Not first thing in the morning. Ugh, please. I need some Sea Captain's choice or Salmon Dinner."

With a sigh, Ellie pushed up to her elbows. Lola glanced up at her, her forehead wrinkling. "I could use a trip to the potty, too."

"Okay, okay, I'm up."

Cleo leapt off Ellie's chest and paraded across the bed

63

before hopping down to the floor and sauntering to the door. Ellie pulled on her robe and slid her feet into her slippers.

"I hoped to be cured by today."

"Cured of what?" Cleo inquired as they padded down the stairs. Ellie let Lola out into the front yard before she plodded to the kitchen.

"Catch you at the back door," Lola called as she hopped down the steps.

Cleo led the way to the kitchen, leaping onto the counter. "What did you hope to be cured of?" she inquired again as Ellie pulled a can of food from the cupboard. "Oh, not to be a pain, but not Ocean Whitefish today."

Ellie flicked her gaze to the cat, her eyebrows raised. The black cat's shoulders wiggled as if in a shrug. "I just had it yesterday. A little variety, please."

"This is unbelievable," Ellie murmured under her breath as she shoved the can back into the cupboard and selected another. She showcased it like a model on a game show. "Will this work?"

The cat's eyes narrowed at the can. "Yeah, Salmon dinner, that'll work."

With a huff, Ellie peeled the can's lid back and dumped the contents into the bowl before stalking to the back door to let the dog in.

"Ah, excuse me," Cleo said when she returned.

"Now what?"

"You didn't smoosh it up. It's in a lump. I'm not a barbarian."

"You can talk, why can't you mush up your own food?"

Cleo waved a paw at her. "No thumbs, duh."

Ellie grabbed the paw-shaped serving spoon and squashed the food into the bowl. "Happy?"

"Very," Cleo said before diving into the bowl.

Ellie flicked open the food bin containing the dog food

and poured a scoop of food into Lola's bowl. The dog hurried toward the little pink dish and scooped out a few kernels of food, crunching them before sticking her head into the bowl for more.

"Mmm, now what do you need cured of?" Cleo inquired, her mouth full of food.

"Talking to you two," Ellie said. "And if Aunt Susie talked to you, didn't she ever teach you not to talk with your mouth full?"

"She complained about it all the time. Cleo never listens," Lola informed her. "Mind if I have a few bones?"

"What kind of cat would I be if I did what I was told?" Cleo asked, mouth full of food again. "And why would you not want to talk to us?"

"Seriously?" Ellie asked.

A wrinkled expression covered Lola's face after she gobbled the small treats Ellie tossed in her bowl. She sank to her haunches. "Do you not like us?"

"No, I… " Ellie groaned. "This is not normal."

"Says who?" Cleo demanded.

"Says me and just about every other normal person in the world."

Cleo licked her paw and dragged it over her face. "Oh well, tough luck. Besides, we have more important things to worry about. Susie was murdered! We have to figure out who did it!"

"The police will figure out who did it," Ellie answered as she cracked a few eggs into a frying pan.

Cleo stopped her grooming and stared wide-eyed at Ellie before she flicked her gaze to Lola. Lola's eyebrows shot up before they both started to laugh. Cleo nearly knocked herself off the counter chuckling.

"What's so funny?" Ellie inquired as she buttered two slices of toast.

"The police will figure it out," Cleo mimicked in a high-pitched tone. "Who, Rick?"

Lola shook her head. "I wouldn't count on that."

Ellie furrowed her brow. "Why?"

Cleo shrugged as Lola explained. "He's a nice enough guy. He always gives me a nice pat on the head when he visits, but he's not that smart."

"He seemed capable to me."

"Capable of being a cat-killer, maybe," Cleo shot back, leaping to her feet.

"Cool it, Cleo," Lola said, sidling up to Ellie as she sat down with her breakfast. "He's not a cat killer."

"We don't know that," Cleo countered, leaping gracefully from counter to table.

"Hey, I don't think you should be on the table," Ellie said.

Cleo slowly eased her backend into a sit, her eyes never leaving Ellie's in an emboldened stare.

Ellie puckered her lips in an unimpressed expression. "Fine, do what you want."

"I usually do."

"It's true, she does," Lola confirmed. "And just because Rick doesn't bother with you doesn't make him a cat killer."

"It could. And besides, how do we know he's not Susie's killer?"

"Sheriff Rick? No, he's a nice man."

"He isn't!"

"You hiss at him every time he comes. That's why he doesn't like you. Try being a little friendly."

"Oh, this coming from Barky McBark. Every time the mailman drops a package, you go wild."

"It could be anything," Lola argued.

"It's the same person every single time." Cleo rolled her eyes.

"You never know when he may try to break into the house!"

"And you never know when Sheriff Rick may snap and kill a cat."

"Okay, enough, you two. Look, I want to know who killed Aunt Susie as much as you, I'm just not sure we should be digging around in a police investigation."

"Like I said," Cleo replied, "if you want to know who did it, you'd better dig around. Sheriff Rick isn't going to find anything. He couldn't find his way out of a wet paper bag."

Chimes floated through the air. Lola squealed out a panicked bark, followed by a few loud woofs, spinning to stare at Ellie.

"Doorbell," Cleo announced.

"Yes, I know what it is," Ellie answered.

"I meant that for the dummy." Cleo nudged her chin in Lola's direction.

"Hey, there's no need for that." Ellie rose from her chair and pulled her robe tighter around her as she glanced into the hall.

Cleo leapt from the counter, landing gracefully on her feet and sashaying into the hall. "She barks every time."

"We have no idea who it is," Lola answered. "It could be an ax murderer."

"It's not an ax murderer," Cleo said as someone rapped on the door.

Another round of barks emerged from Lola.

"Stop that!' Ellie shouted. "It's not an ax murderer! It's Mac."

"Oh," Lola said, her tail wagging, shaking her entire rear with it.

"Dummy," Cleo muttered as she sashayed past Lola and toward the door.

Ellie sighed as she stalked to the door and pulled it open.

Mac stood on the other side of the screen door. He waved a flat box.

"Morning," he said with a nod. "Hope I didn't wake you. I brought donuts."

"No, that would have been Cleo," Ellie said as she pushed the screen door open and motioned for him to enter. "And donuts are always welcome."

"Hi, Mac," Lola said with a wag of her tail.

"Bet he's here to tell us they know nothing about Susie," Cleo said.

Ellie eyed the two animals and gave a slight shake of her head.

"Good, good. Well, I hope it's not too early to stop by."

"Not at all. I was just having breakfast. Come in, I've got coffee on."

"Sure," Mac said. "I'd love a cup. Right after I say hello to Big Lol!" He squatted down and gave Lola an ear rub.

A groaning sound emerged from Lola. "Ohhh, that's the spot," she said.

Cleo raised her back and rubbed Mac's leg. "And hello to you, too, Cleo." The black cat let out a meow.

"Morning, Mac," she said.

Ellie made her way down the hall to the kitchen. "Do you take cream and sugar?"

"Nah, I'm good without!" Mac called into the kitchen.

"You sure? A very nice man went shopping for me and I'm pretty sure he stocked me up." Ellie searched the cabinet above the coffee pot, pulling down a large mug. She sloshed the dark brown liquid into the red cup and waddled to the table with the pot still in her hand.

After a refresh of her cup, she slid the pot back into the maker and sat down across from Mac who had collapsed into a chair against the wall. Lola sat at his feet.

"Just wanted to check in on you, after the news yesterday," Mac explained after a sip of the dark aromatic liquid. Cleo sauntered in and hopped to her perch on the counter.

"Mmm, thanks," Ellie answered. "Yeah, I'm okay. It was a shock, but I'm okay. I do hope they catch the person who did it."

Mac nodded as he sipped at his coffee again. Ellie pulled open the box of donuts and selected a chocolate creme-filled pastry. She stood and tore two paper towels from the roll on the counter. She handed one to Mac who had snagged a jelly donut before the lid closed on the box.

"Do the police have any leads?" Ellie asked.

"Well," Mac began with a mouthful of donut, "I spoke with Rick this morning—"

"The answer is no," Cleo said.

"And he'd done some preliminary work—"

"Did they find anything?" Lola asked.

"And, well—"

"It's a no," Cleo repeated.

"The long and short of it is he doesn't have any leads."

"Told you," Cleo said.

"Really?" Ellie inquired before licking the powdered sugar off her fingers.

"No."

"No way to trace the poison?"

"It's not too hard to get your hands on."

"What about who she had lunch with?"

Mac shrugged. "There's no way of knowing that."

"You could ask us," Cleo said.

Ellie glanced at her before returning her gaze to Mac. "Well, did she have any enemies?"

"Of course not," Lola said.

Mac offered a mouth shrug before he said, "I suppose we all do."

"What does that mean?" Ellie inquired.

"Look, Ellie, Susie was invested in a lot of different things in town."

"So?"

"So, when you own half the town, not everyone sees eye-to-eye with you."

"So, she did."

"If you can call it that. Sure. Plenty of people disagreed with her on things and she had a few people who preferred her to stay out of their business. Even asked her to take a step back."

"And she didn't?"

"Susie had her opinion and she did own a lot of stakes in various businesses. She never backed down. She didn't get to where she was by being a shrinking violet. A lot of people don't like that. But that doesn't mean any of them killed her."

Ellie sighed as she bit off another chocolatey piece of donut.

"Told you," Cleo repeated. "Sheriff Rick couldn't find the killer if they were standing over Susie's body with a box of poison in their hand."

"We've got a nice little town here," Mac continued. "And despite our disagreements, I can't imagine any of them would have killed her."

"Any of her business partners, you mean?"

Mac nodded as he took a big bite of his donut.

"Had she argued with any of them recently?"

Mac snorted a chuckle, his mouth still full of the delectable pastry. "All of 'em," he admitted.

CHAPTER 8

"*A*LL of them?" Ellie repeated.

"Mmm-hmm. That's right."

"What? Over what?"

"Oh, anything. Everything. I told you, Susie had a mind of her own. She had her own ideas on what constituted good business moves and she never backed down."

"Is that what Hazel meant yesterday about not everyone being happy with the B&B reopening?"

"Sort of. A few people had their knickers in a twist over bringing tourists back into town. Not everyone is tourist-friendly. A few of the locals downright hate tourist season. Just an FYI, since you'll likely face the same opposition when you try to reopen."

"Surely people see how good tourism is for the town. And the area is fantastic! Skiing in the winter, the lake in the summer. It's beautiful here. It's natural people would want to share that."

Mac shrugged. "Some people don't see it that way. They moved here for unspoiled beauty and they don't want anything, well, spoiling that."

"It's a selfish view, but I guess people want what they want," Ellie said with a shrug.

Mac nodded as he polished off his donut.

"Well, I still plan to open the B&B. I was hoping there would be some news on Aunt Susie before I plowed forward, but it doesn't look like that's going to happen."

"Maybe something'll break, but I wouldn't hold my breath. Town like this isn't used to murder. We just don't deal with it."

"Just the bickering, huh?"

"Usually that's about it. This is going to raise a lot of eyebrows around Salem Falls." Mac slapped his hand on the table. "Well, I suppose I ought to let you get back to enjoying your morning. If you need anything, give me a holler."

"Oh, it's no bother," Ellie said, standing with him. "I'll walk you out."

They stepped into the hall and strolled toward the door. Cleo and Lola followed.

"You're leaving on Sunday?"

"Yeah, but I'll be back Friday, if not before then."

"Great. Let me know when you're back in town. I'll take you out for dinner. Give you a proper welcome."

"You've already done that," Ellie said.

"Well, we'll call it an official welcome to Salem Falls permanently."

Ellie smiled and nodded in silent acceptance of the offer as they reached the door. Mac pushed open the screen door.

"Hey," Ellie said before he stepped onto the porch, "did Susie ever mention anything weird about the animals?"

"Weird?"

"Yeah, you know, did she say they had any weird quirks? Or anything like that?"

"Not that I know of," Mac said with a frown. He scratched his head. "She mentioned Cleo being a water buffalo."

"I am not!"

"And Lola being a little barky."

"It's called being protective," Lola said.

"But other than that, nothing I can think of." He furrowed his brow and glanced at Ellie. "Why? Is there a problem or something you're concerned about?"

"Oh, no," Ellie said with a shake of her head. "I think they may be missing her."

"We are," Cleo said.

"I'm sure they are. She loved those little fur balls. Talked to 'em like they were her kids."

"We were her friends," Lola said.

Ellie nodded, realizing she talked to them because they talked back. "It's almost like they talk back to you."

Mac burst out laughing, slapping his thigh as he chuckled. "You know, that's exactly what Susie used to say. You're more like her than you know, Ellie. She'd love that you're here and taking over the place, along with taking care of her babies."

"Well, I'm glad to be here. I feel at home here. I just wish it wasn't at Aunt Susie's expense."

Mac shook his head and clicked his tongue. "It's a real shame about Susie. She'll be sorely missed. But we're glad to have you here. I'm glad this old place will have someone who loves her here." Mac stepped onto the porch and Ellie caught the screen door before it swung shut.

"Thanks, Mac. And thanks for stopping by. Let me know if you hear anything else from the Sheriff, huh?"

"Will do." He offered a salute and skipped down the stairs.

"Have a good day!" Ellie called. He gave another wave before he slipped behind his wheel and fired the engine. With a quick toot, he swung the car around and headed down the driveway. Dust from the gravel filled the morning air.

Ellie let the door swing shut and pushed the front door closed.

"I told you Sheriff Dummy wouldn't have any leads," Cleo said, pacing the wood floor of the entryway.

"That's not nice, Cleo."

"Listen, I call a spade a spade, okay? And we have bigger fish to fry."

"Oh?" Ellie inquired.

"We're having fish?" Lola asked.

Cleo stopped her pacing and squeezed her eyes shut. "We're not having fish, Lola. It's a figure of speech."

"Oh, right."

"It means we have other things to discuss. Like who killed Susie and how we're going to find out."

"I'm still not sure we should pursue this on our own," Ellie argued as she swept down the hall and back into the kitchen. Lola and Cleo followed her. She plopped into the kitchen chair and grabbed another donut.

"Hey, I could use some thinking food, too."

"You've got a bowl full of dry food, eat that," Ellie said with a mouthful.

"I'd like a treat," Cleo said. "You have a donut, it's only fair."

"Ohhh, treat, treat, treat," Lola said. She quickly sat on the floor, her tail wagging furiously.

Ellie set her donut down on the paper towel and groaned as she climbed to her feet. "Fine."

"Creamer, please," Cleo said.

"Seriously?"

"Yeah, I love it. Susie always kept a small creamer in the fridge just for me."

With an arched eyebrow, Ellie pulled the creamer from the refrigerator and poured a small amount onto a saucer, setting it in front of Cleo. She lapped at it while Ellie grabbed a few milk bones.

"Not those," Lola said.

"What do you want?"

Ellie frowned, dropping them back in the jug. "The good treats. The Pupcorns. In the bin." Lola nudged her head toward a basket of treats on the counter. She found the red bag filled with dog-shaped treats labeled Pupcorn and grabbed a few. She offered one to Lola who crunched it down in seconds.

"Mmm, I love the Pupcorn."

"Everyone happy?" Ellie asked, collapsing into the chair and taking another bite of her glazed donut.

Cleo finished lapping up the milk. She licked her chops before settling into a sit and licking her front paw. She rubbed it over her face a few times before yawning.

"Mmmm, I could use a nap."

"I thought you wanted to figure out who killed Susie," Ellie asked.

"I do. But I can't think when I'm this tired. We'll have to reconvene after my nap." Cleo yawned again. "We also need to discuss your departure."

"My departure?"

Cleo leapt onto the floor and sauntered toward the door. "Yep. Your plan is no good. We need an alternative," she shouted as she sashayed into the hall and disappeared.

Ellie shook her head and sighed before she settled her gaze on Lola. "What about you? Do you need a nap, too?"

"I could use one. We've been up for over an hour and a half already."

"Wow, crazy."

"I know. When Susie was alive, I'd already be asleep while she had tea in the sunroom."

Ellie glanced over her shoulder at the sun-filled room. "You want me to take my coffee out there?"

"If you wouldn't mind. I always sleep better in the morning sun."

"All right. Just let me grab the folder of B&B ideas."

"Meet you there." Lola rose and sauntered into the sunroom. Ellie wandered down the hall, finding Cleo sprawled on the back of the couch, eyes squeezed shut. She hurried up the steps and snatched the folder from her bedroom before she returned downstairs.

With a fresh cup of coffee, she shuffled into the sunroom and found a comfortable rocker. Lola lounged on her side in the morning sun. She side-eyed Ellie before she offered a sigh and squeezed her eyes shut.

Ellie stared out at the morning sun, bathing the leaves of the deciduous trees in its golden light. Why hadn't she visited her aunt in the last few decades of her life? She guessed life had gotten away from her. She'd gotten so wrapped up in her marriage and making her way, she'd forgotten to take the time. And now the woman was gone. Murdered. And according to Mac, they'd likely never find the culprit. Though according to the talking animals, a development that still disturbed her, they could find the wrongdoer and bring them to justice.

Ellie crinkled her brow as she sipped at her coffee. Was she really about to believe a talking dog and cat? Her life had taken a turn for the worse recently, but this was outrageous.

She glanced down at the folder in her lap. With a flick of her finger, she opened it and looked at the plans. *Reopening Plan for Salem Falls B&B* was written across the top. Ellie scanned the items listed before turning the page to review the Murder Mystery weekend feature.

Before she got too involved in the details, her phone

jangled in her pocket, vibrating against her leg. Ellie dug the phone out and swiped to accept the call from Mia.

"Hey, Mia."

"Hey," Mia answered through the phone's speaker. "Did I imagine it or did you say you were in Salem Falls and moving there?"

"You didn't imagine it, I'm still up here. And I'm moving this week."

"Okay, so I didn't go crazy. I was talking to Joe last night, and it just sounded so nuts coming out of my mouth!"

"Speaking of, hope he's okay with your weekend away because I'm going to need the help!"

"Oh, yeah. I promised hubby-dearest a fishing weekend in return and he's thrilled. I just can't believe you're moving!"

"Wait 'til you see this place," Ellie said, balancing the phone on her shoulder as she closed the folder. "It's fantastic. And not just the house. The town, the area. I'm telling you, you're going to want to move, too."

"Really? I don't mind Winwick. It's nice."

"It's nothing compared to Salem Falls. I'm telling you, just wait until next weekend. You'll see."

"I still can't believe it. Quaint, lovely town or not."

"Well, quaint and lovely, yes, though there is a darker side."

"Ohhhh, what's that mean?"

"I got some unexpected news yesterday. My aunt didn't just die. She was murdered."

"What? Okay, now I'm really concerned about your decision. Do they have any suspects?"

"No. The police seem to be at a loss, but I'm still hoping they'll find the killer. I feel terrible about this."

"No wonder. You just settled yourself into moving and now this?"

"No, I feel good about the move either way. But I feel awful that someone murdered Aunt Susie."

"Oh, right. Yeah, that's awful. I hope they catch whoever did it. It'll help put your mind at ease."

Ellie nodded and opened her mouth to speak when a crash sounded followed by a shriek and startled meow. "What was that?" Lola leapt to her feet, floppy ears back and forehead wrinkled in panic. "Cleo!" she shouted, scrambling from the sunroom into the house with a series of sharp barks.

"Huh?" Mia asked.

"Something just made a huge crash here. Must have been the cat. I'd better go see what it is."

"I'll let you go. Talk tomorrow about Monday?"

"Sure, I'll call you once I'm home."

Ellie ended the call and shoved the phone into her pocket. "Lola! Cleo!" Ellie called.

Lola continued barking as Ellie crossed the kitchen.

"Ellie! Hurry!" Lola shouted. She appeared in the hall beyond the kitchen, her mouth forming an "o" as she sucked in a breath to power another loud bark.

"Okay, okay, what is it?" Ellie inquired as she quickened her step.

"Help! Help! Helpless animal down! I'm under attack. Taking fire!" Cleo shouted.

Ellie's eyes went wide and she jogged down the hall in her slippers. As she turned the corner, rounding the steps, she spotted the source of the commotion.

The lace curtain covering the front window wafted in the morning breeze. Jagged glass formed what remained of the window. A large chunk of glass was missing from the center. It lay scattered across the floor. A brick wrapped in paper sat on the floor next to the couch.

Ellie shoved her hair behind her ears as she hovered over

the offending red rectangle. "Cleo?" she called, glancing around the room.

A mewl came from under an armchair. Lola followed Ellie into the room. "No, stay back, Lola. I don't want you to get cut."

Lola backed up a few steps. "Where's Cleo?"

"I'll find her," Ellie promised. "Just wait there."

"Cleo?" Ellie said again, skirting around the glass and past the sofa. Another soft meow.

Ellie knelt on the floor and leaned her head close to the ground. Two glowing green saucers stared back from under the chair.

"Are you okay?"

"What do you think?" Cleo snapped.

"Did the brick hit you? Do we need to go to the vet?"

"What? No! Why would you even bring that up?"

"You said you were hurt!"

"I didn't say that. I said I was under attack and taking fire!"

"And when I asked if you were okay, you said what do you think? I thought you were hurt!"

"I'm not hurt. Only my pride."

"Just come out."

"Cleo?" Lola called from the foyer.

"I'm okay, Lola," Cleo called as she slinked out from under the armchair. She rose, her back arching high and her tail standing stick straight as she stared at the broken window.

Ellie ran her hands over the sleek black fur. "You seem okay. No blood or glass in your fur."

Cleo spun around, tiptoeing in the opposite direction. "I didn't get hit."

Ellie climbed to her feet and scooped Cleo into her arms. "Careful!" Cleo shouted. "I'm delicate!"

"You're fine, Cleo," Ellie said. "I don't want you walking across the glass and hurting your paws."

Lola stared at them from the foyer. Her tail wagged as she spotted Cleo. Ellie dropped the cat off next to her canine pal. Lola nosed her. "Are you okay?"

Cleo ducked away from her. "Yes, get your big nose off me. I'm fine. You're gonna get my fur riled."

Ellie wandered back into the living room and stooped over the brick. "What is it, Ellie?" Lola inquired.

"Just stay back," Ellie said, waving her hand at the two animals behind her. She carefully picked up the brick with her thumb and forefinger. Tape held a piece of paper to the building block. She peeled it back, tearing the paper in one spot. After she set the brick on a nearby table, she unfurled the note.

Her jaw dropped open as she read the message, written in letters cut from a newspaper.

Leave now or you'll end up like Susan.

CHAPTER 9

*E*llie stared at the threatening note for a moment.

"Ellie? What is it?" Lola questioned again.

"What does it say?" Cleo inquired.

Ellie shuffled into the foyer and swallowed hard. She flashed the note at the animals. Cleo eyed her. "I can't read. I'm a cat."

"How was I supposed to know that? You can talk!"

"Just tell us what it says," Cleo answered.

"It says leave now or you'll end up like Susan."

Lola gulped, her eyes wide. "You mean…dead?"

"Of course it means dead," Cleo said. "It's a threat."

"But… you're not going to leave, are you, Ellie?" Lola asked. She stared up at Ellie with big brown eyes. Her mouth formed its usual frown and her forehead wrinkled with concern.

"No, of course not."

"Oh good," Lola answered, sinking onto her haunches. "I can't take another loss."

Cleo glanced at Lola, then Ellie. "But you are leaving. Tomorrow."

"Just temporarily," Ellie said.

"Susie thought she was leaving temporarily, too," Cleo lamented, her eyes sinking to the floor below.

Ellie rubbed the fur behind her ear. "I know it'll be hard, but I'll be gone less than a week. I won't disappear, I promise."

"How can you be sure?" Lola asked. She bumped her nose against the paper Ellie held in her hand.

"I'll be careful."

"What about us?" Cleo asked. "Someone busted the front window! We could be hurt, catnapped, or worse! I could wander out the broken window and become lost!"

"For that to happen, you'd have to leave willingly."

"You never know what could happen! I could hit my head and lose my senses," Cleo argued.

"And what if someone attacks us while you're gone?" Lola added.

"I will board up the window and call the police about this."

"Sheriff Cat-Hater isn't going to look out for us!" Cleo huffed, pacing the floorboards.

"I'm sure Mac will," Ellie answered.

"Mac only comes by two or three times per day," Lola said.

"We could be dead for hours before he knows it!" Cleo wailed.

"Okay, okay, just calm down. I have to go home and pack. It'll be less than a week."

Cleo ceased her pacing and stared at Ellie. "You could take us with you."

"Ah—" Ellie said.

"Yeah," Lola agreed. "You could take us with you. Then we'd all be safe."

Ellie shook her head and stared down at the furry faces.

Cleo's eyes were wide as saucers and Lola gave her best sad puppy dog look. "Please?" they said in unison.

Ellie huffed and squeezed her lips together as she fluttered her eyelashes. "Okay, fine. I'll take you both with me."

Cleo breathed out a sigh of relief as Lola's tail wiggled. "Go?" Lola said. "In the car?" Her tail wagged even more.

"Yes, in the car, dummy, we aren't gonna walk!"

"Yes, go in the car. Tomorrow, not now. Don't get so excited." Ellie pulled her phone from her pocket. "Now, I'm going to call the police and report this."

* * *

A knock sounded on the door. Lola let out a screech at the sound followed by several sharp barks.

"Lola! Will you stop that barking?" Ellie asked as she skipped down the steps.

Lola spun to face her, eyes wide. "It's the police!" Ellie said. "No need to bark."

"Could have been anyone," Lola answered.

Cleo stalked into the foyer, rubbing her tail against the doorway leading to the library as Ellie pulled the door open.

Rick stood on the other side, hat in hand. "Sorry to meet again under these circumstances," he said as she pushed open the screen door.

He stepped inside glancing down at Cleo and Lola. Cleo narrowed her eyes and offered a hiss. Rick winced and chose to offer Lola a pat on the head.

"Here's the window," Ellie said, motioning to the living room. "I moved the brick so I could retrieve the note." Ellie motioned to the brick on the table and the note lying next to it.

Rick picked up the note and studied it. He pulled a notebook from his pocket and clicked his pen. "Did you see anyone?"

"No. I was on the phone with a friend when I heard the crash. I came in here and found the window broken and the brick on the floor."

Rick nodded and puckered his lips as he stared at the mess on the floor and the note. "Any idea who may have done this? Anyone confront you since you've been in town?"

"No," Ellie said. "I haven't met many people but the people I have met have been nothing but nice."

"He's lost," Cleo said. "He has no idea what to do next."

"He's thinking," Lola said.

"He's too dumb to think."

Ellie glanced at the animals and gave a slight head shake.

Rick rubbed his neck.

"Not many people are even aware I'm here," Ellie added. "Like I said, I haven't met many people."

"Well, that doesn't mean much."

"What do you mean?"

Rick shrugged and arched his eyebrows as he tapped his pen on the notepad. "I mean, everyone in town knows you're here."

"How?"

"It's a small town, Ellie. Word gets around fast."

"So, you're saying this could have been anyone because everyone knows I'm here."

Rick let his mouth hang open a moment as his head bobbed up and down in a slow nod. "Yep, that's what I'm saying."

"Dope," Cleo said.

Ellie shot her a warning glare.

Ellie waved her hand at the note. "This is a definite threat. Do you think it could have come from the killer?"

"It's possible."

"Possible!" Cleo shouted.

"I'm starting to agree with Cleo. He has no clue how to solve a crime," Lola said.

"I think it's more than possible," Ellie said. "Why would someone kill my aunt and then a different person threaten me. Doesn't it make sense that the person threatening me is the killer?"

Rick put his hands on his hips and pursed his lips. "Yep, probably you're right."

"Well, do you have any leads?"

"Not many. I'm working on it, though."

"Who do you have so far?"

"I can't comment on an active case—"

"You're kidding me. I was attacked! I have a right to know."

"I don't have anything firm. I can't give out details like that."

"Bull! He doesn't know. His suspect list is empty," Cleo said, rising to her feet and stalking around the foyer.

"But I assure you we're working on it, night and day," Rick said.

Ellie drew the corner of her mouth back in an annoyed expression. "Okay."

"Listen, I'll have a patrol car out here every hour until we get this solved."

"So you do think you can solve it?"

"Nope, he can't," Cleo said.

"We're going to try."

"Okay. Well, I'll only be here today. I'm leaving tomorrow to pack up my place in Winwick. I'll be back Friday."

"Oh, okay. Well, we'll be sure to keep an eye on the place while you're gone. Check in on the animals." He glanced to Lola with a nod and then to Cleo with narrowed eyes.

"Did you see how he looked at me?" Cleo exclaimed. "Cat-hater."

"I'm taking them with me."

"Oh," Rick answered. "Great. Good."

"We're not staying here with you in charge, cat-hater!"

Ellie widened her eyes at Cleo in a silent warning. "I didn't want to leave them alone after Aunt Susie's death. They've been through enough."

Rick nodded. "I'll get our glass man out here to help you with this."

"Thanks. In the meantime, I'll patch it up with some plywood."

"I can take care of that," Rick said.

"I can do it," Ellie said with a wave.

"Oh!" Rick exclaimed, surprise in his voice.

"I'm pretty handy."

He flashed a smile at her. "That's good. You may need to be in an old place like this."

They stood for a few moments in silence before he added, "Well, I'll get out of your hair then. I'll take the brick and note with me for analysis. I doubt we'll find anything, but you never know."

"You couldn't find your way out of a wet paper bag," Cleo shot back.

He used a handkerchief to load the two items into evidence bags. "I'll let you know if we find anything on these."

"Okay, thanks, Sheriff."

"Please, call me Rick."

"Okay, Rick," Ellie said with a nod as she walked him to the front door.

Cleo glared at him as he passed through the foyer and onto the porch. Ellie waved as he pulled away in the police cruiser. She pushed the door closed and turned to find two faces staring at her from the floor.

"I don't like him," Cleo said.

"You don't like anyone," Lola retorted.

"That's not true," Cleo answered. "I liked Susie and I'm fairly sure I like Ellie."

Ellie made a face at the cat. "Fairly?"

"Jury's still out. We'll see how it goes after you move here."

Ellie stared at the ceiling in a silent plea for strength. "And I *don't* like the way Sheriff Cat-killer looks at you."

"What?" Ellie questioned. "And cool it on the cat-killer thing. I don't think he's killed any cats."

"Maybe he has and maybe he hasn't, doesn't change that I don't like how he looks at you."

Ellie strode down the hall and retrieved a broom and dustpan from the pantry.

"And how does he look at me?" she asked as she swept the glass strewn across the hardwood into a pile.

"Like he likes you," Cleo said, leaping onto the top of the couch after Ellie cleared the floor.

"Please," Ellie said with a roll of her eyes. "That's the last thing I'm looking for."

Lola's face wrinkled with confusion. "Why, Ellie? Sheriff Rick seems nice."

"You're an idiot," Cleo shot back.

"She's not an idiot," Ellie said. "And the truth is, I'm just getting over one relationship. I do not want or need another."

Lola meandered into the room, tapping Ellie's leg with her paw. "What happened?"

"Oh, nothing," Ellie said with a sigh.

Cleo stalked toward her, wiggling her tail. "Tell us. We want the juicy details!"

"Fine. My husband, after fifteen years of marriage,

decided he preferred a waitress to me. He cleaned out my bank account, packed up his things, and walked out on me, leaving me with a house I can't afford and a mountain of debt. So, no, I'm not looking for a relationship right at the moment. Possibly not ever."

Cleo shook her head. "The scum."

"Sorry, Ellie," Lola said. "That stinks. And if it helps, I think he was crazy."

"Thanks. I appreciate that. I can't believe it's coming from a dog, but I'll take what I can get."

"It's best you move here, then," Cleo added. "We'll take care of you. And I'm glad to hear Sheriff Ca—" Cleo paused. "Eh, Sheriff Rick won't be moving in anytime soon."

"Pass," Ellie said as she scooped the dustbin off the floor. "I'm looking for a fresh start and I want to do my own thing this time. Wait here while I dump this and find some wood to close that window."

"Susie kept some in the shed out back!" Cleo called after her.

In short order, Ellie had the window boarded up. As she pounded the final nail into the temporary covering, a knock sounded at the front door. Lola's boisterous bark filled the air as she bounded across the living room, charging toward the door.

"Ellie? It's Mac!" Mac's voice hollered.

"Coming!"

Ellie tossed the hammer on the table and hurried to the door. She twisted the lock and pulled it open. "Hey, Mac."

Lola stood at the door with her tail wiggling back and forth.

He stepped into the foyer, gulping in breaths. "Are you okay?" he questioned. "Rick told me."

"Yeah, we're fine. Word really gets around fast, huh?"

He puffed out another few breaths as he answered. "It's a small town. I'm sure everyone already knows."

"Well, thanks for checking on us."

"No problem. And don't worry, I'll check every few hours while you're gone. Especially with the animals here."

"Oh, I'm taking them with me. And I'm going to try to get back here earlier than Friday."

"Oh. Well, I could watch them, no problem. If you feel more comfortable, I can take them to my place."

"Pass," Cleo said.

"I love Mac but I don't want to go with him," Lola added.

"Thanks, but I think they've been through enough. I'd rather them get used to me and my routines."

"Understood," Mac answered. "Well, I'll still check on the house. And do you need the window boarded?"

"No, I just took care of that," Ellie said. She waved her hand at the boarded up window.

Mac lifted his eyebrows as he eyed the hammer on the table. "Oh! Handy, huh?"

"A little. Also, determined to stand on my own two feet."

"Will you be okay here tonight?" Mac asked.

"I think so. Hopefully, it was just an attempt to scare me off and nothing more."

"Well, I hope it didn't."

"Nope. My plans haven't changed. Just as soon as I can pack up my things, I'll be back."

Mac smiled and nodded. "Good. Say, how about a little lunch. My treat."

"If you let me do the treating, we have a deal."

"Oh, ah—"

"Now, if it's not my treat, the deal's off."

"Well, okay," Mac said, giving in to her demand. "How's the diner?"

"Perfect. Let me grab my purse."

Ellie bounced up the stairs and retrieved the leather bag from her bedroom, shoving her cell phone inside as she descended to the first level.

"Hey, how about bringing something back for us?" Cleo inquired.

"I'll take a burger," Lola said.

"Milkshake, vanilla, extra whipped cream," Cleo demanded.

Ellie slung her purse strap over her shoulder. "Did Susie usually bring back food for the animals?" she inquired.

"She did. Usually stopped at Salem Scoops and got—" Mac rubbed his chin.

"Vanilla soft serve doggie dish," Lola said.

"A doggie dish for Lola," Mac reported, pointing at the dog.

"Vanilla scoop with extra whipped cream," Cleo said.

Mac eyed the cat. "Vanilla soft serve covered in whipped cream for Cleo."

"No burgers or milkshakes, huh?"

Mac burst into laughter. "No, but she said they always asked her for it. She was a real character your Aunt Susie."

"Okay. Well, I'll be sure to stop by the ice cream shop on my way home." Ellie glanced meaningfully at the two animals.

"I'm sure they'll love you for that."

"Be back soon, guys. Behave."

"Yeah, thanks for leaving us alone here. Unprotected after the incident this morning!" Cleo shouted as the door closed.

"I think Cleo's upset," Ellie said, ambling down the stairs.

"Oh, I'm sure. Susie always said they gave her hell when she left 'em. I'll drive."

Ellie slipped into the passenger's seat of Mac's car and, in minutes, they were pulling into the diner's parking lot.

The scent of sizzling burgers and fried food filled the air

as they stepped through the door. Mac waved to Val who bustled behind the counter, grabbing full plates to deliver to the waiting patrons.

"Hey, Mac," she said as she skirted past them. "Take any seat you'd like."

Mac led Ellie to the booth they'd sat in two days ago. Ellie slid into the same side as Val dropped menus off and poured a coffee for Mac.

"Coffee, honey?" Val asked Ellie.

"No, thanks. But I will take a chocolate shake."

"You got it, honey. You ready to order or do you need a few minutes?"

"They got a great brunch here," Mac said.

Ellie puckered her lips in thought. "I'll need a few minutes. I can't decide between the brunch and the burger."

"Burger's a great choice, too," Mac said.

"But I've already tried it," Ellie answered as she scanned the menu. "Eggs and waffles, huh?"

"Oh, Val makes a mean waffle. And she gets locally sourced maple syrup. None of that high fructose crap they sell at the store."

"You've sold me!" Ellie said.

Mac waved Val over and they placed their order. The bell over the door jangled as Val collected their menus with a promise of food coming right up. A woman in a bright red blazer and matching red lips stepped inside. Her skinny jeans ended in spiked red heels. Dark sunglasses shielded much of her face which was framed by thick dark hair.

She scanned the interior of the diner before arching a perfectly shaped eyebrow at Ellie.

"Uh-oh," Mac said. "Looks like you caught Scarlett's eye."

"Scarlett?"

"Mmm-hmm," Mac said, keeping his head down and avoiding eye contact with the diner's latest arrival. "If we're lucky, she'll go somewhere else. Though I doubt it. With you being new and all, you won't escape the attention of—"

The woman's shadow loomed over the table. "Hi, there." She flicked her gaze between the two of them.

"Hey, Scarlett," Mac said, a grin on his face. "Fancy meeting you here!"

"Aren't you going to introduce me, Mac?" She stared at Ellie.

Ellie smiled at her and extended her hand as Mac introduced her. "Scarlett, this is Ellie...uh." His voice faltered, unsure which last name to use.

"Byrne," Ellie said. "Ellie Byrne."

Mac nodded. "Ellie, this is Scarlett O'Hara. She's a reporter with our local newspaper, The Salem Falls Herald."

"I'm also part owner," she said as she stared down her nose at Ellie.

"Great. I'll have to make sure I subscribe."

"Susie had a subscription. I'll move your name to it since the address is the same."

"Perfect."

"Susie was the other owner," Mac explained. "The majority owner." He flicked his gaze to Scarlett. "Which makes Ellie your new boss, I guess."

Scarlett offered a disingenuous smile that bordered on a smirk to them. "I don't suppose you'd be interested in selling? What would you want with a boring old newspaper?"

Before Ellie could answer, Mac stepped in. "Let her settle in first, Scarlett, before you're pestering her for business meetings."

"Well, she really should make a decision. Running a newspaper isn't a spectator sport." Scarlett pulled a business card from the red leather bag slung over her shoulder and tossed it onto the table. "Call me. Even if you're as stubborn as your aunt about selling, we'll need to discuss operations. I'd like to make some changes."

The woman spun on a spiked heel, her perfectly coiffed hair flying in near slow motion like a bombshell in a movie. The sound of her heels pounded across the tiled floor as she retreated to the counter, grabbing a menu to flip through.

"Wow," Ellie said as she stormed away.

"Scarlett is tenacious. Typical reporter."

"Tenacious is putting it mildly." Ellie leaned closer and lowered her voice. "And is her name *really* Scarlett O'Hara?"

Mac offered a low chuckle. "Yep. Her parents had a real sense of humor. Got so famous for it, she kept it even after she got married."

Ellie glanced over her shoulder at the woman who detailed her list of demands to Val. "Burger, well done, not burnt, but not too juicy. Sesame seed bun lightly toasted. Fresh lettuce, only the leafy bit. How are your tomatoes today? Are they pale or red?"

"Who would marry her?"

Mac snorted another chuckle. "Someone not willing to stick to his word. He left her two years ago."

Ellie glanced down at her folded hands. "Well, I don't envy her that. It's not fun."

"Ellie, the man who left you was a fool." His gaze flicked to Scarlett who continued to discuss her order with Val.

"Two cherries and only one squirt of whipped cream," she babbled.

"The man who left her was likely a very wise man."

Ellie chuckled despite herself. "What did she mean about Aunt Susie being stubborn?"

Val arrived with their meals. She set a fluffy Belgian waffle in front of Ellie along with two over-easy eggs and three slices of crisp bacon. "Your Aunt Susie was a barracuda in business," she answered as she slid a plate of steak and eggs in front of Mac.

"Oh, really?"

Val nodded. "Oh, yeah. Scarlett wanted to buy her out of the newspaper a bunch of times." Val shook her head. "Susie wouldn't have it. Said she was the only thing keeping the newspaper honest. It frustrated Scarlett to no end." She unloaded the ketchup, syrup, and a caddy of varied jellies onto the table.

Ellie nodded at the response.

"Need anything else?" Val questioned as she scanned the table.

"Don't think so," Mac said. "Thanks, Val."

The sweet scent of the waffle made Ellie's stomach rumble in anticipation. She drenched a quarter of the waffle with the thick syrup and dug in.

"Careful what you take as gospel in a small town like this," Mac said in a low voice as he sawed at his steak.

"Is she embellishing?"

"No. Scarlett and your aunt did argue over the newspaper several times. But Susie argued over business with a lot of people. Val included."

"Really?" Ellie asked as she waited for the syrup to stop dripping from her freshly cut piece of waffle.

"Oh, yeah. Val also wanted to buy Susie out. Wanted to open a speakeasy in the basement. Susie wouldn't hear of it."

"A speakeasy, huh?"

"I'm sure you'll be hearing about it soon," Mac said. "Val'll want to buy you out or ask you to give your blessing on her speakeasy."

"Why didn't Aunt Susie?"

"Susie didn't want the trouble of it. Thought it carried a certain negative vibe and would detract from the place."

"Ah. Well, I guess she has a point, but it could also give the place a fun side."

"That's what Val thought. She and Susie argued about it for months."

"Really? Friendly sparring or bitter arguing?"

"It got kind of heated. But don't go jumping to any conclusions. Val's the sweetest gal. She wouldn't hurt a fly."

Ellie nodded as she chewed another piece of syrup-laden waffle.

"I'll reserve my judgment for my own interactions with Val."

Mac smiled and nodded at her.

CHAPTER 10

S tuffed to her tonsils, Ellie waddled out of the diner and into Mac's car. The conversation about the two women her aunt had sparred with played across her mind. Could they have killed her?

"Boy, if I keep eating like this, I won't fit into any of the clothes I'm heading home to pack."

"Ah, you'll get plenty of exercise around here. Susie used to walk to town. Always kept her trim."

"Aunt Susie walked to town?"

"Every day."

"Wow. Okay, I'm embarrassed that she was probably more fit than I am."

Mac chuckled at her statement as he pulled into the driveway. "Here we are."

"You should have made me walk," Ellie joked.

"You can walk next time," he promised. "Now, you're leaving tomorrow but will be back Friday, right?"

"Yep. Leaving tomorrow, taking Cleo and Lola. Oh, shoot, I forgot to ask you to swing by the ice cream shop for their treats."

Mac fired the engine. "I'll take you back."

Ellie waved her hand at him. "No, no. I'll grab Lola's leash and take her for a walk. It'll be good exercise for both of us."

"Hey, there's the spirit. You sure I can't drive you? It slipped my mind, too."

"Nah. It'll be a nice way for me to explore the town. Anyway, I may be back early. I'll let you know when I'm back in town."

"Back early, huh?" Mac asked, ducking his head to see through the door as Ellie climbed out.

Ellie poked her head inside the car. "Yeah. I just don't see the point of hanging around Winwick. And I can't wait to get started on my new life."

"We can't wait to have you. Let me know when you return."

"Will do." Ellie shoved the door closed and waved as he swung around and headed down the driveway.

She climbed the stairs, her purse bouncing off her hip, and unlocked the door. Two furry faces waited inside, staring expectantly. Cleo searched her hands as she entered.

"Where's my ice cream?" she whined.

"And mine!" Lola added, though her tail wagged anyway.

"I—" Ellie started.

"Forgot. You forgot," Cleo said.

"You forgot us?" Lola asked.

"No!" Ellie fibbed. "I just... remembered after we were already in the car. And in the driveway."

Cleo narrowed her eyes at Ellie. "You forgot."

"Well, I had another idea. A better idea."

"You get me a milkshake and Lola a burger?"

"No. But I thought Lola and I could take a walk into town and get the ice cream. And you, Cleo, could take a nap! And when you wake up, I'll be here with ice cream."

Cleo stared at her for a moment before she rose to her

feet and stretched. With a big yawn, she stalked toward the living room. "Don't forget the extra whipped cream," she called as she hopped onto the couch and curled in a ball.

Lola wagged her tail as Ellie stared down at her. "This is a good plan. We going for a walk!"

"Yes, we are," Ellie said. "Isn't it exciting?"

Lola trotted next to Ellie as she searched out a leash and collar from the pantry. "Yes. You're right, this is a way better plan."

"I thought you might enjoy it." She slipped the collar around Lola's neck and clipped on the thick pink leash. "Ready?"

"Yup," Lola answered.

Ellie led her onto the porch, locking the door behind her and tossing the keys into her purse. She slipped on a pair of sunglasses and stepped into the bright afternoon sunshine.

Lola sniffed the ground for a moment before Ellie tugged on her leash. "Come on."

They strolled down the driveway. A robin hopped around at the edge of the road. Lola darted toward it, pulling Ellie along with her. Sharp barks filled the air as she charged toward the small bird. It fluttered its wings and rose to a nearby branch, squeaking its annoyance.

"And stay away!" Lola said as she stared after it.

"Lola!"

Lola spun to face Ellie, her tail wagging.

"Why did you do that? It's just a bird! Leave it alone."

"Who knows what it was doing here? Could have been anything. Ellie, it could have attacked you."

"I think I'll survive a robin attack."

Ellie tugged her leash and they stepped onto the road. A biker approached. Ellie waved as Lola lunged at him with a barrage of barks.

"Lola! Stop barking at everything and everyone!"

"I'm sorry, I can't help it. It's in my job description."

"Did you do this when Susie walked you?"

"Susie never walked me to town," Lola answered.

"Why not?"

"Because I barked at everything and everyone."

Ellie's shoulders slumped and she shook her head. "We really need to work on that."

They continued along the deserted road until the sidewalk began at the edge of town. Ellie meandered through the streets, noting the location of several things like the grocer, hardware store, and pet store.

The quaint shops of Main Street appeared before them as they rounded a corner. The bright sunshine beamed down on the waving flags and banners that lined the street. Several shops had their doors open, welcoming visitors. A swinging sign announced the location of Salem Scoops.

"Behave in there," Ellie warned as they approached. She pushed through the door. A jangling bell announced their arrival.

A dark-haired woman with a sleek ponytail and a visor emblazoned with the words SALEM SCOOPS in bright pink lettering stood behind the counter.

"Hello, come on in," she said with a smile.

"Is it okay to bring the dog?" Ellie asked, hovering in the doorway.

"Absolutely. We're pet friendly. You'll find most places in Salem Falls are."

Ellie tugged Lola's leash as she strode over to the creamery case. "So, you're Susie's niece?" the woman, whose name tag read Sam, asked.

"Wow, news travels fast, huh?"

"Well, you've got Lola, so it's not hard to figure out."

"Oh, I was under the impression Lola didn't come into town much."

"She didn't, but we still all know her. I'm Sam. Susie owns a small interest in the creamery. So, I've met Lola lots of times before."

"Hi, Sam," Lola said, her bottom teeth showing above her frown-y lip.

"Oh, boy," Ellie said, bending to study the flavors. "Did you and Susie get along or was she quashing your dreams to expand your business, too?"

"Met some of the other business owners, already, huh?" Sam asked with a chuckle.

"I have," Ellie answered with a chuckle.

"Don't let them bother you. Everybody in Salem Falls has got an opinion, you'll find."

"Well, that's everywhere."

"So, where are you from?" Sam asked. "Oh, and if you want a sample of anything let me know."

"Winwick, over toward Pittsburgh. I'm actually here for the dog and cat but thought I might splurge."

"Oh, I can get their orders ready whenever. I think it's soft serve vanilla for both, whipped cream for Cleo, and a biscuit for Lola."

"I'd like mine now," Lola said.

"She ordered that a lot, huh?"

"All the time," Sam said. "All the flavors in the case are homemade."

"I think I'll try the Chocolate Moose Tracks," Ellie said. "Plus the animal order."

"Can I get that, too?" Lola inquired. Ellie shook her head at the dog.

"Waffle cone, cake cone, or bowl?"

"Waffle cone," Ellie answered.

"Coming right up. And I'll bag Lola and Cleo's for the road."

"Thanks. So, you didn't have any of the issues with Susie

the other business owners had?"

Sam bent over the dairy case as she filled a waffle cone with the creamy dessert. "Not really. Sometimes we had a difference of opinion, but it wasn't anything major. And I usually found out she had a point in the end.

"I think some of the other business owners she worked with just had to have their way."

Sam wrapped the cone in a napkin, stuck a spoon in the candy-filled ice cream, and handed it over to Ellie. She bustled around behind the counter, grabbing two styrofoam bowls and approaching a large machine.

"So, are you here to sell the manor?"

Ellie licked the turned-over spoon of chocolate-y ice cream as she shook her head. "No, I'm going to move here."

Sam's eyebrows raised. "Oh! Well, welcome neighbor! I live down the road from you, though you can't see my house from the manor."

"Thanks," Ellie said. "Yeah, I— well, it'll be a nice change."

"Not digging Winwick anymore?" Sam stuck a few dog bones into the soft serve before snapping a lid on top.

"Not so much," Ellie admitted. "I'm looking forward to the change. And the property is fantastic."

"I agree. Susie was thinking of reopening the B&B there."

Ellie licked at the sweet ice cream. "That's what I heard. I found her plans and I must say, they really are solid."

"Any chance you'll become the newest business owner in town?"

"A very good chance. I'd really like to open the place up."

"Great!" Sam said as she sprayed a generous layer of whipped cream on the white ice cream. "I'd love to discuss collaboration. Ice Cream Sundae Saturdays or something."

"I saw a note about that in the reopening plan. As soon as I settle in, I'll pick your brain for ideas."

"Perfect!" Sam stuffed the two to-go dishes of ice cream into a baggie and handed them over the counter.

Ellie dangled the bag's handles around her wrist as she reached for her purse.

Sam waved her away. "No charge. Consider it your welcome to Salem Falls."

Ellie slouched her shoulders and cocked her head. "No, come on, at least let me pay for mine or the animals."

"Nope, free of charge."

Ellie dropped her purse at her side. "Well, thanks!"

"No problem." Sam gave her a wide grin before she reached over the counter and tossed a dog bone Lola's way. Lola caught it mid-air, chomping it down in seconds.

"Thanks, Sam," she said with a toothy grin.

Ellie offered her thanks a second time and tugged on Lola's leash. "Come on, Lol, let's get home. Cleo is waiting." She waved as she stepped through the door onto the sidewalk.

They meandered away from Main Street as Ellie polished off the ice cream in her waffle cone.

"She seemed nice," Ellie said as they approached the outskirts of town.

"Sam is very nice. Aunt Susie liked her."

Lola stopped to sniff a fence post and Ellie tugged on her leash. "Come on, what are you doing?"

"I smell something. Dogs. Lots of dogs." She gave the post another big sniff before she trotted after Ellie. "Gee, I hope Sam didn't kill Susie."

"Why would Sam kill Aunt Susie? She seems to have liked her."

Lola's forehead wrinkled. "Why would anyone kill her?"

"Well, it sounds like more than a few people didn't like her because of their business ties. But Sam wasn't one of those people."

"Susie liked Sam."

"Did Sam meet with Aunt Susie the day she died?"

"Yep."

Ellie's eyebrows raised. "When?"

"Ummm." Lola's ears wobbled as she tried to recall.

"Never mind, I'll ask Cleo. I'm sure she'll remember." Ellie bit into her cone, crunching a large piece.

"She probably will, yeah. Can I have a taste of that?"

"No, it has chocolate."

"Oh, come on. It won't hurt me. Take some off the top part."

"You're a pain," Ellie said as she broke off a small piece and handed it to Lola.

"It's so small," Lola retorted after she swallowed it. She eyed the cone again.

"No more. You have your own ice cream, stop stealing mine."

They stepped off the sidewalk at the edge of town and continued along the winding road. The heavy foliage shaded most of the pavement from the sun. They arrived back at the driveway after one more barking fit from Lola as a bike zipped past.

"Will you quit that?" Ellie begged as she tugged her down the driveway toward the house.

"Sorry. Those things come out of nowhere and they're so fast. And that noise they make! It drives me nuts."

Ellie led her up the stairs and pushed through the front door into the darkened foyer. "Cleo! We're back. I got your ice cream."

Ellie set the bag on the nearby table and pulled off Lola's collar.

"Cleo!" Ellie called. She returned the leash and collar to the hook in the pantry with Lola following her. "Cleo?"

Her heart skipped a beat. Where was the little fur ball, she pondered? She glanced into the living room. The wood remained fastened over the broken window.

"Where is she, Ellie?" Lola asked.

"I don't know," Ellie murmured as she scanned the room again. "Cleo?" She turned to face Lola. "Does she have any favorite spots?"

"Umm. The couch. The cat tree in the sunroom," Lola began.

Ellie hurried down the hall and through the kitchen, peering into the sunroom. The cat tree sat empty.

"The chair in the library."

Ellie raced toward the library, calling for Cleo and scanning the space. No Cleo.

"Susie's bed."

Ellie took the stairs two at a time, sucking in breaths as she clutched the door jamb, swinging into the room to glance at the bed. No Cleo.

Lola galloped up the steps. "Reading nook."

With a sinking feeling, Ellie hurried up to the third floor and checked the space. Cleo's words rang in her mind about being left alone and disappearing. Had someone silenced the small animal?

CHAPTER 11

*E*llie found no trace of the tiny cat upstairs. She stumbled down the stairs at breakneck speed to grab her phone from her purse, intending to call Mac for help. As she whipped around the banister and stumbled onto the foyer's floor, a black form slinked into the room.

Her red tongue appeared as she offered a massive yawn. With bleary eyes, she sat down and swiped a paw over her face. "Hey, Ellie. Got my ice cream?"

Ellie set her jaw, shoving her phone back in her purse and placing a hand on her hip. "Where have you been?"

"Napping," Cleo said. "Woo! I was out. I really needed that rest. Anyway, got the ice cream? I hope you remembered the extra whipped cream."

"Sam remembered," Lola said.

"Oh, good."

"Napping where, Cleo? I've been racing through the house searching for you. I thought something happened to you."

"Wouldn't you like to know?" Cleo said, arching her back

as she stretched and stalked to the kitchen. "Where's the ice cream?"

Ellie shook her head and grabbed the bag, lumbering into the kitchen with Lola at her heels. She popped open the two containers, placing Cleo's on the counter and Lola's on the floor.

The black cat's eyes widened before she dove into the thick layer of whipped cream. Lola crunched on the bones before biting the ice cream. She'd wiped out the soft serve in seconds and chased the cup around the floor as she licked it clean.

"Oh, Cleo," she said as she finished and licked her chops. "Did Sam meet with Susie the day she died?"

"Hmm?" Cleo glanced up, her pink tongue making a swipe on either side of her face. "Oh, yeah, she did."

"When?" Ellie inquired.

Cleo polished off another tuft of whipped cream. "Around ten-thirty," she mumbled as she licked the ice cream, pulling back with a wrinkled nose at the coldness. After a second, she gave it another try.

"Ten-thirty," Ellie repeated as she mentally calculated the hours between her visit and Susie's death. "So, in theory, she could have killed Aunt Susie."

"No," Lola answered. "Not Sam!"

Cleo's green eyes glanced up at Ellie. "What?" Ellie questioned.

"Nothing. I agree. She could have killed Susie."

"Cleo! How can you say that?" Lola questioned. "Sam is so nice."

"It's the nice ones you got to watch out for," the cat spat back.

"Did they eat anything when Sam came?"

"Yep," Cleo answered. "Susie had tea and those rectangle cookies."

"Shortbreads," Lola clarified. "Susie always gives me a bite."

"Right, those."

"So, Sam met with Susie at ten-thirty, they ate, and a few hours later, Susie died of poisoning."

"Sam couldn't have done it!" Lola insisted.

"Someone poisoned her," Ellie answered.

"But it couldn't have been Sam!"

"Did she meet with anyone else that day?"

"Sure, tons of people. It was Grand Central Station around here the day Susie died."

"Really?" Ellie said.

"Yep," Cleo answered, lapping up some of the melted ice cream at the bottom of the cup. "Lola never stopped barking. She'd just get done barking at one person and then another one would come and she'd be at it again."

"Why didn't you tell me this before?" Ellie questioned.

"You didn't ask," Cleo said. She sat up straight and cleaned her face.

"Well, we need to make a list of all the people she met with and start from there."

"I thought you didn't want to solve the mystery, Ellie," Lola said.

"Now that someone's thrown a brick through the window, I do. I want this person caught so they don't kill me, too!"

"And Sheriff C— er, Rick isn't going to do it," Cleo added.

"Can you help me make a list?" Ellie asked.

"We'll try!" Lola answered.

Ellie raised her eyebrows at Cleo. "Cleo?"

Cleo stared down at the white cup. "Cleo?" Ellie asked again.

Cleo reached her paw out and batted the empty ice cream cup from the counter. It bounced around on the floor before rolling back and forth on its side. Lola raced over to lick it.

"Was that called for?"

"What?"

Ellie glared at the cat as she swiped the two containers off the floor and stuffed them in the trash. She grabbed a pen and notepad from the counter and plopped down at the table.

"Okay, who else did Susie see on the day she died?"

"Sam," Lola said.

"Yes, I know that."

The dog stood on her hind legs, tail wagging, with her front feet on the table. She stared at the paper. "Write it down."

Ellie jotted the number one and the name "Sam" on the paper and the time of her visit next to it. "There, happy now?"

Lola's tail wagged faster. "Yep."

"Okay, who else?"

"Mac," Cleo said.

"Oh, right, Mac," Lola said.

"Mac? Do you really think he did it? What time did he come by?"

"Eight," Cleo said. "Brought donuts."

Ellie nodded as she jotted it down. "Okay, Mac, 8 a.m., brought food. Okay, who else?"

Cleo glanced at the ceiling in thought. "Rick."

"Sheriff Rick came by?"

"Yes, he did," Lola said, sinking to her haunches. "He stopped in because he wanted to talk to Aunt Susie about a mean note someone left her."

"Someone left her a mean note?"

"Someone left her a bunch of mean notes," Cleo answered.

"Why didn't you tell me this before?"

"You didn't—"

"Ask, right. I know. Okay, does Sheriff Rick have the mean notes?"

"I don't know what Susie did with them," Lola said.

"How did she receive them? In the mail? Or did someone drop them off?"

"They came in the mail."

"But there was no stamp," Cleo added.

"And what did they say?"

"Mean stuff," Lola answered.

"What kind of mean stuff?"

Cleo scrunched down, holding her paw out, her claws gleaming in the light. "Give me what I want or else," she growled before returning to her normal posture.

"Demanding notes. Okay, that's something to work with. I'll ask Sheriff Rick about them." Ellie jotted a note at the bottom of the page.

"Won't help," Cleo said. "He'll just stare at you like you're speaking another language. He has no idea who sent them."

"Is that what he said to Susie before she died?"

"He said he was trying really hard to find who wrote it but it might be impossible," Lola answered.

"Okay, well, maybe he's made some progress. Can't hurt to ask. Who else came that day?"

Cleo yawned. "Getting tired. May have to pick this up later."

"Seriously? You want me to solve this murder but I can't make a list of who was here because you need another nap?"

"I have been up for nearly forty-five minutes."

"Just give me at least one more name before you slink off to a dark hiding spot."

Cleo stretched, her rear end high in the air before she pulled her shoulders forward, stretching her back legs long behind her. She offered another wide yawn, blinking bleary eyes. "Val," she said as she hopped off the counter and stalked across the floor. "Came tearing in here screaming that Susie would get what was coming to her."

The little black cat disappeared into the hallway. Ellie stared after her. "Seriously? She drops that bombshell and leaves?"

She flicked her gaze to Lola. "Do you remember this?"

"Yeah," Lola answered. "She was really mad. They argued for a while and Val stormed off."

"Okay, but did she bring anything for Susie to eat?"

"No, not that time."

Ellie jotted Val's name on the paper but wrote the words "no food" next to it. "Do you know what time she came?"

"Mmmm," Lola murmured, "nine."

"Okay," Ellie said with a nod as she jotted it down.

"The first time."

"What do you mean the first time?"

"She came back later."

"When?"

Lola's eyes lifted to the ceiling. "After lunch. Maybe around one."

"Did they argue again?"

"No, Val said she was sorry."

Ellie nodded, noting the second visit.

"Then she gave Susie a strawberry pie."

"Did Susie eat any?"

"Yeah. Val insisted. She said she wanted her to try it."

"Did Val eat it?"

"No, she said she couldn't even think of eating a piece because she'd tasted it too much while baking it."

Ellie's eyebrows lifted. "So Val threatened Susie, then came back with food and made sure Susie ate it?"

"Yep," Lola confirmed and followed up with a big yawn. "Do you mind if I head in for a nap, too?"

"No, go ahead," Ellie answered with a pat on the dog's head. "We'll talk about this later."

The dog slogged her way from the kitchen toward the living room.

Ellie put a star next to Val's name. A clear suspect had emerged from the afternoon's discussion. Val had argued with Susie on a number of occasions before, according to Mac. And the day of her death, they'd had a whopper of a fight. She's returned, hat in hand, but was the apology legitimate or merely a way to ensure her threat was carried through?

Ellie tapped her pen against the pad as she parsed through the information. Did Susie still have the threatening notes? They may help in identifying the culprit.

Ellie rose from her chair and scanned the kitchen. She pulled open several drawers before she stumbled upon the junk drawer. She pawed through it, finding a few sticky notes, none of which contained a threatening message.

About to toss them back in the drawer, she took the random notes and dumped them in the trash can. She spun and placed her hands on her hips, puckering her lips at the space. After a moment of thought, she left the room and made her way upstairs, climbing to the third floor.

She ducked into the office and scanned the small rectangular room. Her eyes centered on the desk. She crossed to it and searched through the drawers. It took an hour to sort through the papers, but when she finished, she had found no such notes.

She eyed the file cabinet, wrinkling her nose at searching through it. After a glance through the drawers, she found no folders marked "threatening notes" and no loose papers.

With a sigh, she plopped onto the desk chair. Maybe Aunt

Susie had given the notes to Rick. That would have made the most sense. She reached in her pocket, intent on phoning the sheriff to ask. Her hand hovered over her lock screen until the display died out. She stared at her own reflection in the black mirror.

"This is crazy," she said aloud. "I'm not calling the sheriff to ask if I can see these notes."

With a deep inhale, she pulled herself up and strode from the room and down to the second floor. Ellie glanced over the banister into the foyer. All remained quiet on the floor below.

She stretched and glanced into the master bedroom. The bed tempted her to lie down for a nap along with her two furry friends. She strode inside, intent on climbing under the covers.

A quick glance around convinced her to skip the nap and begin clearing space for the items she'd bring from Winwick at the end of the week. She wrinkled her nose as she searched for a starting space, finally deciding the short dresser would be a good enough item to tackle.

After retrieving bags from the pantry, she pulled open the top left drawer and began to empty it. A melancholy feeling settled in the pit of her stomach as she bagged her aunt's things. Her poor aunt's life had been snuffed out and now any traces of it would be removed from her home.

As she cleared the camisoles from the drawer's bottom, an envelope dropped onto the flowered drawer liner. She spotted her name scrawled across the white container.

Ellie dropped the black plastic bag to her feet and snatched the envelope. Staring at it, she stumbled toward the bed and sank onto the soft mattress.

After a moment, she spun the envelope around and flipped open the flap. With her hands shaking, she slipped a folded note from inside. Flicking it open, she scanned the scrawled handwriting.

Dear Ellie,

It's been a long time since I've seen you. I hope you're doing well but I have a sense that maybe you're not doing as well as you could be. That's why I left you the Manor. I hope it helps.

And I hope you won't sell it. Out of everyone in the family, you and I were always alike. So, I think you'll take your inheritance in stride and make something out of this old place.

If you're reading this, I'm not here to tell you anything about running a B&B. Though I sincerely hope I'll be able to discuss this with you before I die.

I'm not so sure, though, I've had a few strange incidents crop up. So, if you're reading this note, well, I'm gone before I expected.

In any case, Ellie, open the B&B. Build something from it. Use it to make your life what you want. I hope you have a ball with the place.

Yours,
Aunt Susie

P.S. Please take good care of Cleo and Lola. They're special.

"You aren't kidding they're special," Ellie murmured as a tear rolled onto her cheek. So, her aunt suspected something may happen to her and wrote Ellie a letter to ensure she knew she wanted her to open the old bed and breakfast.

Ellie pressed the note against her chest as she squeezed her lips together and another tear fell onto her cheek. Aunt Susie had thought enough of her to leave her a beautiful estate and she'd never even taken the time to call.

She pulled the letter away from her chest and stared at it. A tear dropped onto the paper, creating a wet splotch that blurred the edge of the final word. She wiped at her face and sniffled.

With a deep breath, she pushed her shoulders back. She'd not only make something of the B&B, but she'd also find out who put an untimely end to her aunt's life.

Ellie slipped the letter back into the envelope and slid it onto the night table. She flicked her long hair over her shoulder and climbed to her feet. "Four more drawers," she mumbled to herself as she stalked across the room to the dresser.

She sniffled a few more times as she settled her emotions before diving into the next drawer. Cleared of clothes, she pulled open the bottom drawer on the right side of the low chest and emptied it.

A variety of items met her gaze as she pulled open the top left drawer. With a sigh, she dove into the varied personal items. She set aside the perfume bottle, enjoying the scent and choosing to keep it. She found three dollars and seven cents in change scattered around the drawer as well as a small sewing kit. A few dresser scarves in various patterns were stuffed at the back.

As she pulled them free, a few scraps of paper fluttered to the floor. She shoved the scarves into a bag before leaning over to collect the three papers that had scattered across the room.

Ellie gathered them up, spotting handwriting on one of them. She turned it over and glanced at the words before she pitched them in the garbage bag.

As she settled back onto the floor and pulled open the second drawer, she froze. Her mind traveled back over the note she'd just scanned. Had she read it correctly?

She dropped the sweater in her hands and dug through the bag in search of the scraps of paper. She retrieved one and read it.

Stop ignoring me. I have the power to ruin you.

CHAPTER 12

*E*llie read the threatening words again. This must be one of the mean notes Lola and Cleo were referring to! She dove into the bag in search of the others. She snatched the other two from within the tangle of discarded items and scanned them. One read: *Give me what I want or you'll regret it... in more ways than one.*

And the other read: *I'm getting impatient. I'd better see results soon. Or else.*

"I found them!" Ellie shouted. A bark sounded from downstairs. "Oh, stop it. It was me!"

After a final grumble, the house went quiet again. Ellie stared at the handwritten notes. She wondered what Rick had to say about them.

Steadying herself against the dresser, she climbed to her feet and found her cell phone. After a text to Mac, she sat on the bed waiting for a response.

Her phone rang moments later. "Hey, Mac," Ellie said. "Thanks for calling, though you could have just sent the number via email."

"Just wanted to check. I know you said it wasn't an emergency, but I wanted to know why you needed the number for the police station. Call me nosy, but I just wanted to be sure you're okay."

"I'm fine. But I found a few notes while cleaning out some of Aunt Susie's things. They seem threatening. And I understand she'd been being threatened for a while before her death."

"Who told you that?"

"Uh," Ellie murmured, trying to come up with a response. Learning the information from the dog and cat in the house wasn't going to suffice. "I found a letter addressed to me among Aunt Susie's things. She mentioned it. And then I found the notes."

"Oh, ah, well, Rick is aware of it."

"Okay. I wanted to follow up. See if he'd found anything. These are handwritten so we may be able to match the handwriting if we had some samples."

"I'm sure if he knew anything, he'd have said something. Does it match the note you received?"

"No, mine was in magazine cutouts. These are written."

"Maybe it's not related."

"Really? The threatening note I got after someone threw a brick through my window is unrelated to the slew of threatening notes Aunt Susie received? I'd also like to ask the sheriff why he never mentioned the notes Susie received when I spoke with him earlier."

"He may have assumed it was unrelated."

"These notes sound personal," Ellie said, reading them over again. "Aunt Susie never said anything to anyone about who did this?"

"If she did, it wasn't to me."

"Okay, well, I still want to talk to the sheriff."

"I understand," Mac said, passing along the number for the station. Ellie jotted it down and they ended their call.

She swiped into her keypad and entered the number. After a few rings, Hazel's bubbly voice answered.

"Hi, Hazel. It's Ellie… Byrne. Susie's niece."

"Oh, hi, Ellie. Oh, no. You didn't get another rock through your window, did you?"

"No, no more rocks, but I wondered if Rick had a minute to discuss something."

"Oh, let me see. Just a minute."

"Sure."

A scratching sound raked across the receiver and she heard Hazel holler, "Sheriff? Do you have time to talk to Ellie Byrne? Susie's niece."

"Did she get another rock through the window?" Rick's voice answered.

"No. She said she wanted to discuss something."

"Sure, I'll take the call in my office."

"Okay. I'll patch her through." Another scraping. "Hey, Ellie? It's Hazel. Are you still there?"

"Hi, Hazel, still here."

"Okay. Sheriff said he can take your call now. I'm going to patch you through."

"Okay, thanks."

Another commotion sounded along with the screeching sound of buttons being pressed. Ellie held the phone a few inches from her ear.

"Oops, sorry, Ellie, I forgot to hit the transfer button first. Just a second."

A rustling of papers sounded and Hazel's voice spoke to no one. "Transfer, extension, transfer. Okay, transfer—" The line went to elevator music before it started to ring.

"Rick, here," Rick's voice said a moment later.

"Hey, Rick. It's Ellie. Listen, sorry to be a pain, but I just found some threatening notes among my aunt's stuff. I wondered if she'd told you about them?" Ellie waited, knowing the answer to the question, but wanting to hear it from the sheriff anyway.

"Oh, yeah. She did tell me about those. In fact, I think she received another the day she died."

"And did you ever find anything out about them? Did you follow up on the lead?"

"I did, I wasn't able to find much."

"They were handwritten. Could you match the handwriting to someone?"

"Well, I asked Susie about it. Thought maybe she'd recognize the handwriting. She said she didn't. I was surprised by that. The notes sounded very personal. She also refused to let me keep them."

"Why did she report them if she didn't want you to follow up on them?"

"She said she wanted me to know in case she turned up dead. Said to be sure to do an autopsy because if she died in the near future it would be murder."

"What?" Ellie questioned, her voice shooting an octave higher.

"That's what she said. And one of the reasons we did the autopsy when we found her. It looked accidental but I thought it was too much of a coincidence."

"No kidding," Ellie said. "Well, whoever wrote these notes is likely the culprit."

"That's a fair bet, yeah. Of course, it could have been someone blowing off steam. There's no direct threat."

"No direct threat? 'I'll ruin you,'" Ellie read, shuffling from one note to another, "'You'll regret it.' 'Or else.' Sounds threatening to me."

"Or it could be or else I'll never speak to you again. People threaten all sorts of things."

"But this time a woman wound up dead."

"Well, I can't argue with you there. Listen, why don't you

bring those notes by so I can have a look at them. Keep them in the case file as evidence."

Ellie considered it for a moment. "Sure. I can drop them off on my way out of town tomorrow morning."

"I can pick 'em up if you'd like."

"No, that's okay. I'm sure you've got better things to do than come by to pick up a few notes. I'll drop them off before I leave tomorrow."

Rick chuckled. "Well, there's not a lot that happens in Salem Falls on a regular basis, but sure, if you'd like to drop them off tomorrow, that's fine."

"Sure. Thanks, Rick."

"Anytime. And I'll have a patrol car out watching the house tonight. I don't expect any trouble, but better safe than sorry."

"Thanks, I appreciate that."

Ellie ended the call and glanced down at the papers. She furrowed her brow at them before she rose from her perch on the bed and climbed to the office on the third floor. She crossed to the all-in-one printer and swung open the top.

With all three notes on the glass panel, she pressed the copy button. A warm sheet of paper shot out of the printer and landed at her feet.

She grabbed it and studied it. Satisfied, she folded the paper and placed it in her sweater pocket before retrieving the originals from the scanner. She searched through the desk drawer for an envelope and shoved them inside then sealed it.

After dropping the envelope into her purse, she finished cleaning out the remaining two drawers of the dresser before she hauled the filled bags downstairs.

As she plopped the last bag down in front of the front door, Lola appeared, her tail wagging.

"What's that?" she asked.

"Oh," Ellie said as she wiped a bead of sweat from her brow and fanned herself. She winced. "Some of Susie's things."

Lola sniffed at the bags then lifted her wrinkled face to Ellie. "Are you going to throw it all away?"

"No," Ellie said. "I thought maybe I'd donate it. The clothes are in good condition."

Lola glanced at the bag again. "Poor Susie."

"I know. I feel the same way." Ellie rubbed the dog's head. "But someone can use these. It may help someone out. So it's like Aunt Susie's last kind act."

Lola wagged her tail at the idea.

"Oh," Ellie said, "I found the mean notes you and Cleo told me about."

"You did?" Lola questioned. "Where?"

"In a drawer upstairs while I was cleaning."

Cleo appeared in the foyer. She swiped her body against the doorway to the living room, yawned, and stretched. "Told you."

"I called the sheriff. We'll drop them off tomorrow morning on our way out of town for him to look at. I think they're related to the case."

"Oh, well, may as well burn them," Cleo said.

"What's that mean?"

"You're giving them to Sheriff Dummy. He won't be able to help."

"Well, he needs them for evidence."

"Evidence of how dumb he is? Because he won't be able to track down the killer from those."

"No evidence for when *we* track down the killer," Ellie said.

Cleo's eyes widened and Lola's bottom wagged along with her tail.

"Do you mean it, Ellie?" Lola asked.

"Yeah, do you promise?" Cleo inquired.

"I do. While I was cleaning, I found a note from Aunt Susie. And I feel I owe it to her to find her killer."

"Now you're talking," Cleo said. "What are we going to do first? Get some rope and tie someone up? I'll claw a confession out of 'em." She brandished a sharp claw.

"No. But the first thing we need to do is finish our list of people Aunt Susie met on the day she died. And then I'm going to do some investigating on handwriting to see if any of them match those notes."

"And then when you find a match," Cleo said with her eyes narrowed, "I'll pop a claw in their a—"

"No, you won't," Ellie finished before the cat could. "No one is popping any claws in anyone's anything."

"You're no fun," Cleo said with a wrinkled nose.

"Come on, let's go finish our list of people before dinner."

Cleo and Lola followed Ellie into the kitchen. Ellie plopped onto the wooden chair and slid the list in front of her. "Okay, I've got Mac, Sam, Rick, and Val so far. Who else?"

Cleo glanced up to the ceiling as she pondered the question. Lola followed her eyes. "Is something up there?" Lola asked.

"I'm thinking, nincompoop."

"Cleo, that's not nice."

"Nobody ever accused me of being nice." The cat stood and paced the countertop. "Now, let me think. Let's see. Scarlett."

"Scarlett? Okay, what time?" Ellie inquired, jotting the name down next to the number five.

Lola nodded and stood on her hind legs, her front paws on the table. "Oh, yeah, Scarlett. She came before lunch. I remember because Susie didn't eat yet and Scarlett had on lots of perfume and it made me sneeze a lot."

"Yeah, you were blowing snot everywhere," Cleo said.

"I was not. And I couldn't help it. She had some kind of smell. It was awful."

Ellie jotted down the time. "Did they eat anything?"

"Susie had tea," Lola said. "I wondered if it tasted like perfume."

"Did Scarlett?"

"No, she just wanted to holler," Cleo said.

"She hollered at Susie?" Ellie asked, making a note of it.

"Oh, yeah," Cleo said. "I barely got to nap that day because so many people were yelling at Susie."

"Poor Susie," Lola said.

"What did they argue about?"

"The newspaper. Scarlett wanted Susie out of it. Said she wanted to run it on her own and do things her way," Cleo answered.

"And Susie didn't back down, I'm guessing," Ellie said.

"Nope, not Susie. Said she was half owner of that paper and it was going to stay that way," Cleo said, pounding her paw against the counter.

"She said if Scarlett took over, she'd run it aground," Lola added.

"Into the ground, d—" Cleo stopped mid-word and flicked her gaze to Ellie. "Lola."

Ellie gave her a smile and a nod. "It's nice to be nice, isn't it?"

"I'm not seeing the appeal," Cleo answered with a flick of her tail.

"Okay, so she's argued with Val and Scarlett. And she had visits from Mac, Sam, and Rick, too, but she didn't argue with them."

"She told Rick he was a dummy," Cleo said.

"Really? She told the sheriff he was stupid?"

"More or less."

"She said he'd better do his job because she was afraid someone may try to harm her," Lola answered.

"So, he could have *killed* her," Cleo shouted.

"I doubt that but I won't cross him off. Anyone else?"

"Bill from the hardware store," Lola said. "He brought me a dog bone."

"He didn't bring me anything," Cleo said. "He probably killed her."

Ellie sighed at the accusation but noted it. "What time?"

"He came at one-thirty," Cleo answered. "They didn't eat though. He just brought her some samples. Susie wanted to redo one of the bedrooms before she opened the B&B again."

"No arguing then?"

"No, she got along with Bill," Lola said.

"Oh, there was one other person who came by that day," Cleo said. "Andy from Salem Grocery. They argued, too."

"Geez, did she argue with the whole town that day?"

"No," Lola said, "we already told you she didn't argue with Mac or Sam. And Delilah came by and they didn't argue either."

"Who's Delilah?"

"She owns Right Meow," Cleo said. "The pet store."

"She brought us treats," Lola said with her tail wagging.

"Yeah, and me, too. She brought me a wand with a feather on the end. I ripped that feather off and tore it to shreds. Best gift ever."

"Okay, and they didn't argue," Ellie said as she noted it on her paper.

"No, she just asked Susie for money," Lola said.

Ellie furrowed her brow.

"Yeah, she didn't yell or anything but she said she needed some money and if she didn't get it, she'd be in real bad trouble," Cleo said.

Ellie wiggled her eyebrows and jotted it down. "Is that everyone?"

"I think so," Cleo said. "Read me the list." She eased herself to sitting and licked her front paw, rubbing it across her face.

Ellie pushed it away and studied it.

"Mac, early morning, didn't argue, brought food. Sam, no arguing, brought food. Rick, no arguing. Hey, you didn't give me a time for Rick."

Cleo narrowed her eyes. "Ten."

Ellie nodded and noted it. "Okay, Rick at ten, no arguing. Val came twice, argued on the first visit, and brought food the second time.

"Scarlett, before lunch, Susie had tea and they argued. Bill, no arguing, no food. Andy argued with her. Did he bring food? And what did they argue about?"

"Yes, he brought her some things from the store," Lola said.

"They argued over money, too," Cleo added. "He wanted more money to expand the store. Susie wasn't sure it would make more money, though, so she said it might not be worth it. She asked him to run some numbers."

"Okay, got it." Ellie added the information to the list, then continued reading. "Delilah, no arguing, no food, but asked for money."

"Yeah, that's right," Cleo said.

Ellie sucked in a deep breath and stared down the list.

"Which one of them did it, Ellie?" Lola asked her.

"I'm not sure. There are probably a few people we can say are less likely, but I'm not striking any from the list yet."

"Now what are we going to do?" Cleo asked. She narrowed her eyes and flexed her claws. "Capture them, tie them up, and scratch a confession out of someone?"

"No, of course not," Ellie said. "I'm going to try to get

some writing samples from a few of these people, particularly the ones who argued with Aunt Susie. If anyone of them matches, I'll take it to Rick."

Cleo wrinkled her furry nose.

"But first," Ellie said. "We're going to eat and get some sleep for the trip back to Winwick tomorrow."

"Dish, dish, dish, dish," Lola chanted.

"All right, all right, I'm getting it," Ellie said as she darted into the pantry. This proved to be a huge change in her life, she reflected, as her mind turned to the task of cleaning out her house in Winwick. It didn't stay there long before it ran through the list she'd made courtesy of Cleo and Lola. Plenty of people could have killed her aunt. But which one did the deed?

CHAPTER 13

*E*llie knelt on the thick rug and stared under the chair, her eyes narrowed. Two green eyes stared back.

"No," the cat growled.

"Cleo, come on, get out here."

"I said no," Cleo repeated.

"It's not that bad!" Ellie said.

"Come on, Cleo," Lola called. "We're going in the car!"

"No, you're going in the car. I'm going in a carrier. I won't do it."

"Do you want to stay here by yourself?" Ellie asked.

"No. But I don't want to go in the carrier."

"It's for your own safety. I don't want you to get hurt climbing around in the car."

"Why doesn't Lola have to go in one?"

"Lola has a seatbelt for her collar."

"Then I'll wear a seatbelt."

"You don't have a collar. I checked."

A low growl emanated from the cat as Ellie reached her hand under the chair. She hissed and smacked at it.

Ellie yanked her hand back and frowned. "I'm two seconds from leaving you here, Cleo."

"I will sit on my own in the car."

"Fine," Ellie said. She stood from the floor and brushed her pants off. "Come on out and I'll carry you to the car."

"I can walk."

"I wouldn't want your feet to get dirty."

"They'll be fine," the cat answered as she slinked from under the couch. "A little dirt won't—"

Her voice cut off as Ellie grabbed hold of her with both hands. The cat whipped her body back and forth in a frantic struggle to get loose.

"Help! HELP! I'm being hurt! I'm being killed!" Cleo screamed. Her paws flailed as she writhed in Ellie's grip. She swiped at her, trying to scratch any flesh she could find. White fangs sought to dig into any surface. "I'll kill you! I WILL KILL YOU!"

Ellie shoved the cat into the carrier, flipping the lid closed and zipping it as quickly as she could. She stood and wiped a beat of sweat from her brow as she blew out a breath.

Lola glanced wide-eyed at her. "Is she okay?"

"No, I am not," Cleo answered. "I'm being held captive in a box. I was manhandled and shoved inside. I will be filing a complaint with the ASCPA. This is animal cruelty."

"Oh, you're fine," Ellie said as she slung the carrier's straps over her shoulder and grabbed her keys and purse. "Come on, Lola."

The dog hurried after her, scurrying through the door and onto the porch. She trundled down the few steps to the grass below, sniffing around as Ellie locked the door. With a final jimmy to ensure it held, Ellie let the screen door swing closed and carried Cleo's carrier down to the car. She set the carrier in the backseat, swinging the seatbelt over it to hold it on the seat.

"I hate you," Cleo said, narrowing her eyes at Ellie through the mesh.

Ellie slammed the door on any further comments and hurried to the other side, opening the rear door and ushering Lola into the car. With a tentative leap, Lola dove into the car, her rear end dangling she struggled to pull her girth inside. Ellie shoved her all the way in and clipped the seatbelt on her collar before sliding behind the wheel.

She fired the engine and pulled down the drive.

"WHOA!" Cleo shouted from the backseat. "Slow down. You're driving like a maniac."

"I am not," Ellie answered. "I'm not even going fifteen."

"Well, I can't tell. I'm stuck in this crate and pinned against the seat."

Lola sniffed at the carrier, sticking her nose against the mesh.

"Stop blowing on me, you big lug," Cleo grumbled.

"Pipe down back there, you two," Ellie said with a glance in the rearview mirror.

She swung the car onto the street housing the police station and in minutes, she'd eased into a parking space in front of the tan brick building.

"I'll be right back," she said, swinging the door open and climbing from the seat.

Ellie stepped into the cool morning air and retrieved the envelope from inside the car. She slammed the door shut as Lola stared at her, fogging the window with her breath. With a wave to the dog, she strode up the few concrete steps and pulled the door to the building open.

No one sat at the desk blocking the entrance to the rear. Ellie approached, finding a bell and a note. She crinkled her brow at the unmanned police station as she tapped the bell with her palm.

She sucked in a deep breath and drummed her fingers on

the Formica counter as she waited. A tall, dark-haired man hurried from the offices in the back.

"Good morning," he said as he crossed the room, fiddling to re-attach his weapon's belt around his waist.

Ellie raised her eyebrows at the lax protocols in the department.

"Good morning. I have something for Sheriff Rick."

"Oh, okay," the man answered. "Uh, is this in regards to—"
"

"Susie Byrne's murder. I'm her niece, Ellie." Ellie set the envelope down and stuck her hand out.

The man accepted it and gave it a shake. "Oh, nice to meet you. I'm Nathan, one of the deputies in town." He glanced behind him and thumbed toward the office. "We don't get a lot of crime around Salem Falls, so Sunday mornings aren't really all that exciting. Hence my time in the office."

"Ah," Ellie said with a nod, "well, I suppose that's a good thing." He nodded and smiled at her. Ellie waited a moment, then continued. "Well, I've got the threatening notes my aunt received before she died. Rick said to drop them off and he'd keep them as evidence."

She slid the envelope across the counter toward Nathan. He patted it.

"Got it, thanks. I'll put it on Rick's desk and he'll get it first thing tomorrow."

"Uh, shouldn't you log it as evidence? I mean, if they were to go missing, that wouldn't be good."

"Oh, right, yes, I can do that. And then I'll just let him know they're in evidence. Though again, Salem Falls is a pretty sleepy town, so I'd be surprised if they went missing from the Sheriff's office." He offered an amused grin as his head bobbed up and down.

"Well, you did have a murder, so let's not take any chances."

"That we did, yes. Well, I will put these right into evidence."

"Great, thanks."

"And you take care now. Will we be seeing you around more?"

Ellie backed toward the door. "Oh, yeah. I'm moving up here. I'm just headed home now to pack a few more things."

"Great. Well, I'll see you around then."

Ellie smiled and waved before pushing through the door into the misty air. A late morning fog had settled over the town, shrouding its buildings in a fluffy white blanket and reducing visibility drastically.

Ellie smoothed her hair behind her ears as the damp weather wreaked havoc on it in the few seconds it took her to race to the car. She slid inside and slammed the door shut, locking out any of the moisture.

"Where did this fog come from?" she asked as she fired the engine.

"I don't know where fog comes from, Ellie," Lola answered.

"Let's hope it lifts once we're out of town. Otherwise, it's going to be a miserable drive."

"It already is," Cleo lamented.

"It hasn't been that bad," Lola answered.

Ellie backed from her space and swung onto the road, careful to check for cars hiding in the dense soup.

"What are we going to do when we get there, Ellie?" Lola asked, her nose reaching into the front seat. "Can we take a nap on your bed?"

"As tempting as that would be, we probably should get a start on organizing a few things so the packing goes quickly."

"Okay," Lola said.

"Ugh," Cleo answered. "Pass. I will take the nap. You organize."

Ellie shot a glance in the rearview mirror and shook her head. "I wouldn't expect anything less."

Her forehead crinkled and she did a double-take in the mirror. A car hovered behind her. Its headlights did little to pierce the heavy fog.

"Why is this guy so close?" Ellie murmured.

Lola glanced behind them. "Should I bark?" She glanced at Ellie, her frowny mouth forming an "o" as she prepared to howl.

"No, don't bark. It won't do any good." Ellie flicked her gaze to the road ahead. "Must be a local. He's probably impatient because I'm driving so slow."

Ellie slowed more and inched to the shoulder.

"Now you're driving even slower," Cleo said.

"Yes, I know. He can go around me if he wants."

The tires hit the rough gravel on the side of the road. Ellie depressed the window button and waved her fingers out the slit, motioning for the other driver to pass her.

"Go!" she yelled as the car hovered behind her.

With an exasperated huff, she glanced in the side mirror before motioning again, this time in a larger fashion. "GO!"

The car refused to inch around her, instead, slowing to match her pace as she rumbled along the road with two tires on the berm.

"Fine, it's your funeral," she grumbled as she accelerated and swung back onto the road.

As she did, the other car shot around her.

"What an idiot," she shouted, waving her arms in the air as she slowed again. The car cut her off, nearly crinkling her front bumper in the process.

Ellie slowed again, shaking her head at the incident before she glanced in her mirrors and continued down the road.

"I'm really starting to wonder about this town."

"You're still going to move here, aren't you?" Lola asked.

"Yes, I'm still going to move here, but some of these people are idiots."

"You don't have to tell me twice," Cleo agreed. "And make that most of them."

The car continued to meander down the road through the thick soup, passing several cross streets. As she left one cross street behind, headlights appeared in her mirror.

The other car swung behind her and accelerated until it hung on her back bumper.

"Again?"

Lola glanced behind. "It's the same car, Ellie. I can smell it."

"Yeah, I thought so."

The road hugged the stream, making it impossible for Ellie to move to the side. The car continued to tailgate her. She flicked her gaze between the road ahead and the car behind.

As they reached a stone bridge where the road crossed the stream, the car shot into the other lane. It pulled level with her as their front tires vibrated across the metal slats.

"What the—"

With a sudden jerk, the car fishtailed in front of her. This time it made contact. The sickening scrape of metal on metal tore through the air. Ellie slammed on her brakes and swerved. The other car continued to push her. She smashed into the stone side of the bridge before she came to a halt.

The other car sped away, tires squealing, as her engine sputtered and died.

CHAPTER 14

The seatbelt jerked against her neck and she bounced between it and the seat from the impact. Lola lost her footing and tumbled onto the floor. Cleo's carrier remained snug against the back seat.

"Ugh," Ellie groaned. She pried her shaky hands from their white-knuckled grip on the steering wheel. With a glance over her shoulder, she scanned the back seat. "Is everyone okay?"

Lola's wrinkled face stared up at her. "I think so."

"Cleo?"

"Yeah, I'm fine. Terrified, but fine."

"Now you see why I insisted on putting you into the carrier. You could have been seriously hurt if you were out."

Ellie swung the car door open. "Stay right there a minute."

She stepped into the damp air and surveyed the damage. Scrapes creased one side of her bumper. The other side had been smashed into the hood, which also sported a crinkle. Part of the bumper bent back, threatening to scrape against the tire. Steam rose from the hood.

Ellie's shoulders slumped as she surveyed her damaged vehicle. She could likely drive it back to the manor but definitely not across the state to Winwick.

She slid behind the wheel again and grabbed her phone and pulled up the number for the police station.

"Is it bad?" Cleo asked.

"It's not good," Ellie answered as the line trilled.

"Salem Falls Police Department. This is Nathan."

"Hi, Nathan, this is Ellie Byrne. We just met about twenty minutes ago."

"Yep, I remember. I logged that into evidence just like you asked. Don't worry."

"Thanks, this isn't about that. Someone just ran me off the road over on Stonewater Bridge."

"Oh, no. Is everyone okay and do either of the cars need a tow?"

"It was a hit-and-run. The other driver took off. We're all okay in the car. I'm not sure if I can drive mine. Maybe."

"Okay, well, you sit tight and I'll be right there. Stay in the vehicle, okay?"

"Sure. Thanks."

Ellie ended the call and glanced over the gently flowing stream below her. "Thank goodness the wall held," she murmured, imagining her car taking a plunge into the icy waters.

"This car couldn't crash through a stone wall," Cleo said. "It's too cheap."

"Thank you, peanut gallery," Ellie said, shooting an annoyed glance into the back seat. "It was the best I could afford, okay?"

"Well next time you're planning on taking us on a road trip, at least buy a decent vehicle. I like to travel in style."

"I'll keep it in mind," Ellie said through clenched teeth. She toggled on her cell phone's display and checked the time.

It had been less than two minutes since she'd placed the call. It felt like time was standing still.

She glanced at her door. The lock mechanism stood up after she'd popped the door open to assess the damage. She swatted it down before she checked the time again.

Within another minute, red and blue lights flashed behind her. A patrol car raced toward the bridge, swinging sideways on the street to block access to the road. Nathan climbed from the car and hurried toward the scene.

Lola reclaimed her stance on the backseat and barked at the uniformed officer as he approached. "Stop that," Ellie hissed before she swung her door open.

"Hey, Ellie," he said as he rounded her vehicle and glanced at the damage. He winced. "That doesn't look good."

"No. I haven't tried to start the car. It stalled when I hit the bridge."

"Your bumper might be rubbing your tire. I'll call a tow truck."

"Oh, well, I can try to drive it. I've got the dog and cat with me."

"Oh," Nathan said, raising his eyebrows. "Well, I can take you all back to the manor."

"Okay, thanks," Ellie said as he called a tow company.

After ending the call, he flipped open a notebook. "Did you get the plate?"

"No, I didn't. I was so stunned."

"Anything distinctive about the car?"

"Umm, it was black. Dirty. I'm not sure of the make, but it was like a small SUV. A crossover maybe."

Nathan nodded as he jotted it down.

"I didn't see the driver at all," Ellie added.

"Okay, no idea if it was a man or woman?"

Ellie shook her head with a wince. "No. I couldn't see

anything. It was like they were wearing a hood or a hat or something."

"Got it," Nathan said, making another note. "Tow truck should be here soon. Why don't we get the animals moved to the cruiser."

"Okay," Ellie said. She pulled open the back door to a cacophony of barking. "Stop that barking."

She offered a nervous smile at Nathan as she clipped Lola's leash on her and tugged her out of the vehicle. "Come on, Lola, you've got to go in the back of the police car."

As Ellie walked the dog to the cruiser, she heard Cleo shouting from the back seat.

"Officer? Officer! I'd like to report a crime. An assault. I was minding my own business when suddenly I was grabbed from behind. The perpetrator shoved me into this black bag and pinned me against this seat. I—"

"Come on, you," Ellie said as she released the seatbelt and pulled the carrier from the seat.

"Good thing you had them secured. They could have been seriously harmed, even in a minor crash like this," Nathan said.

"Tell that to the cat. She fought me the entire way."

Nathan chuckled as Ellie shoved the carrier into the backseat of the police car. She swung the door shut as the black cat continued her protests.

A tow truck rumbled toward them moments later. A grizzled fellow with an unlit cigar clenched between his teeth leapt from his perch in the truck. His grease-stained uniform sported a name tag that read "Tony."

"Hi, Tony," Nathan said. "Wanted you to take a look at Ellie's car here. Someone rammed her into the bridge. It may be drivable, but I didn't want her to take the chance."

Tony grunted a response and nodded his head at Ellie.

"Hi, I'm Ellie," she said, opting for a wave rather than a handshake.

The man offered another unintelligible groan before he waddled his pot-bellied body over to the car. He frowned at it, bending over to peer underneath before he straightened.

"She run?"

"I'm not sure. It stalled after I hit the wall. I haven't tried it."

He raised his eyebrows. "Either way, she'll need to come into the shop to be fixed."

"Right," Ellie said.

"I can tow it there now, save you the trouble of bringing it by later or towing it if she don't make it."

"Okay, that's fine. And if you could get me an estimate, I'll call my insurance company."

He offered her a salute before he lumbered back to the tow truck and climbed inside. After a few minutes of maneuvering, he leapt from the truck and hooked the car up.

"Won't have an estimate until late tomorrow," he shouted as the car's front end rose in the air.

"That's fine. Thank you!" Ellie called back over the whine of the tow truck's motor.

"Thanks, Tony," Nathan said. "Ready to head back to the manor?"

Ellie nodded and climbed into the front seat. Lola pressed her nose against the wire cage separating them. Ellie gave the cold, wet skin a tap. "It's fine, Lola. We'll be home soon."

"Poor animals," Nathan said as he killed the flashing lights and swung the car around toward the manor. "They were probably frightened."

"They'll be happy to be home," Ellie agreed.

Within ten minutes, the now-familiar form of the sprawling manor appeared between the trees. The police cruiser bounced up the gravel drive before easing to stop near the porch.

The gravel crunched under Ellie's feet as she stood and tugged open the back door.

Lola's tail wagged. "We're home!"

Ellie pulled her from the car while Nathan grabbed the cat carrier.

"I can take that," Ellie said.

"I've got it."

"Don't let him drop me!" Cleo warned.

"Thanks."

Ellie dug in her purse to find the keys as she trotted up the stairs to the porch. Within minutes, they were settled in the house and the police cruiser was pulling away in a cloud of dust.

Ellie unzipped Cleo's carrier. The black cat zipped out of the bag and ran, belly scraping the floor, under the nearest chair.

"What now, Ellie?" Lola asked.

"First, I'm going to call Mia and tell her I'm not coming back to Winwick this week. And then I'm going to start trying to figure out who killed Aunt Susie and who is trying to kill me."

Ellie pulled her phone from her purse before tossing the leather bag onto the couch. She scrolled to Mia's name and pressed the call button.

The line trilled a few times before Mia picked up.

"Hey, you home already? What did you do? Drive at 500 miles per hour?"

"Hey, Mia. No, I'm back at the manor. I won't be making it home this week."

"What? Why?"

Ellie sighed as she paced the floor. "I was in an accident. I'm fine, but the car is wrecked."

"Oh no! Ellie! Are you sure you're okay? Did you go to the hospital?"

"No, I didn't go to the hospital. I'm fine. It wasn't *that* bad, but bad enough that I couldn't drive across the state."

"What happened?"

"Someone ran me off the road."

"WHAT!" Mia shouted. "Ellie, you need to get out of there. It's not safe there."

"No, it isn't. It wasn't for my aunt and now I'm being targeted. Someone threw a rock through my window yesterday and today I was run off the road. But I'm not leaving. I'm going to solve this."

A shuffling sounded on the other end of the line. "Please tell me you at least called the police."

"I did. They brought me home. They're aware of everything that's happening."

"Okay, well, I'm coming up there."

"No, you don't have to."

"Ellie, I'm coming. I'm just tossing a few things into a suitcase and I'm in the car, okay? You can't do this alone."

"You've got work, Mia."

"I'll take some time off. I'm not going to let you go through this alone. I'll text you when I'm on the road. Don't do anything until I get there, promise?"

"I won't do anything dangerous," Ellie promised.

"Close enough. I'll be there in a few hours."

"I'll get a bedroom ready for you. Outside of the death threat looming over me, you'll love this place."

"We'll see."

The link clicked on the other end and Ellie ended the call. She blew out a breath and rubbed her forehead with her palm.

Lola shuffled into the foyer and stared up at Ellie. "What now?"

"Mia's coming to help us," Ellie said.

"Who's coming? Friend? Friend is coming?"

"Yes, a friend is coming."

Lola's tail wagged furiously. "I like friends. I like who's coming. It's exciting."

"Yes, it is. It would be more exciting if we weren't just run off the road, but I'm excited for Mia to see this place." She stared up the stairs. "Come on, Lola. Let's get a bedroom ready for Mia."

Lola bounded up the stairs behind her. "Okay!"

"Which one should we pick?" Ellie passed up the master bedroom and continued down the hall, peeking into the bedrooms on the second floor. She picked the large octagon at the back of the house and pulled sheets off of the furniture.

With the bedding gathered, she waddled downstairs to freshen it in the laundry. After tossing it into the washer, she wet a rag and headed back up the stairs to dust the room. When she had it halfway presentable, she did a quick clean-up of the bathroom.

She tossed the bedding into the dryer before she collapsed onto the couch. Lola leapt up next to her, settling down at her side.

Ellie patted her flank. "Whew, maybe I don't want to reopen the B&B. This is hard work!"

Lola yawned and settled her head on her front paws. "Yeah, it was."

"You barely did anything!"

"I went up and down the stairs every time you did!" Lola said as her eyes began to close.

"Right. Well, you go ahead and take a snooze while the bedding dries."

* * *

Ellie raced through the trees. A thick fog clung to the forest. Leaves crunched under her feet as branches tore at her arms and face. Tears streamed down her cheeks as she ran. Overhead, a bird cawed as it circled above the treeline.

Footsteps followed behind her. The sound of a gun cocking echoed.

Ellie froze, her eyes wide. She ducked behind a tree and held her breath. Her teeth dug into her lower lip as she prayed she wouldn't be spotted.

She clutched at the rough bark behind her as footsteps approached her location.

"I'll find you," a voice said.

Ellie's breath caught in her throat. Then another noise broke through the air. A shrill ringing.

Her eyes grew to the size of saucers. Was the sound coming from her? She grabbed at her pockets. The sound rang through the air again.

Ellie felt herself slipping away as the world melted around her.

* * *

Ellie bolted up, gasping for breath as she awoke. She glanced around the room. The floral print of the armchair met her gaze along with the white trim of the fireplace. She blew out a long breath. It was nothing more than a dream.

Her phone chimed. She swiped it from the coffee table. A missed call message slid onto the screen as she toggled it on. Mac's name appeared. She pressed the button to return the call.

"Ellie?" he gasped, answering on the first ring.

"Hi, Mac. Sorry, I dozed off on the couch and didn't get the phone in time. What's up?"

"Are you okay? I just heard about the accident."

"Yeah, I'm okay."

"What happened?"

"Some idiot ran me off the road and I crashed into the bridge. I'm fine. The same can't be said for the car."

"Aw, shucks, Ellie. I'm sorry to hear this. I guess that ruins your plans to go home, huh?"

"It sure did that. That's okay. I'd rather stay and figure this out."

"Do you need anything?"

"Uh, no. I have a friend coming over to stay with me. I was just about to head into town after I finished cleaning up the bedroom for her to grab some groceries."

"I can make the run for you."

"No, Mac, it's fine."

"Well, the least I can do is drive you to the store."

"That's ridiculous. The walk won't kill me."

"A drive out of town nearly did!"

"Good point. Well, I hate to take up your Sunday afternoon, but—"

"Don't think anything of it," Mac said. "I'll be right over."

"Okay, take your time. I've got to get the sheets out of the dryer and the bed made."

"No problem. I'll let myself in. Though by the time I get over there, you may be finished."

Ellie dragged herself from the couch with a stretch. Lola lifted her head. "Just stay there, I'm going to make the bed."

With a sigh, Lola laid her head down. Ellie hurried into the laundry room and pulled the bedding from the dryer. She waddled upstairs with the load and hurried to make the bed.

A loud barking downstairs announced Mac's arrival. Ellie heard his booming voice moments later. "Hiya, Big Lol!"

Ellie smoothed out the fresh duvet and fluffed the pillows before striding from the room. She bounded down the stairs. Mac knelt on the ground with Lola, her tail wagging at him.

"Hi, Mac," Ellie greeted him. "Thanks for this. Let me grab my purse."

"No problem," he said, rising to his feet. "And no rush!"

"Are we going somewhere, Ellie?" Lola asked.

"Okay," Ellie said, slinging her purse over her shoulder. "She gave Lola a pat on the head. I'm just going to run to the store with Mac before Mia gets here. You sit tight and watch the house, okay?"

Mac chuckled as she pushed the screen door open. "You remind me so much of Susie. She used to talk to those animals the same way. Like they could understand her."

Ellie offered an amused giggle. "You don't say."

As they drove into town, Mac asked more about the accident. Ellie explained it again.

"Did you get a look at the car?"

"No," Ellie said. "Outside of it being a dirty black car, I have no idea."

"Gosh, Ellie, I'm sorry about this. I never expected this to happen when I sent that letter to you and encouraged you to come."

"Don't be. You couldn't have known. Heck, you didn't even know Susie was murdered when we first spoke."

"Maybe I ought to stay at the house, too."

"I'll be okay. As soon as Mia gets there, we'll be okay. Plus, we have Lola. She barks at the drop of a hat, so nothing will get past her!"

Mac offered a boisterous chuckle. "That she does. Susie said the same thing." He swung the car into the parking lot of the small grocer and eased into a spot.

"I'll just be a few moments."

"I'll come in with you," Mac said. "I need to pick up a TV dinner or two."

"Ugh," Ellie said as she climbed from the car, "tell me you're joking."

"I'm not. Why?"

"Those things are disgusting. Come on, Mac."

"They're fast and easy. And they aren't half bad. I splurge on the Stouffer's though. Only downside is that they don't come with the little brownie bite for dessert. So I have to buy Hostess."

Ellie shook her head but laughed as she jiggled a shopping cart loose from the stack of them and pushed it into the produce section. Mac picked up a small basket and let it swing from his fingers.

"Put that down. You can eat with us this week."

"Now, I'm not going to put you out, Ellie."

"And I'm not going to let you eat TV dinners all week. I'll be cooking for Mia anyway."

Mac shook his head. "Well at least let me bring a dessert."

"As long as it's not Hostess, fine." Ellie stuffed leafy lettuce into a produce bag.

"I'll splurge for a pie over at Salem Sweets."

"On most days, I won't say no to a Ho-ho, but I'm trying to raise the bar." She selected a variety of colorful peppers and added them to the cart.

Mac studied the fruit selection.

"Can you grab a container of the strawberries?" Ellie asked.

Mac added a large plastic bin of berries to Ellie's cart and they continued through the aisles. "So, Susie was an investor in this place, huh?" Ellie questioned.

"Yeah, she was."

Ellie added a freshly baked baguette to her cart. "And she wasn't getting along with the owner."

"Where'd you hear that?"

"Uh, around," Ellie said. "Andy's the owner's name, right?"

"Uh—" Mac began when another voice entered the mix.

"Did I hear my name?"

Ellie twisted to face a stout middle-aged man. With thick black glasses and his blonde hair slicked neatly into a side-parted style, he stood a hair taller than Ellie. Ellie stared at the polka-dotted bowtie poking from under the collar of his blue shirt.

"Andy!" Mac said with a broad smile. "How the heck are you?"

"Getting by." He studied Ellie with his green eyes. "I don't think we've met."

Ellie stuck out her hand. "Ellie Byrne. I'm Susie's niece."

"Oh!" Andy said, his eyebrows shooting upward and his lips forming an "o." "Well, a pleasure to meet you. My condolences on your loss."

Ellie arched an eyebrow at the empty statement. His words sounded hollow. She didn't imagine anything he'd just said was true.

"Thanks," she offered.

"So, Mac, what'll happen to all of Susie's things? Did she have a will or—" He let his statement hang as he cocked his head at Mac.

"You're looking at her!" Mac said, motioning to Ellie.

Andy's eyes went wide before he quickly covered his reaction. His expression turned neutral after the momentary expression of surprise.

"Oh," he said, his voice clipped. "And you'll be disposing of them, certainly?" He offered a chuckle before continuing. "You won't be moving to a backwater burg like Salem Falls, surely."

"Actually, I am!" Ellie answered.

"You're looking at Salem Falls' newest resident!" Mac added, clapping his hands on Ellie's shoulders. "She's moving into the manor. May even reopen the B&B."

Ellie smiled at the man. A bead of sweat appeared at the edge of his perfectly coiffed hair. His lips formed a sour smile. "Well, I guess we'll be business partners then. Unless you'd be interested in selling your portion outright?"

"Let's let her settle in first, Andy."

"Of course," he said with a wrinkled nose. "Let me know when you want to talk. Either way, I hope you're a little smarter than your aunt. Otherwise, you may end up like her."

CHAPTER 15

*E*llie stood wide-eyed, following the departure of the
man who had just threatened her as he strode away.

"Wow, he's a little much," Ellie said, shoving the cart
ahead of her as she continued down the aisle. "Did he just
threaten me?"

"I wouldn't take anything he says too seriously. Andy's—
tightly wound," Mac settled on.

"And obviously he didn't like Aunt Susie."

"They had their differences," Mac admitted.

"I heard they were arguing over an expansion of the store.
Is that true?"

Mac sucked in a breath, his shoulders rising toward his
ears. "Yeah, they were. It's true. Andy wanted more money
and wanted to expand. Susie considered it a bad idea. She
thought he was overextending. Thought it would thin the
profit margins."

"Was she right?" Ellie inquired.

"Hard to say. Andy didn't have any real numbers. I'd
recommend you go over the numbers when you get a

moment before you agree to anything with him. Actually, before you even discuss anything with him."

Ellie flicked her eyes over to Mac, her brows raised. She set a box of Rosemary flavored crackers into the cart. "So, you don't trust him?"

"I didn't say—" Mac held up his hands. "Just take your time with everything. With you taking over all Susie's investments, everyone will want a piece of you. And they'll think they stand to get it because you're new."

"And Andy will try to take advantage of that?"

"Not just Andy."

"So, I'm moving into a town of pariahs, huh?"

"We're a nice town, Ellie. But that doesn't mean people won't try to take advantage of a situation."

"A situation one of them created." She browsed the cheese selection.

"I can't believe that."

"Someone killed her, Mac. And I'm going to find out who." Ellie added a few items to her cart before she pushed it away to another aisle. "He ought to expand his cheese selection."

They completed their purchases and climbed into the car. After a stop at the pie shop, Mac aimed the car for the manor. Ellie waved to Mac as he pulled down the drive with a toot, promising to return for dinner around six.

She hauled the groceries inside, finding a dog with a wiggling bottom waiting in the foyer. "Ellie!" Lola shouted as she stepped inside. She hopped onto her hind legs and danced around with excitement.

"Hi, Lola. I told you I wouldn't be long."

Cleo stalked from the living room. "Did you bring us anything?"

"No, I didn't."

The cat wrinkled her nose. "Of course, you didn't. And you owed us. At least me."

Ellie schlepped the bags down the hall and into the kitchen. "I owed you, huh?"

"Yeah. After you assaulted me and then nearly killed me in the car crash."

"I'm not sure I'll be able to handle all your drama, Cleo," Ellie answered as she stowed the produce in the refrigerator.

The doorbell rang through the house, sending Lola scratching her way across the hardwood and toward the front door with a boisterous bark.

"Can you handle Lola's?" the cat shouted over the din with narrowed eyes.

Ellie offered an unimpressed glance as she strode past the cat toward the door. "Lola, enough!" she shouted.

"Someone's at the door!" Lola yelled, punctuating the statement with another bark.

"Yes, I heard that, thank you. Sit down."

Ellie glanced through the peephole above the frosted glass insert. A lanky young man stood outside with a messenger bag slung over his chest and hanging at his side. He rocked on his feet with his hands shoved in the pockets of his gray khakis. A lock of his thick, dark hair escaped over his forehead, threatening to poke his eye.

"Who is this?" Ellie murmured.

"I don't know. I can't see," Lola said. "But it could be a killer."

"He's not a killer. He doesn't look like he could hurt a fly."

"Those are the worst kind," Cleo said as she darted past in search of a hiding spot. "Got to watch out for those quiet ones."

Ellie tugged the door open and greeted him through the screen door. "Hello, can I help you?"

"Uh, hi," he answered as Lola barreled toward the door.

"Lola, no!"

"It's Jake! Hi, Jake!" Lola exclaimed as she nosed open the screen door and leapt onto the long-limbed twenty-something.

He chuckled and rumpled the dog's ears. "Hi, big Lol."

"Want to come in?" Lola asked. "We can play!"

Ellie ignored the dog's commentary. "Sorry, she gets a little excited about people."

"It's okay. I'm used to her," Jake answered. "I'm Jacob Braedon. Call me Jake. From the Salem Falls Herald. I'm really sorry to disturb you, but Scarlett sent me over."

Ellie crossed her arms over her chest. "Oh, she did, huh? Is this about selling the paper?"

"No," he answered, scratching his head as he wrinkled his nose. "We, uh, heard about the accident this morning. She sent me to get the scoop on the breaking news."

"You're kidding," Ellie said.

He pursed his lips and shook his head. "No, sorry."

"Slow news day?"

"Every day is a slow news day in Salem Falls," Jake answered.

"Well, I guess I shouldn't make you waste the trip. Come on in," Ellie said, holding the screen door open.

"Sorry about this," Jake said as he stepped into the foyer. "I hate to bother you but Scarlett insisted."

"I'll bet she did. Can I get you something to drink?"

"No, thanks. I'm fine."

Ellie motioned to the living room. "Grab a seat in here. What can I tell you about the incident?"

Jake plopped onto the couch. Lola leapt up next to him, her tail wagging. He gave her another pat on the head before he tugged a notepad and pen from within the confines of his bag.

He flipped it open and clicked the pen. "Nathan said it was a hit-and-run?"

"Yes," Ellie said as she eased into the armchair across from him.

"Hey, watch it, I'm under here," Cleo's muffled voice shouted.

Ellie bounced around on the chair a few times for good measure.

"Jerk," Cleo huffed.

The edges of Ellie's lips curled upward before she answered. "Yes, the person was following me and then pulled around me and cut me off. I ended up crashing into the stone bridge."

"And did you recognize the car?"

"No," Ellie said with a head shake.

"Any description?"

"It was a black car. It was dirty." Ellie chuckled. "Sorry, it's not much of a description."

"Were you alone in the vehicle?"

"No, I had the dog and cat. I was on my way home to Winwick for the week to start packing for the move here. The animals convinced me to take them." She chuckled at the statement. "So, I loaded them in the car for the drive."

"Everyone was okay, right?"

"Oh, yeah. I was just a little rattled, but I had Lola seat-belted in the backseat. She just slipped off the seat. Cleo was in her carrier—"

"Still mad about that," Cleo added.

"—so she was fine."

Jake nodded as he continued to make notes on the page.

"What time was this?"

"We left around eight-thirty and I made a stop at the police station so I'd say it was around nine."

Jake lifted his eyebrows as he wrote. "You stopped at the police station?"

"Yes."

"Was there a reason for that?" he questioned.

"There was," Ellie said with a slow nod. She pondered sharing the information, weighing the odds of divulging it to the reporter. It would come out eventually, she figured. "I found a few threatening notes among my aunt's things. I took them to the police department to help with their investigation into her murder."

Jake lifted his eyebrows. "Threatening notes, really?"

Ellie nodded. "Yes. I assumed they may be connected to the murder and felt it was best the sheriff had them as evidence."

"I see," he said, scratching on his notepad. "Can you tell me what they said?"

"Demands, threats like you'll regret it if you don't give me what I want. That kind of thing."

"Were they handwritten or typed or—?"

"Handwritten," Ellie answered.

"So, we could potentially match someone's handwriting to the notes and find the source."

Ellie nodded. "Yes. At least, that's what I hope. And that may give us some clue about who murdered her."

He scanned his notes before he flicked the notebook closed. "Well, I think that does it. I'll follow up with the police about the notes, but I have all the information I need about the accident."

Ellie stood as he did. "Hopefully that's enough to appease Scarlett."

"Nothing's ever enough to appease Scarlett," the young man said as he stepped toward the foyer. "But I have enough for a story."

"Great. I'll look for it on the front page tomorrow," Ellie joked.

"Speaking of, is there a photo you like for the spread?"

"Are you serious? It was a hit-and-run. I was joking about being on the front page."

Jake winced. "I wasn't. The newest member of the Salem Falls community targeted in a hit-and-run after her aunt was murdered is going to make the front page, above the fold."

Ellie's eyes widened as she lifted her eyebrows. "Just put a picture of my smashed car," she suggested.

"Oh, great idea. Is it over at Tony's?"

"It is."

"I'll stop by there and grab a few shots of the wreckage. That kind of carnage will really draw readers in."

"I'll bet."

Jake offered her a smile as he pushed the screen door open and stepped onto the porch. "For what it's worth, I hope they find the person who killed Susie. She was always really nice to me. She's the reason I have my job."

"Oh, really?"

"Yeah, she hired me. I'm not sure I had Scarlett's full approval, though she doesn't seem to mind now."

"Well, I'm sure Aunt Susie picked you for a reason. You must have deserved it."

He nodded and smiled at her. "If there's anything I can do to help, let me know."

"Actually," Ellie answered before he let the door go, "I don't suppose you could get me a sample of Scarlett's hand-writing."

Jake's eyebrows raised toward his hairline and his forehead pinched. "Do you really think she may have killed Susie?"

Ellie shrugged. "First of all, the person who wrote the notes may not be the killer. Second, I could use it to rule her out if the writing doesn't match." She shrugged again as she crossed her arms. "I just—I know they argued before Aunt Susie died. So, I'm comparing anyone who had a beef with her to the notes."

He wiggled his eyebrows as he stared out over the wooded lot. "Scarlett definitely had one of those. Though, to be fair, she's got a beef with almost everyone in town."

Ellie chuckled at the statement, certain he wasn't embellishing. He thrust his hands into his pockets and nodded. "Anyway, yes, I'll try to get you something."

"Thank you," Ellie said. "Really, I appreciate this. And I hope to just rule her out."

"Should I just stop by with it when I have it?"

"Sure. Ah, just a second, I'll give you my number and you can text me."

They exchanged contact information. The young man nodded at her and offered a tight-lipped smile before he bounced down the stairs and climbed into his crossover.

A plume of dust followed in his wake as he blazed down the driveway. Ellie rested her chin on her cell phone, pondering if her trust in him was misplaced. She glanced down at Lola, who wagged her tail.

"I like him," Lola said.

"I do, too," Ellie answered as she pushed the door shut. "But can we trust him?"

CHAPTER 16

"Susie always trusted Jake," Cleo's voice called as she stretched out from under the armchair.

"That's a start, I guess." Ellie raised her eyebrows. "Maybe I put him in too tight of a spot, asking him to spy on his boss."

"She deserves it," Cleo said.

"And you said it was just to rule her out," Lola said.

"She was lying, dummy. If that handwriting matches, guess who's going to the slammer?"

"Who?" Lola questioned.

Cleo shook her head and squeezed her eyes shut. "You are so du—"

"Stop, Cleo," Ellie said with a sigh. "If Scarlett's handwriting is a match, yes, I would turn her in. I'd love to rule her out, but I'd also love to find who killed Aunt Susie and if it turns out it's Scarlett, well—" Ellie shrugged and left the statement unfinished.

"We'll tie her to a chair and I'll pop a claw in her a—"

"No," Ellie interrupted. "We'll turn her in and let the police handle it."

"Sheriff Ca— er, Sheriff Du—" Cleo shook her head. "Sheriff Rick can't handle anything."

Ellie raised her eyebrows at the cat. "Great job, Cleo. You only half-insulted him."

"And it zapped all my energy," the cat said with a yawn. "I'm going to sleep."

She stretched, her back arched high before she slinked back under the armchair. The doorbell rang again.

"You've *got* to be kidding me," Cleo groaned as Lola raced to the door, barking.

"Someone's here!" she shouted.

"You don't say," Ellie said with a shake of her head as she followed the dog to the door. "Shh, quiet. Stop barking."

She glanced through the peephole. A blonde in a floppy beanie with a weekend bag slung over her shoulder stood in a pair of leggings, boots, and a comfy tunic. Her hair fell in a braid over her shoulder as she glanced around.

Ellie yanked the door open with a broad grin. "Mia!"

The woman whipped her attention to the front door, her lips forming an equally wide smile. "Ellie!" she exclaimed. "Oh, thank goodness you're okay. I half expected to find you in a sling or with a giant bandage on your forehead."

"I'm fine! I told you that. Come in!"

Lola wagged her tail and sniffed in the air. "Who is this?" she asked.

Mia stepped through the door, her head swiveling to take in the space. "Mia, this is my Aunt Susie's dog, Lola. Well, now she's my dog. And there's a black cat hiding somewhere around here named Cleo. Lola, meet my best friend, Mia."

"Well, hi there, Lola," Mia said, giving the dog a pat on the head. She glanced around the space again. "Wow, this place looks great!"

"Hi, Mia," Lola said. Mia ignored it, unable to hear the dog's commentary.

"Told you," Ellie said, shoving her hands into her back pockets. "I'll show you around, but let's take your bag upstairs first."

Mia nodded as Ellie led her up the wooden stairs.

Lola followed. "She seems nice."

Ellie led Mia down the hall to the octagonal room overlooking the stream in the back. Mia dropped her bag as she stepped onto the hardwood inside.

"Oh my gosh! Ellie! This is amazing!" She hurried to the window to glance out at the tree-lined stream gently flowing through the property.

"I told you. This place is amazing. I'm lucky my aunt left it to me."

Mia's shoulders slumped as she spun to face Ellie. "I'm still bummed your moving."

"Seriously? I'm not that far. And this place is incredible!"

"Still, you're leaving your entire life behind, El. And are you sure you want to be stuck in a small town like this? I mean, your aunt was murdered here. How nice can it be?"

"Hey!" Lola interjected. "Salem Falls is a nice town."

"Salem Falls is a nice town," Ellie echoed.

"How nice can it be? There's a killer loose!" Mia retorted.

"Come on," Ellie said, waving her hand to dismiss the comment, "let me show you the rest of the place."

Mia hefted her overnight bag onto the luggage rack Ellie had placed next to the closet before they left the room. Ellie, with Lola in tow, led Mia around the house. They settled with a hot cup of tea on the patio off the breakfast nook.

Mia sipped at the hot liquid before she set the cup down on her saucer, tracing its outline with her index finger. "Well," she said with a sigh, "I guess I can see why you'd want to stay. The house is beautiful. But still—"

"Still nothing, Mia. I'm broke. Like beyond broke. I paid Luke with loose change, that's how broke. This is a godsend."

"But the move," Mia said with a pout. "You're leaving everything you know. Your friends, your house, your town."

"I'm leaving a house I can't afford in a town that's just okay. The friends part stinks, I agree. But I'll have this fabulous house where you all can come and visit me!"

Mia stared into the amber liquid. She blew out a long breath. "I just hate the idea of you moving five hours away. Especially after your aunt was murdered and now you're being targeted!"

Ellie reached across the table and grasped her hand. "I know. And I appreciate it. But honestly, I can't see a better way."

"What if you just sold this place and took the money? Would it be enough to keep your house in Winwick?"

Ellie pursed her lips as Lola stared at her, awaiting an answer.

"We're not moving, are we, Ellie?" Lola questioned.

Ellie sucked in a deep breath. "The truth is I don't want to do that. I don't want to sell the house and take the cash. Even if it saved the house in Winwick, I just— I don't want to live there anymore. I want a fresh start. And this provides it."

"But you weren't thinking about that before your aunt died."

"No, I was barely keeping my head above water. Actually, I wasn't keeping my head above water. I was drowning. And not just in debt. In everything. In self-pity and feelings of worthlessness. I need a fresh start."

"Can't you get one in Winwick? Sell the house. Get another place. Open a business there!"

Ellie shook her head. "Sorry, Mia. This place meant the world to my aunt. She really wanted me to have it and to keep it. And I'm going to honor her wishes. And besides, it gives me the perfect opportunity to get my life together."

Mia puckered her lips as she sucked in a breath. "I guess I can't change your mind."

"Nope," Ellie said with a shake of her head.

"Okay, well, the least I can do, then, is make sure this crazy town is safe for you. So, what's up with the investigation into your aunt's murder? And what about the accident?"

Ellie took another sip of her tea as Cleo arched her back before stretching her front feet onto the patio and dragging the rest of her body out with her. She leapt onto a chair next to Mia and stared at her.

"Hi, kitty!" Mia said.

"I don't like her look," Cleo said.

Ellie ignored her. "If the police have any leads, they aren't sharing. But I found a few notes among my aunt's things. Threatening notes."

Cleo narrowed her eyes at Mia. "She looks like a weirdo," Cleo added.

"I thought she was nice," Lola said.

"Did you give them to the police?"

"I did. But... I kept a copy." Ellie pulled the folded paper from within her cardigan pocket and passed it over to Mia.

Mia scanned the notes on the paper. Her eyes widened. "Ellie! These are terrible!"

"I'm afraid so." Ellie shrugged. "Maybe they're not connected to the murder, but I'd be surprised if they weren't."

"What else would they be?" Mia asked. She reached over and absent-mindedly stroked Cleo's head.

Cleo ducked away and batted at her hand. "Don't touch me, weirdo."

Ellie shook her head at Cleo as Lola said, "She's nice!" Lola stood and wandered toward Mia, her tail wagging. "You can pet me!"

"Oh, you're a playful little kitty," Mia said with a grin. She wiggled her fingers at Cleo.

Cleo leapt off the chair and disappeared into the house. "Idiot."

Ellie answered Mia's questions with a deep inhale. "Apparently, Aunt Susie had argued with a good number of people before her death. It could have been related to that."

"What did she argue with them about?"

"Money, mostly," Ellie answered. "She was an investor in a lot of local businesses. She didn't always agree with their business decisions."

Mia nodded. "Okay, so who did she argue with right before her death?"

"The list is long and varied," Ellie answered. She held a finger up as she stood from the table and hurried inside the kitchen. She returned with her list and plopped onto her chair.

"She was poisoned by a quick-acting toxin. So, any of the foods she ate that day could have been the source. Around the lunch hour would be the most likely time frame but it really could have been any time that day."

Ellie scanned the list before she spun it so both women could view it.

"So, we've got Mac with donuts but no arguments at eight."

"Donuts could have been laced with poison," Mia noted.

"No way," Lola said. "Cleo may be right about her!"

"I doubt it's Mac," Ellie said. "They were good friends. There's no reason he'd kill her."

"Could be something you don't know. Something not related to money," Mia answered.

"No, no, no," Lola insisted.

"I really don't think so," Ellie said. "Look, you'll get a chance to meet Mac at dinner tonight. You can let me know what you think after. And besides my gut instinct, eight is a bit early to have poisoned her given the time she died. I mean, in theory, it could have happened but it's less likely than some of these others. Plus, I haven't heard anything about any arguments between Aunt Susie and Mac in any time leading up to her murder."

"Okay, I'll keep an open mind on him and let you know my thoughts after I meet this Mac character. Who's next?"

"Sam, from the ice cream shop. They had tea together, but they didn't argue. And from what I understand, Aunt Susie and Sam got along."

"Says who?"

"Sam and a few others who knew Aunt Susie. Sam appreciated her business advice."

"You're too naive, Ellie. It's a good thing I came."

"No, Sam's innocent!" Lola said.

"Who's next?" Mia inquired.

"Sheriff Rick, innocent," Lola answered.

"Sheriff Rick," Ellie said. She shook her head. "Rick. The Sheriff. He brought no food and they had a minor altercation. Aunt Susie informed him of the threatening notes and told him she was afraid it would come to nothing good unless he did something about it."

"And the sheriff had no idea who was doing it?"

"He says Aunt Susie wouldn't let him keep the notes and didn't recognize the handwriting. He hadn't tracked anyone down related to it.

"Wow, he sounds like a real winner."

"Same thing I said. Maybe she isn't so bad after all," Cleo said as she stalked back onto the patio. She leapt onto the chair next to Mia.

Mia reached out to ruffle the cat's fur with a grin. "Let's not go that far," Cleo said.

"Okay, next person."

"Wait, I wasn't done with the sheriff," Mia answered.

"Sheriff Rick didn't kill her. Next person. Val, the owner of the diner. She argued with Susie *then* she returned with a pie and insisted Susie eat it. Val didn't eat any at all."

"Ohhhh, she sounds guilty! Do we have any samples of her handwriting?"

"No, but we should try to get one. Maybe we can stop by the diner for breakfast tomorrow."

"Sounds like a plan. Let's get this lady's signature and see if we can't catch a killer."

Ellie held up a finger. "Before we have her tried and convicted in the court of public opinion, there's more."

Ellie scanned the list. "Okay, Bill stopped by within the time frame but brought nothing but samples from the hardware store for a bedroom redo and they also didn't argue. They got along."

"Could the poison have been on the samples?"

"I'm not sure. I think it has to be ingested. But I suppose it could have gotten on her hands and then into her mouth if she didn't wash them after touching the samples."

"Something to keep in mind."

Ellie nodded. "Okay, here's a more plausible suspect, though. Andy, the local grocer. He brought her a food order from the store and they argued. He wanted more money to expand the grocery store. Aunt Susie didn't agree."

"Okay, so he killed her over it."

"Possibly. Last but not least, Delilah, the owner of the Right Meow pet store. She did not bring food and they didn't argue *but* she asked for money and seemed desperate about it."

Mia furrowed her brow. "How do you have all these details?"

Ellie squeezed her lips together. Lola and Cleo stared at her. "Go on, tell her," Cleo said.

"Yeah, we know everyone who was here that day. Tell her we told you."

"Aunt Susie kept a detailed journal."

Mia nodded. "So, these are her personal notes on what happened that day?"

"Yes, she jotted them down after each person left. I guess she kept records for business interactions and also because she'd received those threatening notes and wanted everything documented."

Mia scanned the list again. "Looks like we have a few people who are more likely than the others, but I wouldn't rule anyone out just yet."

"I asked someone for a sample of Scarlett's handwriting. We need to work on getting Val's and Andy's."

"And Sam's, Mac's, Rick's—"

"Rick did it," Cleo added.

"He did not!" Lola insisted.

Ellie shook her head and held up a hand. "One thing at a time. Let's get those three first and then move on from there."

"Yeah, move on to Sheriff Killer."

Ellie swiped a toy wand from the floor and poked at Cleo with it.

"I'm just saying, it's never the most obvious suspect," Mia said as Ellie discarded the feather-laden wand onto the table.

Her shoulders slumped and she made a face at Mia. "That's only in movies and novels."

Mia shook her head with her chin raised. "Real life, too! Cops are always after the wrong suspects." She grabbed the wand and waved it at the cat.

"Yeah, cops are—" Cleo stopped dead, her eyes narrowing at the wand. She dove after it, climbing onto the table to swipe at the moving feathers. "Got to get those feathers."

"Okay, fine. We'll start with the supposed red herrings and rule them out before we move on to the others."

"You said we're meeting with Mac tonight?" Mia held the wand high overhead jiggling it. Cleo leapt upward in an attempt to grab it.

"What are you doing, Cleo?" Lola asked as the cat swished her tail and eyed the feathers.

"Got to get those feathers," the cat answered through clenched teeth.

"He's coming over for dinner tonight."

"I'll work on getting a handwriting sample from him." Cleo grabbed hold of the feathers and tugged them toward her, pulling the wand from Mia's hands.

"Perfect, then we can rule him out first."

Mia stuck her tongue out at Ellie. "Nice work, kitty!" she said to Cleo, who bunny kicked the wand within an inch of its life.

"We'll see who has the last laugh now, feather wand!" Cleo shouted.

"Speaking of, I'd better get these two fed and start our dinner." Ellie stood and made her way to the kitchen.

Lola raced behind her. "Dish, dish, dish!"

Cleo dropped the feather wand and raced to the kitchen, leaping onto the counter and meowing.

Mia wandered in behind them with the mugs clutched in her hands.

"Just toss those in the sink, I'll get them later," Ellie said as she shook kibble into Lola's bowl.

"I've got 'em," Mia answered. She squirted dish soap into each and adjusted the tap.

Ellie cracked open a can of Ocean Whitefish and emptied it into Cleo's bowl, setting it in front of her.

"You know," Mia said as she sloshed the dishrag inside

one of the mugs. "The handwriting does kind of look more feminine than masculine."

"I agree," Ellie answered. "Which is another reason I can safely rule out Mac."

Mia rinsed the mugs and spun around, leaning against the counter as she dried her hands. "Still, the killer could have disguised their writing."

"What I don't understand is why they didn't type it or use the magazine cutouts."

"Magazine cutouts?" Mia said with a chuckle. "Talk about the stuff that happens in movies."

Ellie shook her head. "No, the note attached to the rock that crashed through my front window was in magazine cutouts."

"You're kidding."

"Nope. What I can't understand is why they used that for my threatening note, but they hand wrote my aunt's."

"Maybe it's not the same person."

"Maybe," Ellie said, handing a few milkbones to Lola. "Maybe it's someone just taking advantage of the situation and had no idea about the original notes."

"El, are you really sure you want to stay here? I mean, either a killer is targeting you or someone's using your aunt's murder to target you. Is this really the kind of place you want to be?"

With a roll of her eyes, Ellie tugged the refrigerator door open and pulled the produce bags she'd stowed there earlier. "We've been over that," she called.

"And I still think you're crazy," Mia answered as Ellie laid the food on the prep island.

Ellie shot her a glance. "Slice the peppers, would you?"

They spent the next hour finishing the dinner prepa-rations. As Ellie mixed the dressing for the salad, the sound of the screen door creaking open sent Lola racing for the front door. She let out a few loud barks before she settled.

"Hiya, big Lol!" Mac's booming voice said in the foyer.

Cleo leapt from her perch and stalked into the foyer to greet the man. "Hey, Mac," Cleo called as she sauntered away from the kitchen.

"Still think he's a killer?" Ellie murmured under her breath to Mia.

The blonde offered her a coy glance as the large man wandered into the kitchen. "Hope I'm not too early," he said.

Ellie spun to face him. "Aww, are those for me?"

Mac clutched a mixed bouquet in each hand. "Brought a set for each of you. Didn't want anyone to feel left out."

Lola wagged her tail at his feet before issuing a sneeze. "They're pretty," she said before another sneeze.

"Thank you, Mac," Ellie said, crossing the kitchen and relieving him of both bouquets. "Mac, meet my friend, Mia. Mia, this is Mac, Aunt Susie's attorney, and friend."

Mac smiled and stuck his hand out. "I'd say friend and attorney, but who's counting. Pleasure to meet you, Mia."

"Nice to meet you, Mac," Mia said, shaking his head. "And thank you for the flowers. That was very kind."

"I'll get two vases!" Ellie called as she stepped into the pantry. She returned with two pink glass vases in hand and filled them with water, cutting the stems of the flowers and arranging them in the glass containers. Mac and Mia chatted at the kitchen table.

She set one vase on the table. "I'll take the other up to your room after dinner."

"Thanks," Mia answered.

"Well, hell of a friend you've got here, Ellie. I understand she's not real keen on your move."

Mia offered Mac a stunned glance. "I didn't—"

"You didn't have to, I'm sharp enough to pick up on a few

comments you made and realize you're not too fond of Ellie's decision."

"Well—"

Mac held up his hand. "Can't say I blame you. I wouldn't want my friend moving away on me either. But I can assure you, she's in good hands here."

"I'm not convinced. In the time she's been here," Mia retorted, ticking off her points on her fingers, "she has found out her aunt was murdered, had a brick thrown through her front window wrapped in a threatening message, and been run off the road."

Mac shook his head. "I understand everything you're saying. The trouble Ellie's had since she's been in town bothers me too. But—"

"But nothing!" Mia interrupted. "It's not safe here! Not for Ellie! She ought to just sell the manor and come back home. That's my opinion. The cops have no leads on this which makes it even worse."

"How do you know she'll be safe at home? She'll still own everything but the manor. Unless that's what the killer was after, we have no reason to believe that will solve the problem."

"Okay, so she sells off the entire kit-and-caboodle! Washes her hands of the whole thing and be done with it."

"Hey! I'm right here and I have a brain of my own," Ellie shouted as she stuck a salad on the table along with plates and cutlery.

"And what are your thoughts, Ellie? Your friend has made a few good points. Are you rethinking your plans?"

"No, I am not," she said, placing plates of spaghetti in front of each of them. "Mia makes good points, but how do we know that isn't exactly what the killer wants me to do? In that case, the killer wins!"

"So, you think the killer is threatening you so you'll sell?" Mia asked.

"Yes! I think they tried to threaten Aunt Susie and when that didn't work, they killed her and then hoped to stand a better chance with the new heir who may just prefer to wash her hands of the whole situation."

"So, you're going to stay out of stubbornness? How is that smart?"

Ellie shrugged as she draped her napkin over her lap. "I didn't say it was smart, but I'm not going to be kicked out of what is potentially the best thing that's happened to me, outside of Aunt Susie's death, because someone thinks they can scare me off."

Mac grinned and nodded at her. "That's what I like to hear." He pointed his fork at her. "Don't you back down for anyone."

"Let's just hope she doesn't end up like her aunt," Mia retorted.

"Can we stop talking about this over our meal?" Ellie requested. "Let's talk about something lighter."

"Just a second," Mia said. "Before we drop the subject. Mac, are you willing to jot a note down for me?"

"A note?"

"Yeah," Mia said. Mia leapt from her seat and grabbed a notepad and pen. "Write something like 'I'd better see results soon.'"

Mac furrowed his brow as he accepted the pen.

"No, don't write that," Ellie said to him.

He shifted his gaze between the two women. Mia focused on Ellie and shrugged. "Why not?"

"Okay," Ellie answered, "just write it and let's end this."

Mac offered a shrug and raised his eyebrows as he jotted the requested words. He shoved the pen and pad across the table toward Mia. "Well? Did I pass?"

CHAPTER 17

*E*llie peered over the salad bowl at the note Mia held. She glanced up at Mac and nodded. "Yep."

"Mind telling me what that was about?" Mac inquired.

"We're comparing handwriting to the notes Aunt Susie received. Yours isn't a match."

"You have the notes?" Mac asked.

Ellie shook her head. "No, Rick has them now, but I made a copy."

"Do you mind if I see them?"

Ellie dug the note from her pocket and handed it to him. "Do you recognize the handwriting?"

"Can't say that I do, but I'm not sure I'd know anyone's handwriting offhand. But now you know it's not mine."

"I had no doubt," Ellie said, shooting a glare toward Mia.

Mia held her hands up. "I take no chances."

Mac gave one of his belly laughs. "You got a good friend there, Ellie. Too bad we can't interest you in moving up to Salem Falls. You'd make a nice addition to the town."

Mia avoided the question, offering a fleeting smile before steering the conversation in another direction.

As the night wound down, Ellie walked Mac to the front door. Lola followed and the man stooped to give her another ear scratch.

"I'll be seeing you, big Lol," he said.

"Bye, Mac," Lola answered.

Mac stood and faced Ellie. "Thanks for the dinner."

"You're welcome. Listen, sorry about Mia. She's not really on board with me moving up here and it shows."

"No problem at all. Like I said, she's a good friend to worry about you like that." Mac pushed open the screen door before hesitating. "Oh, Ellie, please if you're pursuing this be careful. She is right about one thing. There's a killer on the loose. I don't want to see anything happen to you."

"Thanks, Mac. I will be."

The man gave her a nod before heading out into the dusky evening, whistling as he wandered to his car. Ellie pushed the door shut as a cloud of dust billowed behind him and rejoined Mia on the patio. The soft sound of trickling water, the whirr of grasshoppers, and the chorus of pond frogs filled the summer night air.

"It really is peaceful here," Mia said as Ellie regained her seat. Cleo lounged in the grass in front of them, occasionally waving a paw in the air at a lightning bug, but finding herself too lazy to chase after it.

"Yeah, it is," Ellie agreed. "Which is another reason—"

"I know, I know," Mia said, holding up a hand to stop Ellie's speech. "I get it. I do. I don't like it, but I get it."

"Maybe you can retire to Salem Falls."

Mia forced a weak smile onto her face. "Maybe. Until then, I need my job, so I'm stuck in Winwick."

"Oh, stuck, huh? An hour ago, you wanted to drag me back there."

"At least we'd be stuck together, then," Mia said with a chuckle.

"Yeah, but this way, you always have an escape."

"Careful, El, I may be here every weekend."

"Fine by me. I'll keep your room open for you. It's here whenever you want it."

Lola wagged her tail. "Is she going to come all the time? I like her."

"Maybe you can help me get this place up to snuff to reopen the B&B."

"That sounds like a plan."

Ellie reached across the table and clutched Mia's hand. She relaxed back in her chair and pulled her legs up onto the seat, enjoying the summer night.

* * *

Ellie raced through the thick woods behind the manor. Branches tore at her skin and pulled her hair as she gasped for breath, her feet stumbling to find their way through the dense forest.

She bent at the waist, resting her hands on her thighs as she sucked in a breath. She risked a glance behind her. A shadow followed, moving stealthily among the trees.

Ellie pushed herself to continue along the mossy ground. She found a large oak and sheltered behind it as she caught her breath. Her lower lip smarted as she bit into it.

As she held her breath, waiting for the shadow to pass, a sound broke through the silence of the night. The shrill ringing jangled next to her. She searched the air for the noise. It sounded again and Ellie's eyes rose higher.

After a moment, she shifted, batting at the blanket covering her as she startled awake. She glanced around the unfamiliar room before she sucked in a deep breath, realizing her location.

The noise continued and she snapped her head in its

direction. Her cell phone buzzed and trilled, dancing across the nightstand.

"Are you kidding me?" she huffed as she snatched the phone from the table and silenced it.

She flopped back into the pillows, flinging her arm over her eyes. She pulled her arm away as the phone rang again. "Seriously?"

She jabbed at the phone to send the caller to voicemail. Within seconds, the blue light lit the ceiling again and the phone played its tune.

"You've got to be kidding." Ellie swiped the phone from the table and tapped the answer button. "Who is this?"

A robotic voice answered. "Leave Salem Falls or you'll be sorry."

"What? Who is this?" Ellie questioned. She pulled the phone away from her ear and stared at it as the call ended.

"What kind of idiot does this?" she grumbled as she pulled up her recent call list. She jabbed at the last call and hit the call button. The line trilled on the other end but no one answered the call. She tried twice more but found herself ignored both times.

She tossed the phone onto the nightstand and turned to find two sets of eyes fixed on her.

"Who was it, Ellie?" Lola asked.

"Yeah, what kind of idiot calls in the middle of the night? I'm trying to sleep!" Cleo said with a massive yawn.

Ellie swung her legs over the side of the bed. "Some idiot who thought it would be funny to call and threaten me." She slid her feet into her slippers and tugged her robe around her.

"Where are you going?" Lola inquired.

"Nowhere. But I'll never sleep now. I may as well pace the floor until the sun comes up."

"What a silly waste of resources," Cleo said, as she stretched.

"Well, I can't sleep. The phone call has me all stirred up."

"What did they say?" Lola asked.

"They told me to leave or I'd be sorry." Ellie pressed her palm to her forehead as she spun and stalked in the opposite direction.

"Man or woman?" Cleo asked.

"Neither. One of those weird robotic voices. Like a voice changer thing."

"Maybe you should call Sheriff Rick?" Lola suggested.

"And tell him what? That I got a threatening call?"

"Yeah," Lola said.

"Won't do any good," Cleo said. "He won't be able to help. He could be standing next to the person making the call and he'd still not know who did it."

"I don't think he's that bad. And Lola has a point. I should call him, but I don't need to do it in the middle of the night."

"Why not? You can't sleep," Cleo answered.

"Maybe it'll make me feel better." Ellie grabbed her phone from the nightstand. She puckered her lips as she stared down at the device in her hand. Her brow furrowed and she tapped on the darkened screen with her index finger.

"How did they get this number?"

"Huh?" Lola asked.

"This is my cell phone. How did they get this number? I haven't given it to anyone in town except—" Her voice cut off.

"Except who?" Lola asked.

Ellie sank onto the bed. "Mac and Sheriff Rick."

Cleo groomed her side, tossing her head back as she smoothed the fur down toward her tail. "Told you he was guilty," she said between licks.

Ellie shook her head at the cat, though a sinking suspicion grew in the pit of her stomach that Sheriff Rick Crawford may somehow be involved.

CHAPTER 18

*E*llie shuffled around the kitchen in her slippers as she readied a cup of hot tea. Morning sunshine shone into the adjacent sunroom. She returned the kettle to the stove and dunked her teabag in and out of the steaming water.

Mia slogged through the doorway a moment later.

"Good morning, did you sleep well?" Ellie asked.

"Actually, I did, yes. But I still am in desperate need of coffee."

Ellie pointed to the pot in the corner. "Already made."

Mia groaned appreciatively as she wrangled the pot from the machine and poured the dark liquid into the mug.

Ellie handed her creamer before she requested it. With a grateful nod, she poured a generous amount into the dark coffee, turning it almond in color.

Ellie slurped a sip of her hot tea. "I'm heading for the sunroom if you want to join me."

Mia followed with a donut in hand and the two women settled into wicker rockers. Lola side-eyed them before offering a sigh and returning to her morning nap. Cleo lounged on the corner cat tree, bright sunlight streaming onto her black fur.

"Wow, it's great out here."

"It is," Ellie answered.

"You okay?" Mia inquired.

"I'm tired," Ellie admitted. "Rough night."

"Couldn't sleep?"

"I could, but the phone call in the wee hours of the morning ruined whatever chance I had."

"Who called?"

Ellie rolled her eyes. "I don't know. Whoever it was used one of those robotic voice changers."

"What? Some kind of prank call?"

Ellie shook her head as she took another sip of tea. "No, another threat."

"Ellie!" Mia shouted, leaping to the edge of her chair. "Did you call the police?"

"Not yet."

Mia puckered her lips and shook her head.

Ellie held her hand up to stop any comment. "I will, I will."

"How are you so calm about this?"

"I'm not calm, I'm tired. And the thing is—"

"What?" Mia inquired as Ellie's voice cut off.

"Well, only two people in town have my number. Mac and the sheriff."

Mia settled back into her rocker, the wicker squeaking as she leaned against it. She stared out over the sunlit trees as she pondered the new information.

"So—" She allowed the statement to linger in the air without continuing.

"Yep," Ellie answered, not needing the words to be spoken to understand.

"But we ruled out Mac." Mia puckered her lips. "Or did we?"

Ellie shot her a sideways glance. "Let's not go back to that."

"Come on, El, with the latest development, you've got to be thinking he may be involved."

"It could easily be Rick."

"The sheriff in town is a killer?"

"He's as likely as Mac. And what better way to cover up your crime? He's the sheriff. He'll just never solve it."

"Okay, if that's the case, why even admit there was a crime? He could have said she drowned and been done with it. Why send her to the coroner?"

Ellie shrugged. "I don't know. Nothing's adding up. All I know is I haven't given my number to anyone but Mac and I called the sheriff's office, so he'd have it too— ohhhh," Ellie said.

"What is it?"

"I called the sheriff's office. That means the secretary would have it, too. What's her name?" Ellie snapped her fingers in the air as she tried to recall it. "Hazel! Hazel! She'd have it AND the deputy, Nathan."

"So, any of those four could have done this."

Ellie jabbed her finger toward Mia. "Yes, and you said the handwriting looked more feminine."

"Is there any reason this Hazel woman would hate your aunt?"

Ellie narrowed her eyes, staring into space as she tried to recall any details.

"Maybe we should check your aunt's journal," Mia suggested.

Ellie shook her head, trying to cover her lie about the journal. "No, she never mentions her. I guess because they weren't in business together. *But* when I first met her at the police station, Mac said I was thinking of reopening the B&B. Rick said people would be happy to hear that and she said 'not everyone.'"

"Meaning she wasn't?"

Ellie shrugged. "She didn't say that exactly, but she did mention people wouldn't be happy. Rick didn't allow her to continue much further after that."

Mia's eyebrows rose toward her hairline. "Sheriff Rick covering for his secretary? Maybe something going on between them?"

Ellie considered it. Cleo's eyes opened to slits. "Could be," the cat said. "She's as dumb as he is."

"I'm not sure," Ellie answered. "But maybe we should add her to the list and try to get a handwriting sample."

Ellie darted into the kitchen to retrieve her suspect list and added Hazel's name to it.

"We need a plan to get handwriting samples," Mia said, shoving the remaining piece of donut into her mouth.

Ellie scanned the list and winced. "I'm not sure how we're going to pull that off."

"Well, we're heading to the diner today, right?" Mia inquired.

"Bring me a milkshake," Cleo said.

"I'll take a burger," Lola said, raising her head off the floor.

"And we can pop by the ice cream shop after, though I think Sam is low on the suspect list, but we can try to get a sample of handwriting there, too."

"Ohhh, ice cream! So, don't get dessert at the diner?"

"You can get dessert there. You can get ice cream, too, I won't stop you. But I need to get something for Cleo and Lola."

"Seriously?"

"Yes. Aunt Susie used to get them ice cream all the time when she went out."

"She really spoiled them, huh?"

Ellie chuckled as she flicked her gaze between the two animals and smirked. "They're special."

"Must be." Mia slurped the last bits of coffee from her mug. "I'm going to get a refill. You want anything?"

"No, I'm good."

Mia rose and padded into the kitchen. "We've still got a long list of people we need to get writing samples from," she called from within the kitchen.

"Yeah, I know. We've got quite a list here and all we've come up with so far is go to the diner. We haven't even figured out a way to get her handwriting."

Mia shuffled back to her chair and plopped onto it. "Doesn't she take orders when you're there? On one of those little notepads?"

"Yeah, she did, but I don't recall ever seeing it. She doesn't give us a copy."

Mia pursed her lips. "We'll figure something out. Even if it's just a quick glance as she writes up our order. Maybe that'll be enough."

Ellie nodded. "Okay, that leaves Rick, Bill, Andy, and Delilah."

Mia leaned over the chair's arm. "And Scarlett."

"I may have that handled."

Mia raised her eyebrows.

"She owns the local newspaper. Well, part of it. I met one of her reporters and he agreed to get a sample of her handwriting for me."

"Oh, nice. Did he think she could be guilty?"

"I don't think so. He agreed to do it so I could rule her out."

"And what if it provides proof she did it?"

"I'll cross that bridge when I come to it." Ellie glanced at the wall clock in the kitchen through the open French doors. "Our breakfast is going to become a brunch soon."

Mia waved her hand as she sipped at her coffee. "Make it lunch or early dinner as far as I'm concerned. I'm not in any rush. I'm on vacation."

"Vacation, huh? I thought you were supposed to be working to help me move or get the B&B into shape."

Mia lifted a shoulder. "It's still a vacation. I don't have to go to work."

"Speaking of, how'd you get the time off?"

Mia offered her a mouth shrug and shook her head. "I had some vacation time banked up."

"Aw, you didn't have to use your vacation time. What'll you do if you want to go to the beach with Joe or something?"

Mia rolled her eyes. "Yeah, right. Joe has no desire to go to the beach."

"Oh, come on. Okay, any vacation then."

"Probably not happening. It's fine. Don't think twice about it. I'm here for you. So, what's your plan for the week? Other than tracking down handwriting and catching a killer?"

"I found a bunch of plans my aunt had for reopening the B&B. They look great. But I figured we could take a look at the rooms and see what updates are needed. I need to get Mac on finding out what I need to do to reopen with the town. And then I'll need to start working on marketing and a website and all that. That's where you come in." Ellie pointed at Mia.

Mia sucked in a breath, her eyebrows raising and a closed-mouthed grin forming on her lips. "Ohhh, I love building websites! Are you going to keep the name? Salem

Falls Manor? I'm already thinking of design ideas but we need to lock down a domain name ASAP!"

"A what?"

"A domain name! You know, the thing you type into the address bar to get to the page."

"Don't you just type Salem Falls Manor into Google?"

"Maybe, but when you do, you'll get search results. And when you click on one it takes you to a website. And we want the domain name at the top to be something that people will know. Like the name of the inn."

"Should I change it from Salem Falls Manor?"

"It's up to you." Mia pulled her phone from within her robe pocket. "Let me see if that's available as a domain name."

She tapped around on the handheld device. "Okay, the domain name for Salem Falls Manor exists if you want it."

"What about Salem Falls Slumber Inn?"

Mia grimaced. "Sounds like a cheap motel."

Ellie swatted at her. "No, it doesn't! Come on!"

"Sure it does. Why not call it the Salem Falls Cockroach Motel?"

Ellie pressed her lips together and shook her head.

"We don't have roaches!" Cleo retorted. "Call it 'Cleo's place.' That has a classy ring to it."

"But it's not your place, Cleo," Lola answered.

"What about Salem Falls Cozy B&B," Ellie suggested.

Mia considered it while she tapped around on her phone.

"Aww, I like that, Ellie," Lola said.

Cleo yawned. "It's okay. I still think Cleo's place is better. But I guess cozy is nice."

"Well, you'd have to use 'and' rather than an ampersand, but that domain name is available. What do you think? Salem Falls Manor or Salem Falls Cozy B&B?"

Ellie scrunched her eyebrows together and gazed into the

air. "Salem Falls Cozy B&B. I love it. I think it describes the place perfectly."

"It is cozy. All right, Salem Falls Cozy B&B it is! I'll lock up the domain name today and get started with a few website design ideas. I brought my camera. We can get some shots of the property and rooms."

"Oh, Aunt Susie had samples delivered for one of the rooms. We should check those out to get some design ideas. And I want to start the murder mystery-themed weekends, so we'll need something on the website about that."

Mia nodded as she typed on her phone. "Got it. Play up the quiet coziness, murder mystery weekends, anything else?"

"Not that I can think of. That's a good start. I'll review all of Aunt Susie's stuff and we can add prices."

"I can hook up an online reservation system, too."

"Oh, book online, that would be great! I hate calling places."

"That's crazy," Mia said as she added it to her list. "What's the big deal?"

"I don't know, I just prefer clicking my way to a stay rather than calling and fiddling with asking for a room and passing a credit card over the phone and all that."

Mia rolled her eyes and offered an amused smirk.

"Either way, I think booking online is great."

"I'll add both a call us and a book online button."

"Perfect." Ellie wrapped her hands around her mug as she took a final sip. "I'm really looking forward to this."

"Ideas are already flowing. Do you mind if I get some pictures before we head into town for whatever meal we're eating?"

"Not at all. Although some of the rooms still have sheets covering things."

Mia stood from her rocker and grabbed her coffee cup. "I'll start with the outside."

"I'll pull the sheets off and you can get some shots when you come in. Even if they're rough, I can get an idea of how this website will come together."

"Sounds good. And I can always edit out any dust," Mia said with a wink.

"Too bad you can't edit it out in real life," Ellie answered.

The women parted ways, with Mia retrieving her camera and heading outside to get shots of the manor and surrounding area in the morning sunlight and Ellie climbing to the second level to pull sheets from some of the furniture in the guest rooms.

Ellie also swiped a dust rag around the reading room on the third floor and the library on the main floor, figuring they would be excellent rooms to showcase on the website.

After a morning of picture taking, Mia returned her camera to her room and changed for a late lunch at the diner.

"I think I've got enough pictures to get a great start on the website when we get back."

"I'm so excited to see it," Ellie said as Mia navigated the town's streets toward the diner. "I'll start working on my business plan. Mac said it's the first thing I'll need to approach the Commerce Committee with."

"I can't believe you're opening a B&B!" Mia said as she swung the car into the diner's parking lot. "This place looks interesting."

"It's a real 50s diner. And the food is great," Ellie called over the car as they both climbed to their feet.

Ellie pulled the diner's door open and ushered Mia inside ahead of her. Val bustled around behind the counter. She smiled and waved as Ellie walked in.

"Grab any seat you'd like!"

Ellie nodded and led Mia to a window-side booth. They

shimmied into the glittery red seats as Val plopped menus down in front of them.

"Need a minute?" she asked after snapping her gum.

"Yeah, thanks," Ellie answered.

Mia flicked open her menu, pretending to study it. She snapped her eyes up as Val strolled away. "Is that her?"

"Yep. That's Val," Ellie confirmed, paying equal attention to her menu.

Mia narrowed her eyes at the woman.

"What do you think? Does she look like a killer?"

"Maybe. She could have snapped and killed someone, sure. I'd believe it."

Ellie wiggled her eyebrows before she pointed to Mia's menu. "You'd better decide what you want before she gets back here and wonders what you were doing."

"Browsing," Mia said with a wobble of her head. "The menu is three pages long, so I really have to think."

"Ohhh, you're good," Ellie answered.

"What are you getting?"

Ellie flopped the plastic-coated menu shut. "I think I'll go for the burger again. I had it last time and it was perfect."

"Hmm, maybe I'll do the same."

Val returned as Mia closed her menu. "We ready?"

"We are!" Mia announced. "Though I have a special request."

"Name it," Val said, thrusting her hip out and tapping her pencil against her order pad.

"I'm visiting my friend Ellie here for a little vacation and to help her out with her idea to reopen the B&B—"

"Well, my aunt's idea I'm following up on," Ellie explained.

"Oh!" Val said with a broad smile. "You're reopening the Manor? Fantastic idea! We should talk. The diner can provide some catering."

"We'll set something up," Ellie said with a smile.

"Anyway," Mia chimed in, "as I was saying, I'm visiting and whenever I visit somewhere, I always hit a local restaurant. And then I get my order written by the waitstaff as a little souvenir. So, would it be possible for you to give me a copy of your order sheet before we leave?"

Val's eyes rolled from side to side as she considered the request. "Uh, I mean, I don't see why not. Though I've never had anyone ask me for the order check."

"Well, I have a whole stack of them at home and I'd love to add this one. I'm also a photographer," Mia said, patting the camera bag at her side, "so, I'll take a few shots of the place inside and outside, if that's okay with you, and tack the check with the pictures."

Val gave her a mouth shrug and lifted a shoulder in the air. "Sure. Whatever floats your boat."

"Thank you. And on that note, I will have the burger and fries."

"All the fixings on that?"

"Yep."

"Something to drink?"

"Uh—" Mia's eyes darted to the soda fountain behind the counter. "Ohh, Vanilla Coke."

"Great choice." She turned her attention to Ellie. "How about you, hun?"

"Same!" Ellie said.

"Easy enough!" Val said, collecting the menus. "Two burgers, fries, and old-fashioned Vanilla Cokes coming right up."

"Thanks!" Ellie called over her shoulder as the uniform-clad woman strode away.

"This really is a cute place," Mia said. She pulled her DSLR camera from her tote bag and snapped a few pictures.

"Way to make it look good," Ellie said, giving her the a-okay sign with her hand.

"Do you think she'd let us link your B&B site to hers?"

"I don't even know if she has a website."

Mia set the camera on the table and grabbed her phone, tapping around. "Not seeing anything. Well, she should have one!"

"Maybe you can offer your services."

"Oh, don't worry, I plan to."

"Unless she's a killer, right?"

"Even then, I'll take payment from prison."

Ellie chuckled and shook her head at Mia as Val waddled over with a loaded tray. She set the hot food in front of each woman and slid two fizzy Cokes in vintage glasses across the table.

"Need anything else?"

"Nope, I think we're good."

"Oh, and here's your handwritten order check, hun. Hope it's everything you expected." Val gave her a wink and spun to grab the tray from the table behind her before she disappeared behind the counter.

"Mmmmm," Mia said as she sipped her Coke, "this is so good!"

"Wait until you try the burger."

Mia bit into it and groaned with satisfaction. She wiped the corners of her mouth as she chewed and snatched the check from the table. She narrowed her eyes at it.

"Well?" Ellie asked with her mouth still half-full.

Mia stared at it a moment longer. "I can't tell. Do you have your copy of the notes?"

Ellie held up a finger and tugged her purse open. She dug through the contents and pulled out a folded paper.

Mia waved it over as Ellie unfolded it. She slid it across the table and Mia swiped it. She held the check against the paper, her eyes flicking back and forth between the two.

"Well?" Ellie asked.

CHAPTER 19

*M*ia shook her head and crumpled the note into her lap as she slipped the check into her tote. A smiling Val wandered to the table. "How's the food?"

"Oh, so good!" Mia said.

"Anything you need?"

"I don't need anything, but I did have a quick question for you," Mia said.

"Shoot!"

"Well, I checked on my phone while we were waiting for our food, but didn't see anything. Do you have a website?"

Val pulled her lips back and clicked her tongue. "Nope, sorry, honey. Never got around to that."

"You really should have one." Mia dug into her purse and pulled out a business card. "I do some website design. I'll be working on Ellie's B&B. If you'd like me to put one together for you, just shoot me an email or give me a call."

Val studied the pink and black card and bobbed her head. "Okay, I'll give it some thought."

"Great! I'll give you the friends and family rate. It could

be a great boon for your business. We can set up online ordering and everything!"

Val offered another nod. "I'll let you know." She waved the card in the air before she spun on her heel and strode away.

Ellie leaned toward Mia across the table. "Nice cover."

"Do you want to see the note? I couldn't make an assessment in the brief time I had. "

Ellie shook her head. "Shove it in your purse. I'm not taking another chance that she sees those, especially if she wrote them. We can look at them back at the manor."

Mia nodded and slid the paper from her lap into her tote bag.

"You know, you should open your own business, too. Website design."

"I'm thinking about it!" Mia said.

They polished off the burgers and fries in record time after their meager breakfast.

"Thinking about dessert?" Val asked as she dropped by the table.

"Well, I think we're going for ice cream over at Salem Scoops," Ellie said.

"How about a piece of pie for tonight? I can set you up with to-go containers."

"If you don't mind sharing the fridge space, Ellie, I'll go for that."

"I don't mind at all."

"Well, great. Just tell me what you'd like. I've got cherry, apple, blueberry, pecan, French silk, and peanut butter."

"French silk," Ellie said, slapping her hand against the table.

"Ohh, I wish I was that decisive."

"I am NOT turning down a piece of chocolate pie for dinner."

Mia chewed her lower lip as she mulled over the options. "I'll do peanut butter."

"You sure?" Val questioned. "Did you really think about it?"

Mia squashed her lips together. "Y-Yes," she stuttered. "I was between a fruit and peanut butter, but I'm going for the peanut butter."

"You got it. I'll get those boxed for you. Pop 'em both in the fridge when you get home and take them out about twenty minutes or so before you want to enjoy 'em."

"Thanks."

Within ten minutes, they stepped into the fresh afternoon air with two plastic pie containers filled with delicious-looking slices.

Ellie stuck them on the floor of the passenger's side and they left the car behind, choosing to walk to the ice cream shop.

"Whew, after all this exercise, we've earned the ice cream," Mia said as they traversed the sidewalks toward Salem Scoops.

"Mac said Aunt Susie didn't have a car and walked into town all the time."

"What? Wasn't she like... old?"

"Watch how you're defining old. We're not spring chickens anymore either. But to answer your question, she was eighty-two. She would have been eighty-three next month."

"Wow! Eighty-three and walking to town!"

"And ready to reopen her B&B."

"I hope I'm that spry when I'm eighty-three."

"You and me both," Ellie said as she veered onto Main Street. "Though if I keep eating ice cream after every meal, I may not be."

"You'll walk it off."

Ellie waved her crossed fingers as she pulled open the door to Salem Scoops. The bell jingled overhead as the door closed behind them. Sam stood behind the counter, scrolling through something on her phone.

She glanced up and smiled at the two arrivals. "Hey, Ellie! No Lola this time?"

"No Lola. But I will get the to-gos for them."

"And we'll be having something, too," Mia added.

"Definitely! Just let me know what you'd like. I'll get the furry friends taken care of while you browse and stick it in the freezer for you."

Mia approached the cases and squatted to study the flavors. "Oh my goodness, I have no idea what to get."

She straightened as Sam sprayed a generous helping of whipped cream onto Cleo's to-go bowl and snapped the lid on top. "They're all pretty good. If you want to try a sample, let me know."

"I had the Chocolate Moose Tracks last time and it was very good. Very creamy. I think this time I'll go with Cotton Candy."

"Mmm, nice choice!" Sam answered, stowing the to-go bowls in the freezer and grabbing her scoop. "Cone or bowl?"

"Cake cone this time, please."

Sam dug the rainbow confection from the container and squashed it on top of the flat cone. Mia studied the price board on the wall.

"What's a Titanic?" she asked the dark-haired girl.

"It's your choice of three scoops of ice cream. I top it with sprinkles and chocolate and caramel sauces, then I put pirouette cookies in with whipped cream on top for the smoke!"

Mia's eyes lit up and the corners of her mouth turned up. "I'll take that!"

"Mia!" Ellie said as she accepted the cake cone. "That's a *lot* of ice cream!"

"I can handle it."

Ellie widened her eyes and offered her friend an amused smile. Sam grabbed an elongated glass dish. "What flavors?"

Mia scanned the case again. "Rocky Road."

Sam scooped the chocolatey flavor into one end of the dish and raised her eyebrows for the next choice.

"Butterscotch."

"Mmmm," Sam said as she scooped that into the middle. "Last one?"

"Ummm, Reese's Peanut Butter Cup."

Sam wiggled her eyebrows as she dug a large scoop of the candy-laden ice cream from the cooler and plopped it into the glass dish. She dropped her ice cream scooper into a bucket of water and spun to the rear counter.

She pulled a ladle full of steaming fudge from within a vat and drizzled a generous portion over every scoop. She followed it with a warm caramel drizzle. Two spoonfuls of sprinkles covered the sundae.

Sam finished it off with three pirouettes in each scoop and squeezed whipped cream into each. She turned to face them, holding the colorful confection high in the air, with a triumphant grin on her face.

"One Titanic Sundae. Enjoy!" Sam stuck a spoon in the ice cream and handed it over.

"Put them all on one check," Ellie said as she handed over her credit card.

They settled at a table after Ellie paid.

"You are going to be so sick later," Ellie said as she eyed the massive sundae.

"Just wait until I pile that peanut butter pie on top of it."

Ellie grimaced and let her tongue roll out of her mouth. "You're making me sick just thinking about it. I, on the other hand, only had a small cotton candy cone, so my chocolate pie will just hit the spot later."

Mia dug the spoon into the butterscotch ice cream ball. She lifted it, allowing the caramel and hot fudge to drip off her spoon before she slid it into her mouth. "Mmm, this is so good."

Ellie chuckled at her friend as she bit into her cone. She finished the small dessert as Mia continued to work on her massive one.

"You wanna help?" she murmured with a mouthful of Rocky Road.

"No way," Ellie said. "You got yourself into this, you get yourself out!"

"How are we doing over there? Need me to slosh it into a to-go container?"

"Nope, I'm committed."

Ellie shook her head and snatched a soggy pirouette. "Here's my contribution!" She bit into the ice-cream-laden cookie with a smile.

After another twenty minutes and a glass of water, Mia's spoon clattered around the glass bowl as she tossed it into the empty dish.

She raised her eyebrows at Ellie and offered her a triumphant smile. With a pat on her bloated belly, she sighed.

"I did it."

"Yes, you did. Let's see if you're still wearing that smile in a few hours."

"The walk will help!" Mia said as they stood from their little table.

"Oh, hey, Sam..." Ellie said.

Sam waved a white bag at her. "I didn't forget. Here are the treats for the kids."

"Ah, thank you," Ellie said, grabbing the bag. "I had one other thing, too, if you don't mind."

"Name it!"

"Could you jot down a list of your most popular flavors? I'm really thinking about those ice cream socials for the B&B and I wanted to pick a few crowd pleasers."

"Oh, yeah, sure!" Sam said. She grabbed a notepad and scribbled down a few names. "These are easily my top five on average."

Ellie scanned the list. "Wow, lemon, really?"

"Lots of people like a neutral flavor that's a bit more ambitious than vanilla."

"Fair enough." Ellie waved the list in the air. "Thanks!"

"Sure, just let me know what else you need. I'm excited to do ice cream socials at the inn!"

They said their goodbyes and pushed out into the temperate air. The sun lowered in the sky, painting the shops and streets in a deep orange light.

They wandered through the painted streets back to Mia's car at the diner.

"Great job getting the ice cream kid's handwriting sample."

Ellie winked at her. "I don't think it's her. And I really do want to work in ice cream socials."

"Killing two birds with one stone. Good job, El." Mia glanced into a few of the shop windows as they passed by them. "I really need to carve out some time to shop before I leave."

"When do you need to go, by the way?"

"Eh, I'm good for this week at least."

"What? That's crazy. You took your entire week's vacation? Mia! You can't blow all your days on helping me with the B&B."

"I won't. I'll spend some time shopping in town," Mia answered as they reached her car.

Ellie shook her head at the woman as they slipped inside. In minutes, they bounced down the drive toward the house.

Ellie climbed from the passenger seat with two bags of goodies in hand. Lola's barks filled the air, passing through the walls.

"That dog never stops barking," Ellie said. "It's just us!"

She mounted the first step to the porch, ceasing her movement, her back foot dangling in the air. She blinked a few times as she stared up at the door.

"Whoa!" Mia shouted as she crashed into her. "You gotta call your stops, El."

Ellie didn't respond, staring upward, her face a mask of shock. "Is that—" Her voice cut off as she lost the ability to form the words.

Mia followed her gaze, stumbling back a step as her eyes grew wide. "No wonder the dog's barking."

Ellie offered a slight nod as she continued to stare at the scene in front of her. A white paper flapped in the breeze, pinned through the screen to the front door with a large knife. Red letters dripped down the page reading *Leave now or else*.

CHAPTER 20

*E*llie steeled her nerves, squashing her lips together in frustration. She pounded up the steps, the treat bags swinging from her left hand. After snapping a picture with her cell phone, she wrapped the hilt with a tissue and yanked the knife from the door, tossing it on the nearby glass table. It clattered across the surface as she grabbed hold of the paper and studied the letter.

"It's paint," she reported with a shake of her head. "This is ridiculous and look what they did to my screen!"

"Ellie," Mia said, joining her on the porch, "this is getting serious."

"Oh, I'm calling the police. This is beyond ridiculous. This is the second time someone has damaged my property. Look at this door!"

Ellie pulled the screen door open and waved at the splintered wood of the door.

"This is unbelievable," she muttered with a shake of her head as she shoved the key into the lock. "Just unreal."

Mia grabbed the bags from around her wrist as she

pushed in through the front door. Lola squealed inside, rearing onto her hind legs.

"It's me," Ellie said as she stepped into the foyer. "Calm down."

Lola's front paws landed against Ellie and the dog clung to her waist. She whimpered as Ellie rubbed her neck. "It's okay, Lola."

"Someone was on the porch! There was a bang! I barked at them!"

"Good girl. Yes, you scared that nasty person away."

Mia skirted past Ellie who continued to soothe the dog. "I'm going to pop these in the fridge."

"I'm calling the police," Ellie shouted after her. She led the flustered animal into the living room and plopped on the couch. Lola leapt next to her, pressing her body against Ellie's leg.

"It's okay now. Everyone is fine. Just our door is hurt. Did you happen to see the person?"

"No," Lola said.

Cleo dragged herself out from under the sofa. "I didn't see anything either. But I was terrified. A loud bang, then Lola barking. I ran for my life."

Ellie stroked her hand down the cat's back. "It's okay. I'm going to call the police and report this."

She tapped the number for the police station and listened as the phone trilled on the other end.

"Did you happen to remember the ice cream?" Cleo inquired.

Ellie shook her head at the cat. "You're so traumatized, huh? Yes, I got the ice cream."

"I need it after that trauma! My life flashed before my eyes!" Cleo shouted as a female voice sounded on the other end of the line.

"Salem Falls PD, Hazel speaking, how can I help you?"

"Hi Hazel, it's Ellie."

"Oh, hi, Ellie! Nice to hear from you. How was your weekend?"

"Oh, thanks, though, it's not a social call, I'm sorry to say."

"Oh, did something happen?"

"Yes, something happened. I went out to eat and when I got back home, I found a knife and a threatening note pinned to my door."

"Ohhhh my!" Hazel answered. "Gosh, that's terrible. Who do you think did it?"

"I don't know! That's why I'm calling you. The police need to come out and take a look at this and document the damage."

"Okay. I'll send the sheriff out right away. Gosh, I'm so sorry about this, Ellie."

"Thanks, Hazel," Ellie said with a sigh.

"Okay, well, I'm going to tell the sheriff right now. He'll be out just as soon as he can be. Just sit tight, okay?"

"Okay, thanks."

The line remained open. Ellie's forehead wrinkled as she listened. "Hey, Sheriff! Ellie Byrne had another— Oh, shoot!" A loud scraping noise sounded. "Sorry, Ellie, are you still there?"

"I am, yes."

"I forgot to hang up. I got so excited about this I just rushed right off. I'm going to hang up now. Bye, Ellie."

"Bye, Hazel." The receiver clattered to the handset and the call ended. Ellie raised her eyebrows as she stared at the phone.

"What did she say?" Cleo asked.

"She's sending the sheriff out."

"Useless," Cleo murmured. "We may as well track down the culprit ourselves."

Mia rounded the corner and entered the room. "Did you say something?"

"The sheriff's heading out."

"Good. I hope they do something about this."

"I guess I can give these two their treats while we wait."

Lola's stubby tail wagged as she glanced up at Ellie. "Yay, treats!"

"It's about time," Cleo said as she stalked toward the foyer.

Ellie had just set down Lola's dish of soft serve when the doorbell rang. Lola offered a sharp bark. "Shh, that's probably the sheriff. Just eat your ice cream."

Ellie stalked down the hall and pulled open the front door. Rick stood, hands on his hips, surveying the knife sitting next to the front door.

"Hey, Ellie," he said in his Southern drawl. "This the knife?"

"Yep. I didn't touch it. I used a tissue to pull it from the door."

Rick slid on a pair of latex gloves and studied it and the note.

"I'm pretty sure that's red paint," Ellie said as she pushed through the screen door onto the porch.

Rick's head bobbed up and down. "Yep, looks like it. And you didn't see anyone?"

"No. I was out having lunch at the diner and then ice cream at Sam's. I found this when I got home."

Mia appeared at the screen door. "Oh, Rick, this is my friend, Mia. Mia, this is Rick Crawford, Salem Falls' Sheriff."

Rick tipped his hat at her.

"Did you show him the damage?"

"Not yet."

"Well," Mia said as she pushed through the screen door onto the porch, "let me be the first to show you. The door is damaged!" Mia waved her hand toward the splintered wood.

"And look at the screen. This is outrageous. What kind of town do you run where something like this happens *after* her window is broken and you have no idea who it is?"

"We're doing our best to track down whoever did this but these aren't a lot of clues to go on."

"Really?" Mia said, crossing her arms over her chest. "How many criminals is this town harboring that you can't figure out who could be responsible?"

Rick held up his hand to stop her rant.

"I'm serious. First threatening notes, then a murder, still unsolved by your fine department, then a brick through a window, and now this! Not to mention the threatening phone call last night. What sort of town is this?"

"You got a call last night?" Rick asked, turning his attention to Ellie.

Ellie nodded. "I did, yes. At about 2:45 a.m., someone called and threatened me."

"What did they say?"

"Leave Salem Falls or you'll be sorry."

Rick pulled his notepad from his breast pocket. "Was the voice male or female?"

"I couldn't tell. They used one of those robotic voice changers."

The Sheriff adjusted his hat and tapped his pen against his notepad. "Did you recognize the number?"

Ellie shook her head. "No number. It said 'Restricted.'"

"Who's your provider?"

"Telecom."

"Okay, we'll check with the phone company and see if we can get any information on who may have called you."

"You're going to have to do better than that," Mia retorted.

"Look, ma'am—"

"Don't ma'am me," Mia said, her head jutting left and right as she placed her hands on her hips. "Do something to fix this."

Rick offered her an apologetic smile, wiggling his eyebrows as he chuckled. "It's not that easy."

"Maybe you ought to try having a cop out here and then you'd actually catch the person who has sneaked onto this property twice to damage it and once to KILL SOMEONE!"

"Mia!" Ellie shouted with raised eyebrows.

Rick puckered his lips as he shoved the notebook into his pocket. "Okay, I understand how upsetting this is. And I plan on tracking this person down AND providing you with as much protection as we can."

"Thank you," Ellie said. "Yes, this is incredibly upsetting and frustrating. And frightening! My aunt was murdered. I feel that this situation is dangerous enough to warrant concern."

"And I agree. Though we don't know that the incidents are related."

"You've *got* to be joking," Mia said.

Rick held up his hands. "Listen, the other notes were handwritten. The one Ellie received wasn't. This could be a separate person, acting independently from the killer."

Mia wrinkled her nose at the statement.

"He has a point," Ellie said. "But it makes the most sense that this is the same person. They killed my aunt for a reason. What that reason is I don't know. Money? Business? Something else entirely? But whatever it was, it makes sense that they have unfinished business and as her heir, I'm the next target."

"I don't deny that, but I'm trying to keep all the options open so I don't overlook something."

"What have you looked into so far?"

"We're doing a full investigation into everyone Susie had contact with in her final days."

"That reminds me," Ellie said, waving her hand in the air, "I compiled a list of everyone she met with on the day she died. I can make a copy for you if you'd like. I included whether or not they ate anything as best I could since she was poisoned."

Rick's brows knit. "How did you—"

"She had a journal," Ellie interrupted.

"I'd like to see that journal."

"Ah—" Ellie hedged, hesitating as she tried to piece together an explanation of the nonexistent journal. "I dropped it. Into the sink. Which was filled with water. And it's ruined. I tried to dry it but it's all mushy and the ink ran —" Ellie crinkled her nose and shook her head. "It's useless."

"That's too bad."

Ellie smashed her lips together as she nodded. "Yeah. It's really a shame. Well, anyway, I can give you the list I made from it."

"All right, that may be helpful."

"Just a second, I'll grab it and make a copy."

Ellie hurried into the house and retrieved her list from the kitchen table. She hurried up the stairs to the third floor office. As she gulped breaths, she slid the list onto the scanner's glass and pressed the copy button.

The warm paper slid onto the tray and Ellie snatched it and the original list before darting back down the stairs and outside. She sucked in a few breaths, trying to steady her breath, as she strode across the lawn.

She gulped as she held the list out. "Whew," she said as her chest continued to heave, "I really need to get in shape. The stairs are killing me."

"Did you come from a ranch home?" Rick asked as he scanned the list.

"No, just one with a lot fewer steps."

Rick's lips puckered as he scanned down the list.

"Anybody stick out?" Mia asked.

"I can't comment on an ongoing investigation, ma'am."

Mia's eyes widened and she opened her mouth to reply when Ellie cut her off. "We understand. Thanks, Sheriff."

"Thanks," Rick said, waving the list in the air. "I'll make sure to send a patrol car by a few times through the night. Hopefully, these incidents start to die down once they realize you can't be scared off."

"Seriously? That's your answer?" Mia asked. "Hope it all dies down because Ellie's tough and sticks it out?"

"No, that's not what I said," Rick answered. "But if this is just someone trying to scare off the newcomer, it may just die down. And I hope it does, for Ellie's sake. We're not that kind of town."

Mia offered Rick an unimpressed stare. "No, Salem Falls is just the kind of town where people get murdered."

Rick scoffed and shook his head. "Anyway, I'll look into this." He flashed the list as he backed away. "And if you have any other problems, give us a call, Ellie."

"Will do, thanks," Ellie answered.

Rick spun on the gravel and tugged open his car door, sliding inside and slamming the door shut. He fired the engine and backed from the house.

"I can't believe you let him get away with that," Mia said as they stalked to the house.

Ellie mounted the stairs and pulled open the damaged screen door. "Oh, come on, he's doing his best."

"Seriously?" Mia questioned as they stepped into the foyer, her hands on her hips. "Mr. 'I-can't-find-my-way-out-of-a-wet-paper-bag' is seriously who you're pinning your hopes on?"

"That's the same thing I said," Cleo said from her perch

on the third stair. "He is so dumb. Rocks are smarter than he is."

Lola's tail wagged as she stood at Ellie's feet. "What did Sheriff Rick say?"

"I'm not pinning my hopes on him. But he needs to be aware of the situation and I'm sure he's doing his work. But he has to operate in a very specific manner so he doesn't jeopardize the case." Ellie grabbed Mia's purse from the skinny table against the stairs. She grabbed the lunch ticket and copy of the threatening notes and waved them in the air. "We, on the other hand, do not!"

"Ah, yes! Let's take a look at what we have!" Mia said, snatching the papers from Ellie.

Ellie rummaged through her bag and found Sam's popular flavors note.

Lola stood on her hind legs and sniffed at the note. Cleo narrowed her eyes at it. "What's that?"

"Come on, we'll get the magnifying glass from the junk drawer and really study this," Ellie said.

Mia spread the papers out on the kitchen table while Ellie retrieved the large magnifier from the drawer next to the refrigerator.

She joined Mia at the table and scanned the three notes. "Okay, well, even without a magnifier, Sam's is out. No match."

"I agree. Her writing is too bubbly and straight. She also printed, this is written. Unless she disguised her writing here." Mia pointed to the threatening notes.

"Based on her age, I'm not even sure she could write in cursive. Do they even teach that anymore in schools?"

Mia shrugged. "How should I know?"

Cleo leapt onto the table and stared at the papers. "Lemme see." She grabbed hold of Sam's note and pulled it toward her.

Mia gently tugged the note back from Cleo. "Hey, kitty, we need that." She adjusted the notes again and pulled her cell phone from her back pocket, tapping around on it.

"Idiot," Cleo said. Ellie shot the cat a glance. "What? I can help!"

"I can't see," Lola said. She stood on her hind legs, her chin just barely grazing the tabletop.

"Do you want to see, Lola?" Ellie asked. "Here, stand on the chair, but don't fall."

Ellie hoisted her up onto the wooden chair. "My goodness, Lola, I think you'd better stop eating so much ice cream."

Cleo chuckled. "You're fat!"

Lola planted her front feet on the table. "I am not! I'm well-muscled."

Cleo rolled onto her side as she continued to giggle. "You're fat."

"I didn't mean to say you're fat," Ellie answered with a pat on Lola's head.

"Did the dog take exception?" Mia questioned.

"I think so," Ellie said. "Anyway, back to these."

Lola leaned over and stared at the papers. "Ellie, I can't read."

Mia shoved her cell phone into her jeggings. "I couldn't find anything about whether or not schools still teach cursive writing, but I'd be willing to say Sam didn't write these notes unless her writing style and printing style are vastly different."

"Also, she had no motive."

"Or she has a hidden one."

"Not Sam," Lola said.

"For once, I agree with Dopey the dog. Why would Sam kill Susie?"

"If her motive is hidden, it's well-hidden. No one suspects her."

Mia plopped into the chair across from Lola, her finger rubbing her chin.

Ellie studied the note from Val. "What do you make of this one?"

CHAPTER 21

*ia shrugged as she studied Val's note. "It doesn't look that similar but there were a few things that I thought could have matched."

Ellie waved the magnifier over. "The 'b' in burger and better look similar."

"But the 'g' in regret," Mia said, pointing at the letter then using her other hand to point to the other note, "and the 'g' in burger aren't the same."

"Maybe she disguised it," Ellie proposed.

"It's not a slam dunk."

"No. Though she had the strange incident with the strawberry pie. She came back and insisted Aunt Susie eat it and wouldn't eat any herself."

"That is suspect." Mia stared at the paper, her brow furrowing.

"Is there something else?" Ellie asked, returning her gaze to the paper.

"Not with this," Mia answered, "but I think we need to consider people who could also have stuck a knife through your door and thrown a brick through your window."

"What if it's not the same person?"

"What are the chances it's not?" Mia countered.

Ellie shrugged. "Probably slim-to-none."

Mia pursed her lips and nodded at her. "Okay, so could Val have broken the window, called you last night and stuck the knife in your door?"

"No?" Ellie said as more of a question. "She was working at the diner today. Did she leave and run out here, put the knife in my door and go back to the diner?"

"Maybe. She knew we were going for ice cream. Perfect opportunity."

Ellie sank onto the chair behind her. "Good point. We did tell her we'd be away from the house for a bit. She could have taken a break, ran out, and returned with no one any the wiser."

"We could ask another employee at the diner."

"I don't really know any of them well enough."

Mia scrunched her nose up and her shoulders slumped. Ellie raised her eyebrows and her finger, biting her lower lip. "But I know someone who may!"

She hurried into the hall to fish her cell phone from her purse, toggling it on as she made her way back to the kitchen. She tapped around on the display before she tossed it onto the table. "There. Let's see what we can come up with."

Mia offered her a questioning glance.

"I texted Mac. He knows everyone. He may be able to find out if Val stepped out of the diner today in the least suspicious way possible."

Ellie's phone chimed. Mia leaned forward. "What'd he say?"

"Give me a second!" Ellie said as she swiped into her phone. "He's asking why. Val couldn't have done it."

"Oh, bull! If it was up to him, no one could have killed your aunt."

"I told him that and said we just wanted to know to rule her out if we could."

"And?"

Ellie stared at her phone as she waited for a return message. She nodded her head as one flashed across the screen. "He'll do it."

"Good."

"Okay," Ellie said as she scanned the list of suspects. "We can reasonably eliminate Mac and Sam. We're not sure about Val. We need handwriting samples from Rick, Hazel, Andy, and Delilah. Scarlett we have taken care of."

"I have zero ideas for how to get a writing sample from the Sheriff or his secretary. Who are the other two again?"

"Andy owns the grocery store and Delilah owns the pet store."

"Whenever Susie called in an order to the store, Andy always brought it out with a handwritten note stapled to the bag," Cleo said.

Lola agreed. "He did."

Ellie chewed her lower lip. "What if I called the grocery store and gave him a list of things to bring out. Maybe he'd jot them down and we could ask for it."

"You cheater," Cleo said, narrowing her eyes at Ellie. "You stole my idea. Least you could have done is give me credit."

"Would he bring the list?"

"Maybe."

"I guess it's worth a shot."

"It's that or ask for a proposal about expanding the store and I'd prefer not to do that because it sounds like I may be open to considering it and I'm not. At least not right at this moment."

"Do you think that would work for Delilah?"

"I don't know, but maybe I could ask her for some suggestions for a new food for Lola that's better for weight control."

Lola leapt off the chair onto the floor. "Hey! I like my food!"

"Hahaha, she still thinks you're fat," Cleo said with a chuckle, rolling around from side to side.

"I won't change the food, really. Lola seems to like this food. But we could get a list and use it to compare."

"That may work," Mia agreed. "Is the pet store open now?"

Ellie tapped around on her phone. "Ugh, closed Mondays. That'll have to wait until tomorrow."

"Who closes on Mondays?"

"Someone who works the weekends," Ellie answered.

Mia lifted her chin, trying to peer over the top of Ellie's phone. "What's her website look like? Does she need a new one?"

"Seriously? Are you going to offer services to everyone in town?"

"Maybe."

"Why don't you just build an interactive town website that links us all together."

"That's a good idea. Do you think they'd let me?"

"How should I know? I wasn't being serious."

"I was!"

"With your current job, I doubt you'd have time."

Mia didn't respond.

"Anyway, I'm going to call the store and see if I can get a hold of Andy." Ellie rose from the chair and grabbed her cell phone. After a few taps, she placed it against her ear and paced around the kitchen.

A female voice answered on the other end. "Hi, this is Ellie Byrne from Salem Falls manor, Susie's niece. I was wondering if Andy is in?"

"Oh, hi, Ms. Byrne. I'm sorry, Andy's left for the day. May I take a message to pass along to him?"

"Oh, no, thanks. I'll try to catch him tomorrow."

"Okay. He should be in around nine tomorrow morning."

"Great, thank you!"

Ellie sighed as she jabbed at the end call icon. "Well, that was a bust. He's gone for the day."

"We're striking out everywhere!"

Ellie eased into the chair and slumped down, tossing her cell phone onto the table. "Yep."

Mia reached over and grabbed Ellie's hand. "We'll figure it out."

Ellie squeezed her hand and nodded. "Thanks. I just feel stuck. Especially after the knife thing. When is this nonsense going to end? And before you say anything, I know it's only been a few days, but still... I'm over it."

Mia offered her a half-smile and a shrug.

"What?" Ellie asked.

"I didn't say anything."

"You didn't have to. There's something you want to say. Just say it."

Mia's shoulders raised to her ears as she drew in a deep breath. She wiggled Ellie's hand as she pressed her lips together. "I hate to bring this up again, but, Ellie are you really sure about this move? Like really, really sure?"

Ellie focused her eyes on the threatening notes in front of her. After a moment, she slowly nodded her head. "I am. I know it sounds bizarre given what's going on but I want to move here."

"Why?" Mia questioned. "You're leaving everything you

know. You're moving to a new town that doesn't sound all that nice the way we suspect half of it could have done this. I don't get it. If it's the money, I bet you could get a mint for this place and solve most of your financial problems with your current house. Plus, stay invested in the businesses around here for income. And didn't you say your aunt left you a fortune? You don't need this, Ellie."

"I do need this. I can't explain it. And I understand how it looks to someone else. But I need to be here. I need to reinvent myself."

"But you don't *need* to, El. That's what I'm saying."

"Okay, then I want to. You're right. I could take the money and run back to Winwick. But why?"

"Because all your friends are there."

"I will miss you, but I don't have much of a life there to lose. I lost my job. I hate the house because everywhere I look, I'm reminded of my louse of a soon-to-be-ex-husband. My neighbors are a pain and almost all of them somehow blame me for Toby's cheating, as if his decision to fool around with this waitress is due to some shortcoming on my part."

Ellie waved her hands in the air as tears stung her eyes. "I need a fresh start. Away from everything."

Mia frowned. "Away from me."

"You're welcome here anytime."

Mia remained silent for a moment before she sucked in a deep breath. "I guess I give you credit, though. You saw an opportunity and you took it."

Ellie chuckled. "You guess, huh?"

Mia wiggled her eyebrows, avoiding eye contact with Ellie. "I hope I'm as brave as you."

Ellie's forehead scrunched at the statement. She opened her mouth to reply when her ringing cell phone interrupted her. "It's Mac."

Ellie swiped the phone from the table and pressed the answer button. "Hey, Mac. I'm with Mia. Do you mind if I put you on speaker?"

Ellie pulled the phone from her ear and tapped the speakerphone icon. "Okay, go ahead. Did you get any information on Val?"

"I did. But before I tell you, I want to make sure you ladies aren't going to jump to any conclusions."

Ellie shot Mia a glance with raised eyebrows. "We won't," she promised.

"Val's a good lady. And even if she didn't always agree with Susie, well, that doesn't make her a murder."

"But could it make her someone looking to chase me out of town? And I'm guessing from your lead-up, she is unaccounted for around the time that knife was put in my door."

Mac sighed. "Shortly after you left the diner, Val stepped out to run a few errands. Told Shawna she wouldn't be long but she had a few things to handle."

Mia raised her eyebrows at the admission. "So, she could have come out to the manor, stuck the knife with the note in Ellie's front door, and gone back to the diner."

"Appears that way," Mac said. "I asked around a few other places, grocery store, bank, et. cetera, but whatever errand she had didn't have to do with any of those places."

"Are you saying no one saw her around town?" Ellie asked.

"I'm saying she got in her car and disappeared for about thirty minutes at least, yeah."

"More than enough time to drive to the manor and put that note on Ellie's door," Mia concluded.

"I'm afraid so," Mac said with a heavy sigh. "I just can't believe she'd do it."

"We don't know that she did," Ellie said. "We're just trying to vet through people who could have done it versus people who definitely didn't. Someone killed Aunt Susie and someone is threatening me."

"Maybe I could have a conversation with Val. Ask her straight out where she went this afternoon."

"No!" Mia shouted. "Don't do that. If she is our guilty party, we may spook her."

"I'd agree," Ellie said. "We don't want her to suspect we may be on to her. It may make the situation worse."

"How?" Mac questioned. "I doubt she'll continue to harass you if she thinks we suspect her."

"No, she may try to finish me like she did with Aunt Susie." Ellie waved her hand at the phone despite Mac being unable to see her. "Let's just keep our suspicions under our hat for the moment."

"Surely, though, that will only embolden whoever is doing this. I'd hate to see you continue to be harassed, Ellie," Mac countered.

"I'll take a few more days of harassment to prove beyond a shadow of a doubt that we've got the right person. Rick's got the police watching the house. Mia's here—"

"I'm here," Lola said.

"And Lola," Ellie continued. "She'll alert us if anything funny's going on."

Cleo flashed her claws and narrowed her eyes. "And me. Anybody comes in after you, I'll pop a claw in their a—"

"Anyway, let's not panic just yet, and let's not go accusing someone who may be innocent. I plan to live here. I don't want to make enemies of decent folks who may have just had a disagreement with Aunt Susie."

"Well, I think you've got a good head on your shoulders, Ellie. I won't say anything to Val unless she gives us some other reason to suspect it's her."

"Thanks," Ellie said. They finished with a few pleasantries and Ellie ended the call.

"So," Mia said, "looks like Val had the motive, means, and opportunity."

"But did she do it?"

Mia shrugged.

"I hope we figure it out before anything else tragic happens."

CHAPTER 22

*E*llie startled awake to the raucous sounds of Lola's barking. With slits for eyes, she glanced around the room. The dog was nowhere in sight.

"What now?" she murmured as she flung the covers off and swung her legs over the bed.

"I don't know," Cleo hissed from under the bed. "Lola went tearing out of here like the bed was on fire."

Ellie tugged her robe on and shuffled across the room with her eyes half-closed.

"Lola! What are you barking at?" she called over the railing.

Mia hurried down the hall in bare feet. "What's going on?"

Ellie thudded down the stairs. "I don't know. The dog barks at everything."

She reached the landing and swung around toward the front door, continuing down the staircase. Lola paced the floor below, howling and snarling at the front door.

"What are you—"

Ellie froze midstep, still two feet from the lower floor. Her eyes widened. "Lola, get back!" she whispered.

She inched down the remaining two steps and tried to wave the dog behind her, keeping her eyes trained on the front door.

Moonlight streamed through the frosted glass on either side of the wooden barrier. Behind the privacy panel, a dark shadow stood hunched over the lock. A distinctive scraping sounded as tools clacked against the lock.

"Ellie! Someone's out there!" Lola said.

"Yes, I know that!" Ellie hurried back to the stairs and raised her voice just slightly. "Mia!"

"Yeah?" A whispered reply came.

"Call the police. Someone's trying to break in."

"Oh no!" Mia squealed. "Come up here! Get away from the door!"

Footsteps retreated down the hall as Mia raced for her cell phone.

Lola offered a few more harsh barks at the door before she glanced at Ellie who tried to shoo her up the stairs.

"Susie kept a gun in the closet."

"A gun? Loaded?"

"Yep," Lola confirmed. "A hunting rifle. Both barrels loaded."

Ellie nodded and approached the closet next to the front door. The deadbolt on the front door began to slowly slide to the unlocked position.

Ellie darted to the door and swung the chain lock into place before she pulled open the closet door. A double barrel rifle stood inside the door. She grabbed it and aimed at the door as it pushed open, snapping the chain taught.

Lola raced toward the doorway, a shrill bark escaping from her throat.

"Get back!" Ellie shouted. "I've got a loaded gun and I will use it."

The shadowy figure outside the door straightened as the chain went slack. Footsteps pounded across the porch and down the stairs.

Ellie huffed out a sigh of relief as she raced toward the door. She undid the chain lock and swung it open. A dark figure approached the tree line, dashing to be hidden in its cover.

Red and blue lights reflected off the roadside trees as a siren screamed toward them. Lola bolted past Ellie, in full gallop, barreling down the stairs and after the fleeing figure.

Ellie chased after her onto the porch. "Lola! No! Lola, come! Lola! Get back here!"

The police car, siren still blaring and lights glaring, rumbled up the driveway, coming to a stop outside the house.

The siren cut out and Ellie scrambled down the stairs as Nathan stepped out of the vehicle. "Someone was trying to break in. They ran that way! Lola went after them."

She gasped for breath as Nathan nodded and took off toward the tree line. Before he reached it, a single shot rang out in the night. The barking ceased.

Ellie's eyes went wide and her legs felt wobbly. Nathan glanced back at her before he drew his weapon and balanced his flashlight on top, inching forward into the woods.

"Oh, no," Ellie gasped. She hurried into the house and searched the coat closet for a flashlight.

Mia hurried down the stairs in slippers. "What happened?"

"Lola took off after whoever it was. There was a gunshot and she—"

Mia's eyes went wide.

"She's not barking anymore. I have to find her," Ellie

choked. Tears filled her eyes and the flashlight slipped from her trembling fingers as she checked to make sure it lit. She caught it before it hit the floor.

"Just wait a second, Ellie. I'll come with you."

"There's another flashlight in the pantry. I'll meet you outside."

Ellie charged out the front door, gun in one hand, flashlight in the other. She hustled down the stairs and across the gravel. The sharp rocks poked through her flimsy slippers, but she continued, crossing the parking area and slipping into the woods.

Ragged breaths puffed behind her as Mia scurried after her. "Wait up."

"Lola!" Ellie called as she stepped under the canopy of leaves.

"Shh, maybe you should be quiet and not alert whoever she ran after!" Mia whispered.

"To hell with that. I need to find my dog. And if this person stops me, I'll shoot 'em. Who the hell fires a gun at a defenseless dog. If I find this person, I'll tear them to shreds."

Ellie snaked around through the trees. "Lola!"

"Lola!" Mia shouted as she swung her flashlight beam in the opposite direction of Ellie's.

They continued through the woods, each calling out to the dog. Only silence met their shouts. Ellie fought to keep her lower lip from trembling as she searched the area around her. Her voice threatened to betray her upset and she struggled to keep it steady as she called to the dog.

Her stomach tied itself in knots as she imagined the dog hurt or worse. "Oh, Lola," she murmured. Tears blurred her vision.

Even with the distorted sight, movement caught her eye. She swung the gun toward it and blinked to clear her eyes of the burning tears.

Light shone back at her. "Whoa, easy!" Nathan's voice called out as he lowered his light. "What are you two doing out here?"

"Looking for Lola. Have you seen her? After that gunshot —" Ellie's voice trembled and she stopped talking.

"No, I haven't. And I didn't see anyone else either. I heard a car on the road. I'm guessing the person had their car hidden somewhere. I made it to the road in time to see taillights disappear around the bend."

"Which way were they headed? Into town or out?"

"Out," Nathan said.

Ellie nodded as they spoke and then broke into the conversation. "Okay, I'm not worried about which direction they went at the moment. I need to find Lola."

"We'll find her, Ellie," Mia said, rubbing Ellie's shoulders.

Ellie nodded, unable to voice a response. "If the person is gone, maybe we should split up."

"I'll head toward the road," Nathan said.

Mia pointed in the opposite direction with her flashlight's beam. "I'll go this way."

Ellie pursed her lips and nodded. "I'll keep going forward."

They parted ways, each of them calling out to Lola as they moved through the thick woods. Ellie pushed forward, shoving aside branches as she continued to call to the dog.

She stopped and slowly swung the light from left to right, sweeping over the darkened trees and branches. Little moonlight shone through the thick canopy above as she descended deeper and deeper into the thickly wooded area.

"Lola!" she shouted.

A noise sounded to her right. Ellie snapped the beam in its direction. A branch snapped. Ellie peered into the blackness beyond her beam.

"Lola!" she called, her voice lifting with hope.

She took a few steps forward. Another twig snapped. "Lola!" she cried, hurrying forward toward the noise.

She sprinted toward the sound. Branches tore at her hair and skin as she hurried through the trees in a mad scramble to get to the dog. Images raced through her mind as to what she would find. Was Lola hurt? She must be alive if she was moving.

She puffed as she ran. The sound of feet splashing in the stream's water reverberated through the trees.

The woods cleared, opening to the stream cutting through them. Ellie slowed as she reached it, sweeping the beam around. Glowing eyes stared back at her. She focused the beam with a trembling hand. Her heart sank as a white-tailed deer stamped its foot at her before spinning and fleeing into the trees on the opposite side of the creek.

Ellie's shoulders slumped and she let the flashlight fall to her side, the beam directed toward the ground. She gulped in the cool night air as she squeezed her eyes shut. She opened them, continuing to suck in deep breaths as she attempted to piece together a plan.

Light bobbled at her side. Ellie held her hand up in front of her eyes as she squinted at it. "It's me," Mia called. "Did you find something?"

Ellie shook her head as she let her hand fall to the side. "No," she admitted with a sigh. "It was a deer. I assume you didn't find her?"

"No," Mia said as she closed the distance. "No luck."

Ellie scoffed and shook her head, pursing her lips.

"Hey, maybe she went back to the house."

"Maybe," Ellie said.

Mia squeezed her upper arm and offered a weak smile. Ellie avoided eye contact, afraid one glance might start a stream of tears. The water gurgled softly in the late night air as she swallowed the lump in her throat.

"Hey, we'll find her," Mia said.

Ellie bit her lower lip and swiped at a wayward tear that fell from her cheek.

"We didn't find her hurt somewhere or worse. We'll find her. She probably got scared when she heard the gunshot and ran off."

"Yeah," Ellie choked out.

"It's good news we didn't stumble over her anywhere. It means she's alive."

"Or we just didn't find her body. Or she slinked off somewhere and she's hurt or dying." Ellie's voice broke and the tears she'd held back to this point spilled over, staining her cheeks.

Mia reached out and pulled Ellie into an embrace. "You can't think like that. We'll find her."

"I should have been more careful," Ellie sobbed. "I shouldn't have yanked the door open like that. She was so upset. I should have realized she'd run off after the person."

"You couldn't have known she'd take off."

Ellie's shoulders shook with sobs. "I could. That's what dogs do."

"Shh," Mia soothed. "It's not your fault. You've never had a dog before in your life. You couldn't have known."

Ellie leaned back, wiping at her cheeks. "I did."

"When?"

"When I was a kid. And she died. And I got really upset. I never talk about it and I've never had a pet since." She scoffed. "No wonder. I'm a terrible pet parent."

"You are not. We'll find her. But it's impossible in the dark. We can barely see five feet in front of us, even with the moonlight. Let's head back to the house. We'll resume searching as soon as the sun's up."

Ellie did not respond but allowed herself to be led back toward the manor. Red and blue lights still swirled, painting momentary pictures on the surroundings as they approached. Ellie sniffled and wiped at her face as Mia guided her to the stairs.

"Ellie!" Nathan shouted from behind them.

"Go on inside," Mia said, "I'll talk to him."

Ellie nodded and firmed her lower lip in a silent thank you as she plodded up the stairs. She wiped at her tears with the back of her hand as she placed the gun and flashlight in the closet. She closed the door, squeezing her sore eyes shut.

As she spun to lean against it, she popped her eyes open. Cleo slinked down the stairs, her eyes two green saucers in her tiny, furry face.

She stopped mid-stride and stared at Ellie. "Lola?"

Ellie's face twisted into a mask of upset as she shook her head. The cat's head dropped. "Oh, no. Lola." Her tiny shoulders heaved a sigh.

As Mia pushed through the door into the foyer, Cleo darted up the stairs. Ellie wiped at her cheeks again.

"Aw, El. It'll be okay. We'll find her. Nathan said he'll come back in the morning with the sheriff to help search for her."

Ellie nodded as she squeezed Mia in a tight hug.

"Get some sleep," Mia said as she pulled back and squeezed Ellie's arm.

With another nod, Ellie slogged across the foyer and up the stairs. She shambled into the bedroom and threw herself across the bed. Cleo slithered from under the bed and leapt next to Ellie.

She curled in the crook of her arm, her front paw reaching for Ellie's abdomen. "Poor Lola."

Ellie sniffled and nodded at her. "I tried to find her. But it's so dark."

"So dark," Cleo repeated. "And cold. She's probably scared. Maybe hurt. I hope she's not—" The cat's voice cut off and she wailed. "Oh, Lola! You big, dumb lug. Why? Why, Lola?"

Cleo sobbed for a few more moments before she sniffled and shook her head.

Ellie stroked her smooth, sleek fur. "We'll look for her tomorrow."

"I heard the gunshot," Cleo said. "But I never imagined… Oh, Lola!"

"We don't know she's hurt. Maybe she got scared and ran away."

"Yeah. Yeah, maybe she ran away and hid. And she's riding out the night somewhere safe." Cleo sniffled again. "I gotta believe that. She just has to be okay!"

"We'll look for her again in the morning."

"Oh, please let her be okay. I swear I'll never be mean to her again. If I can only look at her stupid, ugly, sweet, wrinkly face again with that frowny mouth and those stupid crooked teeth."

"Don't make promises you can't keep," Ellie warned.

"Okay, I'll be less mean to her."

"Did she ever run away before?"

"No," Cleo answered, "not even when she was a baby. She might run off after a rabbit or something in her younger days, but she always came back in a few minutes."

Ellie smashed her lips together at the news and sighed. She let her eyes slide closed in the hopes of falling asleep.

The incident replayed over and over in her head. In her mind's eye, she pulled the door open. Lola barreled out, barking at full volume. The gunshot echoed in the night air. Lola's barks fell silent.

Ellie tried to imagine anything but the events of the past few hours. She considered her move, mentally cataloging her items. She tried to picture the manor bursting at the seams with B&B guests. At every turn, Lola's face popped into her head.

She snapped her eyes open. Sleep would not come. She gave the black cat's fur another stroke as she slid her arm away from her and rose as noiselessly as possible.

"Are you going to look for Lola?" Cleo whispered.

Ellie sighed, rubbing at her face. "No, but I can't sleep. I was going to head downstairs and pace the floors. Maybe hope I hear her bark or spot her."

"I'll come with you," Cleo said, rising to her four feet and arching her back high in the air. "Hey, maybe if you put a bowl of her food out. Lola loves food."

Ellie stalked down the stairs with Cleo at her side. "Good idea."

She shuffled to the kitchen and shook some kibble into Lola's pink plastic dish. Cleo followed her as she carried it to the front door. The cat stared through the screen as Ellie placed the bowl down on the porch, calling to Lola again.

She scanned the edge of the woods, searching for even the slightest sign of movement. After a moment, she descended the stairs and hurried to the location she'd last seen Lola. She called a few times into the woods, straining to listen for any noise. Only silence met her ears.

With a sigh, she trudged back to the house.

"Anything?" Cleo asked.

Ellie shook her head. "No, nothing."

The cat lowered her eyes to the floor.

"Maybe the food will help," Ellie said as she swept into the house and pushed the door closed. They both stalked into the living room. Cleo leapt onto the window seat and stared out over the moonlit driveway. After a few moments, she settled with her front paws tucked underneath her, her eyes slits.

Ellie arched an eyebrow at the small animal. "Must be

nice," she murmured as the cat's eyes closed. She stared out, searching the horizon for any signs of the white and tan dog.

Nothing moved in the wee hours of the morning. Ellie paced the floor, wincing as she hit every squeaky board on the floor. She pulled the front door open several times to check the food. It remained untouched.

As the grandfather clock in the foyer struck three, a rustling noise sounded.

"Lola!" Ellie breathed.

She raced to the front door and flung it open. Her breath caught in her throat as she spotted movement. A frown formed on her face.

CHAPTER 23

A raccoon climbed the stairs, sniffing in the air at the dog food. Its black-rimmed eyes focused on the pink bowl.

"Get out of here!" Ellie shouted at it.

It crept up another step, nose wriggling.

"I said go!" Ellie pushed the screen door open and stamped her foot on the wooden porch. The raccoon slouched down. Ellie peered over the stair as its head popped up again.

"Get!" she barked again, removing her slipper and waving it at the animal.

The raccoon backed down the stairs and waddled away. It took one last glance back at the house before it scampered away into the woods.

"What'd Roxy want?" Cleo inquired as Ellie climbed the stairs. "Has she seen Lola?"

"Roxy?" Ellie asked, freezing mid-stride.

"Yeah. I smelled her from a mile away."

"Can she talk, too?" Ellie asked.

"Of course, she can. Though she only speaks French."

"Are-are you serious?"

Cleo rolled her eyes and huffed. "No, why would a raccoon speak French? She speaks English like everybody else."

"Well, she didn't say anything to me."

"Mmm, she's probably hungry." Cleo slinked out the door as Ellie pulled it open. "Hey, Roxy! Roxy! You still there?"

The raccoon scurried around the side of the house. "Hi, Cleo," she said.

"Sorry about Ellie, she's new around here."

"Can she hear me?"

"Yeah, she can. Same as Susie."

"Oh, I didn't realize. Most people don't hear us," Roxy said.

Ellie lifted her eyebrows. "Nothing surprises me anymore. Ah, sorry about before. I thought you were trying to steal the food."

"Steal it? I may look like a bandit, but I'm just hungry. I've got four mouths to feed back at home."

"Again?" Cleo said. "Didn't you just have four kids last summer?"

Roxy shrugged, holding her paws out to the sides. "What're you gonna do. Anyway, I figured you put the food out for me."

"No, I put it out for Lola. She ran away earlier. She may be hurt."

"Oh, no. What a shame."

Cleo shook her head. "It's terrible. Have you seen her, Roxy?"

Roxy shook her head. "No, sorry. I just swung by on a pre-dawn forage run. I'll keep an eye out." The raccoon yawned. "But I'll be heading to bed soon."

"Let us know if you see anything."

"Will do." Roxy stood for another moment before her eyes fell to the dish.

"Give her the food, you big dummy," Cleo said to Ellie.

"Oh, right, sorry."

The raccoon clasped her paws in front of her. "Thank you."

"I can get you something else. You can take it back to the kids. How's a hot dog sound?"

Roxy crunched on a piece of kibble, another few clutched in her hand-like paws. "That'd be great."

Ellie entered the house and rooted around in the refrigerator for a pack of hot dogs. She removed two and carried the wiggly sticks of meat to the porch. She handed them off to the small animal who shoved one between her teeth and held the other in one paw. "Thanks," she said through clenched teeth. "Kids'll love these."

"You're welcome."

"Let us know if you see Lola!" Cleo shouted as the nocturnal animal loped toward the tree line.

Ellie sank onto the porch step and cupped her chin in her palm. "This really opens up a whole new world."

"And a fat lot of good it does us if no one has seen Lola."

Ellie squeezed her lips together and shook her head. "Gosh, I hope we find her."

"Me too. I miss that dumb mutt already."

"I'll put some more food out. Hopefully, she'll come home soon."

"Sun will be up in a few short hours. Maybe then," Cleo said.

Ellie scratched the cat's ear and smiled at her before climbing to her feet. She replaced the food in the bowl then climbed up the steps and changed into athletic leggings and a tunic top. She tugged on her sneakers and laced them up as the red digits on the bedside table glowed 4:17 a.m.

Ellie grabbed her phone from the charger next to the clock and tapped around, searching for the sunrise time. With a sunrise time of 5:37 a.m., she had just over an hour to wait to resume the search.

With a deep sigh, she shoved the phone into the side pocket of her pants and plodded down the stairs. Within minutes, the smell of freshly brewed coffee floated through the air as the rich, brown liquid drizzled into the coffee pot.

Ellie breathed in the aroma, hoping it alone helped refresh her. Nervous agitation kept her on edge, unable to rest, relax or sleep until she found the dog. She drummed her fingers on the counter as she waited for the pot to fill.

As it approached half-full, she yanked it from the maker and poured herself a mugful, taking a sip without adding cream or sugar. She grimaced at the bitter flavor as she returned the pot to continue brewing.

She dumped two heaping spoonfuls of sugar into the dark liquid and swished the spoon around before taking another sip.

She'd finished almost three-quarters of the cup when Mia appeared, stretching and yawning in the doorway.

She wrinkled her forehead and offered Ellie a consoling glance. "Did you get any sleep?"

"No, not a wink. I just want to get back out there and search for her. It's getting lighter. I'm going to leave as soon as I finish this cup of coffee."

"Wait for me, please. You shouldn't be out there running around all alone."

"I can at least go out and call for her. I set some food out last night."

"No hits?" Mia asked after gulping down a large sip of coffee.

"Only by a wayward raccoon."

"Roxy isn't wayward," Cleo said as she rubbed against Ellie's legs.

"Are you hungry? I'll get Cleo fed while you fuel up and change," Ellie said to Mia.

She cracked open a can of cat food and emptied it into Cleo's bowl as Mia darted out of the room, coffee mug in hand. Cleo leapt onto the counter and sniffed at the bowl Ellie set out for her.

The cat wrinkled her nose at it and inched away from the dish.

"No?" Ellie asked.

"I can't eat," Cleo admitted. "How can I eat with all this quiet? What I wouldn't give to hear that big lug chomping on her food down below me." Cleo's chin sank to her chest.

"We're going to find her," Ellie said, stroking the cat's head.

Mia appeared in the doorway, hair pulled up into a pony-tail and in athletic clothes. "Aww, not hungry, kitty?"

"No, how can I eat? My best friend is missing. Maybe dead!" The cat glanced at Ellie. "Is she serious?"

"She's too upset to eat. I think she's missing Lola."

"Aww, poor kitty. Do you miss your buddy?" Mia inquired, her voice rising a few octaves.

"Why is she talking to me like I'm a baby?"

"Don't worry, Cleo, we'll find Lola," Ellie answered. She tilted her head as she swallowed the last of the coffee from her mug and set it in the sink. "I'm heading out. If you want breakfast first, I'll stick around the house until you're ready."

"No, I'm good. I'll grab a protein bar," Mia said, ducking into the pantry and emerging with a wrapped oatmeal bar. "You want one?"

Ellie shook her head.

"You need to eat."

"I couldn't stomach it. I'm lucky I got the coffee down."

Mia unwrapped her bar as they trudged down the hall. Ellie pulled the door open and jumped, startled. A figure loomed on the porch in the early morning light.

Ellie pressed her hand to her chest as she blew out a sigh of relief. "Oh, Jake. You scared me."

"Hey, Ellie. Sorry."

"What are you doing here? It's not even six!"

"Yeah, reporters need to start early to get the scoop."

"And you started here?"

"Scarlett sent me. About the break-in and missing dog. Have you found her yet?"

Ellie fluttered her eyelashes at the remark. "No, we haven't. I was just heading out to look for her. I'm sorry, I don't have time for questions right now."

"No problem. I can help search for her."

"You don't have to do that."

"I'd like to help find her."

Ellie nodded, pressing her lips together in a slight, tight-lipped smile. "Okay, that would be great."

"Oh, by the way," Jake said, as the two women stepped onto the porch, "I have the handwriting sample you asked for. Remind me to give it to you when we come back."

"Thanks. Jake, this is my friend, Mia. Mia, meet Jake Braedon, one of the local reporters."

They exchanged pleasantries before descending the porch steps. A marked police cruiser pulled down the drive as they stepped onto the gravel.

Rick emerged from behind the wheel and Nathan popped out of the passenger's side.

"Good morning," Rick said with a wince. "Lola come back yet?"

Ellie shook her head. "No, I put food out on the porch and watched for her all night, but nothing yet."

Rick pursed his lips and nodded. "Well, we'll get on out

into the woods there and see if we can find her. Probably got scared by the gunshot and hid somewhere."

"That's what I'm hoping," Ellie said. "Mia and Jake are going to help look, too."

Another car blazed a trail down the driveway as Rick swung his door shut. The car screeched to a halt and Mac leapt from inside as the car rocked back and forth. "Did she come home yet?"

"No, we were just heading out to look for her."

"Oh, heck, Ellie, I can't believe this. When Rick told me at the coffee shop this morning, I nearly fell over dead. I'll help you look."

"Thanks, everyone." Ellie glanced around. "I guess we should split up. Go in different directions."

Rick nodded. "Nathan, you go west. I'll head toward the south. Ellie and Mia, you take the east, and Mac and Jake can go north."

Everyone agreed and set off in their assigned direction. The women headed toward the rising sun. Mia shielded her eyes from the bright yellow ball peeking over the wooded horizon.

"I think they sent us in this direction because of the sun," Mia lamented as she slid a pair of sunglasses onto her face.

Shouts from the other directions reached their ears. Ellie called out to the dog. Nothing but the singing of birds answered back. She scanned the ground for any sign of paw prints or blood.

"Hey, I hate to sound so suspicious but do you think it's weird that Jake kid showed up this morning and knew Lola was missing?"

"What do you mean?" Ellie questioned as she scanned the area, picking her way through the trees.

"I mean before 6 a.m. the local newspaper already knew

the dog was missing and you had trouble overnight. What are the chances?"

"Mac knew," Ellie answered. "Maybe Scarlett overheard them talking about it."

"Jake got here before Mac. Mac came right after the Sheriff. He probably grabbed a coffee before he came over to your place and Mac followed him."

Ellie furrowed her brow as she considered the timeline. "So, what are you saying?"

"I'm saying is it possible Scarlett knew the dog was missing because Scarlett is the one she ran after. She's on the suspect list."

Ellie stopped walking and stared at Mia before her eyes lifted to the sky. Her eyebrows raised. "Ohhh. Still, would you send the kid reporter out after you knew you did it?"

"Maybe she feels bad about the dog. Or maybe she wants to make it look good? Or maybe she's hoping he gets some information like we know who it is, or we suspect. Maybe she's trying to figure out how much you saw."

"Wow, that's… well, I'm not even sure I know what to say. She has some nerve to send Jake out here if she's the reason Lola's missing."

"I can't wait to compare the writing sample he has," Mia said.

"I can't wait to find Lola."

They continued through the woods, calling to the dog and scanning the area for any clues to her location. After two hours, Ellie stopped walking, leaning her back against the trunk of a large oak tree. She wiped at her brow.

"Maybe we should head back and see if anyone's found anything," Mia suggested.

Ellie scoffed but didn't respond as she stared off in the distance.

"I don't mean give up. I just could use a bottle of water.

And maybe someone else found a sign of her. It would be better if we concentrated our search in an area where she may have been."

"You're right," Ellie said. "I could use a drink too. Let's head back this way. Maybe we'll run into Jake and Mac."

They circled back toward the house, heading north. The men's voices passed through the trees and Ellie and Mia headed in their direction.

As they approached the stream, Mac stood on the banks. Jake waved from the opposite side. Ellie stared down at his soaked cargo pants. He must have waded through the babbling brook to reach the other side.

Ellie waved as they approached. "Find anything?"

"A few paw prints here in the mud," Mac said. "But no Lola."

"Are they fresh?" Mia inquired.

"I'd say they could be from last night," Mac answered.

"Oh, Jake, you're soaked!" Ellie called across the creek.

"It's okay. I don't mind."

"Come back across. Let's regroup at the house. See if Rick and Nathan found anything."

"We can stay out a little longer," Mac countered.

"I'm not planning on staying at the house long. Just enough to grab some waters, maybe a few treats, and head back out."

"You go ahead back. I'll stay out here—" Mac began.

"No," Ellie said. "Look, I understand you want to keep searching. I want to keep searching, too. But everyone needs a minute to sit down, grab some water and create a new plan. We haven't found a trace of her outside of these prints."

Mia crouched over the muddy paw prints. "Maybe we should concentrate our efforts up here where she may have been."

Mac pointed at her. "Good idea."

She stood and wiped her hands against her leggings. "Let's head back and grab the other two."

Ellie stared down at the smudged paw print. She scanned the small rise in the land across the water.

"Come on, El. Just for thirty minutes or so to regroup."

Ellie nodded. Jake leapt into the stream and waded across in the knee-high water. He climbed out, ringing his pant legs out before joining them. The wet khaki material, now a shade darker, clung to his shins.

Ellie stared at the dripping pants. "I'll get you a towel when we get back."

"Oh, it's okay. They'll dry."

"Thanks for helping with the search, by the way."

"Do you need to be getting back to the paper?" Mia asked.

"Oh, no, I can stay and help."

Mia narrowed her eyes at the young man. "How did you find out about the incident anyway?"

"Scarlett heard it on the scanner."

Mia raised her eyebrows. "In the middle of the night?"

Jake nodded as he swiped a hand through his dark hair. "She listens to the thing day and night. I swear she doesn't sleep."

Mia continued to eye him.

"She's serious about her work, huh?" Ellie said to fill the silence. "I can't imagine there's much in a town like this."

"There usually isn't. At least not until Susie died and you showed up."

"Glad to know I can bring the drama," Ellie said.

They emerged from the treeline and strode to the house. Rick stood at the car, speaking into the car's radio. Nathan emerged from the woods moments later.

"Anything?" Ellie called to them.

Rick gave a shake to his head. "Nothing. You?"

"A few muddy paw prints by the stream. We came back to

grab a few bottles of water and regroup. Come on in. I've got coffee on, too."

The group followed Ellie into the manor. "Help yourself to coffee and water in the kitchen. I'm going to run up and grab a towel for Jake."

She hurried up the stairs and grabbed a towel from the linen closet. Cleo peeked from within the master bedroom. "Lola?"

Ellie shook her head. The cat sighed and spun to stalk back into the bedroom. Ellie stared after her for a moment before returning downstairs. As she entered the kitchen, she handed the towel off to Jake.

He pressed the towel against his wet pants. "Thanks. I'll stop at home and change before I head back to the Herald."

"Do you have the note?" Mia asked.

"Uh-huh," he answered, dropping the towel and digging in his bag. He pulled a few sticky notes inside a plastic baggy. Bright red ink stained the white paper.

Mia snatched the bag from his hand and laid it on the table next to the others.

"Comparing writing?" Mac inquired as he sipped at his coffee.

"Yeah," Mia answered, snapping her head back and forth between the new samples from Scarlett and Susie's threatening notes.

Rick approached, balancing the mug in his hand. "Comparing what writing?" His eyes widened and he snapped his head toward Ellie. "Are you kidding?"

"No," Ellie said. "We've been collecting handwriting samples from a few people and comparing them to the notes Aunt Susie received. No matches so far. How's this one looking?"

"There are some similarities. More than Val's, I'd say."

Jake stood and leaned over the table. He pointed at Scarlett's note, then Susie's. "Here," he said. "The p's are similar."

"Yeah, and the r's," Mia agreed.

Rick set his mug on the table and snatched up the loose papers. "This ends now."

Ellie screwed the cap on her water bottle. "What?"

He waved the notes clutched in his hand. "This is a job for the police."

"It won't hurt for us to have a look. And that's my property," Ellie countered.

"I'm taking it," Rick answered.

"No, you aren't."

"You collected writing samples to interfere with a police investigation."

"We're not interfering, we're actually investigating. You should try it sometime," Mia spat back.

"Come on, folks, let's all take a step back here," Mac's voice boomed. The room fell silent for a moment before Mac spoke again. "Now, as far as I can see Ellie and her friends aren't doing anything illegal. It's not illegal to compare people's handwriting."

"Thank you, Mac. It's not." Ellie wrenched the notes from Rick's fingers. "This one is actually a list of ice cream flavors for my B&B reopening research. And this is a souvenir from the diner for Mia. And these are obviously Jake's to-do lists from Scarlett. They are all our property."

"Okay, I get it," Rick said.

"But," Nathan chimed in, "what he's saying is what you're doing is dangerous."

"Searching for the person who did this is dangerous?" Ellie questioned. "I'd say not searching for them is just as dangerous. I want this person caught!"

"So do we," Rick assured her.

Ellie shook her head. "I'm being harassed left and right and now my dog is missing and may be hurt. All because of whoever did this."

"Allegedly," Rick added.

"Oh, please," Ellie said with a roll of her eyes. "I hate that word."

"Either way you slice it," Mia said, "someone is harassing Ellie and someone, perhaps the same person, perhaps not, killed her aunt. And now because of at least one of these parties, the poor dog is missing. We're just trying to narrow down the suspects."

"Fine," Rick said with a tight jaw. "But none of you are handwriting experts. So before you start accusing people, you bring anything to us first, you hear?"

Ellie held up her hands in surrender. "Whoever the person is harassing me came here last night with a gun. I am not going after this person alone, believe me."

"All right, then. With that settled, let's—"

Rick's radio crackled to life. A bubbly female voice broke through the static. "Sheriff? It's Hazel. Hazel Duncan. Your secretary."

Rick pressed his lips together as he reached for the walkie attached to his shoulder and toggled the button. "Yeah, Hazel. Go ahead."

"Oh, hi, Sheriff. Did you find Lola?"

"Not yet. What did you need, Hazel?"

"Oh, right. Uh, Mrs. Patterson called. A few kids rode through her vegetable garden on their bikes and she wants to talk to you."

"Uh, okay. I'll get over there as soon as I can."

"Well, okay, Sheriff, but what should I tell her? She's pretty mad."

"Tell her—"

Ellie waved her hand at him. "It's okay. Go ahead. We'll keep looking."

"Sheriff? Tell her what? I didn't hear you. Can you repeat?"

Rick lifted his eyebrows at her. "You sure?"

"Yeah. If we haven't found her by the time you're finished, come on back. I'll put more coffee on and even rustle up something for lunch."

Rick nodded. "Thanks." He hit the button on his walkie. "Yeah, tell her I'll be right over."

"Okay, Sheriff. Will do." A rustling sounded, then Hazel's voice came over the airwaves again. "Hi, Mrs. Patterson, are you still there?"

"Hazel," Rick said.

"She can't hear you," Nathan said. "She's still holding the button." He held up a finger and pulled his cell phone from his breast pocket. After a few taps, he held it to his ear.

"Oh, hold on, Mrs. Patterson, I have another call," Hazel's voice said. "Uh, hold, line two, answer. Hello?"

Nathan leaned against the sink. "Hazel. You've still got the button pressed on the walkie."

"Huh? Ohhhh, sorry. I always for—" Her voice cut off as she let the button go.

Rick offered a bemused smile at the others before setting his coffee mug down after a final sip. "Keep us informed."

"We will," Mac said.

Nathan ended the call and stuffed the phone into his pocket. "Thanks for the coffee. I hope you find Lola soon."

"Thanks, Nathan," Ellie said as she walked them out.

She returned to the kitchen to find Jake on his phone and, across the room, Mac with his phone glued to his ear. Mia studied the notes.

"No, not yet," Mac said.

"Nothing yet," Jake echoed.

Ellie shuffled to Mia and stared over her shoulder at the papers spread across the table. "None of these really look like a match."

"Okay, Scarlett. See you later," Jake said before ending the call and dropping his cell phone into his pocket. He joined the woman at the table.

"Everything okay with the dragon lady?" Ellie questioned.

"Yeah, she wanted to know if we found Lola yet." He studied the notes. "The s's are completely different."

"Yeah, but that could be because she's disguising her handwriting," Mia answered. "Clearly, she writes very distinctive s's when she signs her name, but maybe she avoided doing that so she couldn't be identified."

Jake rubbed his neck. "I just don't think it's her. I mean, Scarlett can be a pain in the you-know-where but murder? Potentially harming a dog? I don't see it. In fact, she just offered to come out and help us search."

"Yeah, because it's her fault!" Mia countered.

"Well, that'd be real nice," Mac said. "I'm sure Ellie will appreciate it. I know I will."

Ellie wrinkled her forehead as Mac mentioned her name. She glanced at him and shrugged in question. He held a finger up as he finished the call.

After a moment, he pulled the phone from his ear and tapped it with his thumb. "That was Val. She's going to send over some lunch for everyone so we can continue the search. She said she'll stop over after her shift, too, to help.

"Aw, that's nice," Ellie said.

"Unless she did it and she's feeling guilty," Mia said.

"I really don't think anyone we've got samples for so far is guilty. None of the handwriting matches that closely."

"So, it's one of these others," Mia said, picking up the list and studying it.

"We can work on getting a few more samples once we

find Lola. For now, I'm going to concentrate on that and head back out there. I just need another sip of—" Ellie's voice began to slur as she crumpled to the floor.

CHAPTER 24

*"E*llie? Ellie!" Mac's voice called.

"Huh?" Ellie's eyelids fluttered open and she glanced up at the concerned faces hovering over her.

"Easy, now," Mac said. "You fainted."

"What?" Ellie questioned, rubbing her forehead. "Oh, for heaven's sake." She struggled to push herself up to sit.

"Easy, El," Mia said, kneeling beside her.

"I'm fine. I just didn't eat anything this morning and I was up all night. I'm okay though."

She eased herself up to sit.

"Do you feel woozy at all?" Jake asked.

"No. I feel okay."

"I think you should lie down for a bit before Val gets here with lunch," Mac suggested.

"No, I'm okay," Ellie answered. "I really just want to keep searching."

"El, I think Mac's right," Mia said.

"Well, that's a first."

"I'm serious. We've got a few hours before lunch. Eat a protein bar and lie down. Even if you don't sleep, it'll help."

Ellie shook her head. "I want to find her. She's out there all alone, maybe hurt."

"We'll keep searching. Just take an hour."

Ellie reached her hands up to them to help her from the floor. She stood on wobbly legs, concentrating on keeping her balance. Her head pounded at the temples and her vision threatened to close to a pinpoint again as she stood.

She couldn't continue searching even if she wanted to. She clutched Mia's hand as she sank onto the hard kitchen chair. "Okay. I'll eat an energy bar and lie down for an hour. But if you find her, wake me."

"We will," Mia promised as she ducked into the pantry and emerged with a pre-packaged oatmeal square.

Ellie tore open the corner of the package and bit off a chunk. She chewed it, hoping she could find the strength to swallow. She forced it down and chased it with a few swallows of water.

"Come on, El," Mia said. "I'll take you upstairs."

"You know, I probably could go out with you guys—"

"No!" Mia insisted. "You need some rest. Now, up to bed."

"Okay, okay," Ellie said, raising her hands in surrender as Mia led her from the kitchen.

They climbed the stairs and Ellie shuffled into her room and curled up on the bed.

Mia motioned to the window. "Want me to pull the shade?"

"No, I'm fine."

Mia cocked her head at Ellie.

"I'll go to sleep, I promise!"

"Okay." Mia crossed the room and stepped into the hall, pulling the door slightly closed behind her. "I'll wake you if we find anything."

"Thanks."

Ellie stared at the wooden door as footsteps descended

the stairs. Unintelligible voices floated from the foyer to her room. The door opened and closed. Silence fell over the house.

Ellie sighed and pursed her lips, squeezing her eyes closed. A sleek patch of fur swept past her hand.

Her eyes fluttered open to find Cleo staring at her. She smiled at the cat. "Hey, sweetie."

"Nothing yet?"

Ellie shook her head as she ran her fingers down the cat's back. "No. They're out looking now but I could barely stand up."

"You get the vapors?"

Ellie chuckled as she rumpled the cat's fur. "I did."

"Maybe you should take a nap."

"Let's hope when we get up we have a nice surprise."

The cat curled up, pressing her back against Ellie's chest. Ellie wrapped her arm around the fur ball and kissed the top of her head.

Purring filled the air and vibrated against Ellie's stomach. She nestled into the pillow and closed her sore eyes. Within moments, she drifted off to sleep.

* * *

Dark halls spanned in front of and behind Ellie. She stood in the middle, glancing over her shoulder, then in front of her.

"Lola!" she called.

Her voice echoed off walls. Overhead, a fluorescent light flickered before it died. Eerie shadows stretched down the hall. Ellie glanced up and down again before calling for the dog again.

The pitter-patter of claws tapped a tune out on the tile floor. Ellie spun in search of the source. Movement caught her eye down the hall.

Lola hurried away from her.

"Lola!" she called as she followed the dog.

Lola's trot turned into a run and she disappeared around a corner. Ellie hurried toward it, swinging around the edge and staring down the hall. She found it empty.

"Lola!" she called.

The tap-tap-tapping sounded again on her right. She glanced down the first corridor but found it empty. Her eyes flitted between the two halls, trying to find the source of the noise.

"Lola!" She took a few steps down the hall when a screeching resounded from behind her. She spun around and squinted into the darkness. "Lola?"

Ellie took a few steps forward. A nurse in a set of blue scrubs pushed through a door into the hall.

"Excuse me!" Ellie called to her.

The nurse continued walking away from her.

"Hey!" Ellie called again. "Excuse me!"

The nurse ignored her.

"I'm looking for my dog, Lola. Have you seen her?"

The nurse twisted to face her, a cruel smile spreading across her features. Ellie wrinkled her nose at the expression. Her eyes drifted to the blue scrubs the woman wore. Red blood stained them. Ellie's eyes widened and her jaw dropped.

"Is that blood?"

The nurse offered a harsh cackle and continued to stalk away from Ellie. "Is that Lola's blood? Hey! Wait!"

Ellie broke into a run, tearing down the hall after the nurse. The woman disappeared into a room marked with thick bold letters reading O.R.

Ellie slammed into the doors and burst into the operating room. A blood-stained sheet covered a bed in the middle. A bright light shone down on the bed.

A doctor, his back facing Ellie, prepared instruments at a nearby table.

"What's going on here?" Ellie questioned.

The nurse spun to face her. Her stained teeth showed as she offered a devilish grin at Ellie. In her right hand, she clutched a syringe. Liquid sprayed from the top as she approached Ellie.

"No!" Ellie shouted. She tried to run, but the doors were stuck fast.

Ellie spun and pressed her back against the cold metal. "Get away!" she shouted as the nurse continued toward her, syringe raised high.

Ellie held her hands out in front of her to stave off the inevitable attack. The nurse closed in on her, her arm raised high overhead. Hot breath wafted across Ellie's cheek as the nurse swung the sharp needle down toward her.

Ellie screamed as the tip of the needle pierced her skin.

* * *

Ellie's body jolted as she startled awake. She gulped in breaths, glancing around. Remnants of the nightmare still stuck in her mind. Her circumstances flooded back to her, eliciting a sigh. Her heart broke all over again as she recalled the missing dog.

As her heart stopped thudding in her chest, she checked the clock. It read 12:23 p.m. She'd slept longer than she hoped. The silence in the house indicated no one had returned yet. Which also meant they hadn't found Lola.

The black cat next to her stirred. She yawned and stretched her front foot out before rising to her feet and arching her back. "Mmm, what time is it?"

"A little after noon," Ellie reported. She swung her legs

over the edge of the bed and hovered there. Her head still throbbed.

She pressed her hands to her temples and winced. She climbed to her feet and shambled to the bathroom. After tossing back two acetaminophen tablets chased with water, she pulled her hair into a ponytail and headed downstairs.

The front door popped open as she reached the final step.

"Oh, Ellie!" Mac said as he pushed through the door.

"Did you find anything?"

He shook his head, his eyes downcast. "But we'll be right back at it as soon as we fuel up." He held the screen door open.

Val ducked under his arm and entered the foyer, carrying two large bags of food. The scent of French fries and chicken tenders filled the air.

The woman offered Ellie a consoling smile. "How you holding up, honey?"

Ellie raised her eyebrows. "I'll be better when we find her."

Val pulled her lips into a thin line and nodded.

"Here, let me take those," Ellie said.

"I've got it. Can I just set this out in the kitchen?"

"Oh, yes, thank you," Ellie said. "And what do I owe you for this?"

"On the house," Val said with a wave of her hand.

"I couldn't possibly let you do that. This is too much."

"Don't worry about it," Val said as she dumped both bags onto the kitchen table and began to unload them.

Mac shook his head. "Best not to argue with her. Mmmm, that smells great."

"Are Mia and Jake still out there?"

"They were checking out another spot, but they should be back in a few minutes."

"And you found nothing?"

Mac winced. Hushed voices sounded in the foyer before he could answer.

Ellie stuck her head into the hall. "Anything?" she called to them.

"Hey, El, did you get any sleep?"

"Some, yeah. No sign of her?" Ellie persisted.

Jake pursed his lips and stared down at his shoes. Mia joined them in the kitchen. "Food smells great."

"What are you not telling me?"

"Nothing," Mac said. "Other than we didn't find Lola. But we're going to head back out just as soon as we fuel up."

Jake joined them and Ellie stared at him. "Jake?"

"Huh?" he squeaked.

"Did you find something?"

Jake grabbed a paper plate as Val laid them out and used the tongs to grab a few chicken fingers and some fries. He shoved a salty shoestring fry into his mouth.

"Eat, El," Mia encouraged.

"I will as soon as you're honest with me. You found something, didn't you?"

"Unfortunately," Mac answered, "we didn't find anything. No paw prints, no chunks of fur on any trees, nothing. We're not giving up, but we're just not sure where to look next."

"You didn't find anything by the creek where we saw the prints?"

Mia shook her head. "We searched for more prints but we found none."

Ellie nodded as she grabbed a plate. "Well, we haven't found anything definitive yet, so I'm not giving up."

Mia smiled at her. "We'll head back out as soon as we've all eaten something."

"I'll join you," Val said.

"Got the diner covered?" Mac questioned.

"Yeah, I called in Sarah and Amy. They've got it for the afternoon."

"Thanks, Val. I appreciate that," Ellie said.

"You're welcome."

They ate the meal Val provided in relative silence. Ellie's headache dulled as the food pushed the pain relievers through her system. Her heart hung heavy as she considered the lack of clues pointing toward the dog's location. She glanced around at her friends. They'd spent the entire morning searching for the dog and came up empty. She could read the tiredness on their faces and in their bodies. How long could they keep this up? How long before they gave up on her? Twenty-four hours? Forty-eight?

She squeezed her eyes shut and pushed the thoughts from her head as she finished her last fry. "This was really great. Thanks, Val."

"Yeah, really hit the spot," Jake said.

Mac rubbed his fingers against a napkin before tossing his plate into the trash compactor. "Gave me enough energy to get back out there. You ready, Ellie?"

Ellie rose to her feet. "I am." She glanced at the others. "Listen, I appreciate everyone's help but if anyone's tired or—"

"We're fine," Mia said. "We're ready."

"Yeah, I'm all good," Jake said.

"Val, why don't you and I take the area further north on the creek?" Mia suggested. "Ellie, Mac, and Jake can go back to where we found the paw prints in case we missed something."

"Sounds like a plan."

They grabbed bottles of water and headed out the front door. Ellie stopped mid-stride as she stepped down onto the first step off the porch.

A woman dressed in bright red hiking boots, khaki cargo shorts, and a red capelet stood holding a small pooch.

"Scarlett?" Ellie questioned.

She pulled her sunglasses down her nose and stared over them. "I'm here to help!"

"Help with what?" Ellie inquired, still studying her odd outfit.

"With the search, of course! We may not see eye to eye in business, but I have a soft spot for pups." She jiggled the tiny Chihuahua in her arms. "Isn't that right, Pookie?" The dog lapped at her bright red, puckered lips.

"Uh, well, thank you," Ellie answered. "We were just heading out."

"I brought Pookems along. Maybe she can sniff out something to help us."

"Good idea, Scarlett," Mac said. "We found some paw prints this way. Come with us. If you ladies find anything that way, give us a shout and we'll send Scarlett and Pookie over."

"Do you really think that dog can smell out anything?" Mia asked.

Scarlett's posture stiffened and her expression soured. She arched an eyebrow. "Pookie has a very sensitive nose!" She tilted her head to face Ellie. "Lead the way, Ellie."

Ellie offered her a fleeting smile before they set off toward the stream's edge where they'd found the paw prints. Mia and Val headed off in the opposite direction, approaching the stream north of them.

"We concentrated on this side of the stream earlier," Jake explained. "Maybe we should cross it."

Ellie nodded at him. "I'm game."

Scarlett marched next to them with a flamboyant step. "Good thing I wore my hiking boots!"

Ellie glanced down at them, her forehead crinkling at the

fashion boots Scarlett claimed as hiking boots. "You can stay on this side of the stream if you want. Jake was soaked earlier when he crossed it."

"Don't be silly!" Scarlett said with a chuckle. "This is exactly why I wore my boots!"

"Right. Okay, well," Ellie said as they reached the bank, "I suppose I'll just wade in."

"There's a stone up this way," Jake said. "We can hopscotch across. You'll still get a little wet, but at least you won't be soaked to your thighs."

Jake led them a few yards down the bank before he hopped onto a rock. Water flowed over his shoes and lapped at his ankles but stayed below his knees. He leapt across to another stone.

Ellie winced as she eyed the jump.

Jake held out his hand. "Come on."

"Yeah, easier said than done," Ellie groaned.

With pursed lips, she pushed herself from the bank and onto the slick rock. Jake caught her, steadying her as she wobbled to regain her balance.

She puffed out a breath after a second and offered him a smile. "I'm good, thanks."

They hopscotched from stone to stone until they reached the other side. Scarlett sailed across the rocks in her adventurer outfit with no trouble. Mac lumbered behind her, making it easily with his long legs.

"I didn't see anything on this side early this morning, but the light was still pretty dim, so I could have missed something," Jake said. He wandered up the bank. "The paw prints we saw are there. So we should start here to search. She may have crossed here."

"Okay, everyone spread out and start looking," Mac said.

They scanned the bank for signs of muddy paw prints where the dog may have climbed out of the water.

Scarlett branched out from the bank, searching the ground for any tell-tale signs of the dog passing through. She placed Pookie on the ground, allowing the little tan dog to sniff around.

With each footstep that revealed nothing, Ellie's heart sank further. If they couldn't find a clue soon, they may never find the poor animal.

To her left, Scarlett scanned the ground as the Chihuahua nosed around in a pile of decaying leaves. The little dog pawed at them, burying her nose.

"Did you find something, baby?" Scarlett asked.

"Yes," the little dog answered with a whine.

Ellie hurried over toward them when she heard the dog's response. "Did she find something?"

"Here in the leaves," Pookie said, nosing through them.

"Looks like she thinks there's something in these leaves," Scarlett said. "What is it, baby?"

Ellie and Scarlett hovered over the spot, squinting down at it.

Scarlett wrinkled her nose and pushed her chin back. "Is that—"

"Blood," Ellie answered. "Dried blood."

Ellie's heart pounded as she studied the droplets and smearing of the red substance in the decomposing leaves.

Jake approached and stooped to examine the evidence. His head lifted and he scanned the area further up the hill. "There's more!"

Ellie followed the line of his finger and saw the reddish-brown color ahead on a shriveled leaf. She hurried up the hill in search of a trail, though her stomach turned as she considered what a trail of blood may mean. A lump formed in her throat as she spotted more.

They followed the trail uphill, with Mac and Scarlett

scurrying behind them. Scarlett scooped up Pookie as they hurried up the hill.

"If you need Pookie's nose, let me know!" she gasped out.

"Maybe. I don't see anything," Ellie answered as she scanned the area past the last blood spatter.

Scarlett closed the gap between them and set Pookie on the ground. "Where is she, Pookums?"

The dog sniffed around. "She went that way," she said, glancing up the hill. She stalked another few steps up, sniffing again.

"This way," Ellie said. She charged up the hill calling to the lost dog.

"I smell her," the Chihuahua said as she raced up with Ellie. "She's close."

"Where?" Ellie asked. "Lola!"

The tiny dog's nose wriggled in the air. "That way," she said, her eyes narrowing in the gentle breeze.

Ellie pushed on her thighs as she climbed further up. "Lola!"

A twig snapped in front of them. Ellie scanned the rise above her.

A feeble voice called out to her. "Ellie."

Ellie's heart leapt in her chest. "Lola!"

The small form of the dog appeared on the rise. "Oh, Lola!" Ellie called, hurrying up the hill toward her. Tears formed in her eyes.

"Ellie, help," Lola said. The dog tried to walk forward, but stumbled, yelping in pain. She limped another step before she stopped.

CHAPTER 25

"**S**he's hurt," Jake shouted, racing up the hill past Ellie. He scooped the dog's bulky form into his arms and carried her down the hill.

Ellie studied her, running her hands over her back as she lay in Jake's arms. "Are you okay? What hurts?"

Smudges of dirt cover the dog's white fur. Her mouth was caked in dried blood. And her right front paw was swollen to the size of a golfball.

"My foot and my mouth," Lola answered.

"It's okay, we'll get you to the vet," Ellie said. "Oh, Lola, where were you? We were so worried!"

Scarlett caught up to them, scooping the smaller dog into her arms. "I told you Pookie could find her." She offered a triumphant smile.

"Yes, thank you," Ellie answered. "Looks like she needs a vet. Do you—"

"Dr. Meyer in town," Mac shouted, already hurrying down the hill. "Jake, put her straight in my car and we'll take her."

Lola whimpered in pain as Jake jostled her around, hustling down the hill. He waded into the stream, not bothering to find the stones to hop across. Ellie followed him, doing her best to stay dry, but ending up soaked from the shins down.

They met Mac at his car after the trek back. He held the back door open. A towel covered the backseat. "Set her in there. Ellie, you ride with her."

"I'll go tell the others we found her," Jake said. "Let us know when you know anything from the vet."

"Okay," Ellie said as she climbed into the back of the car after doing her best to wring out her clothes.

Mac threw himself behind the wheel and fired the engine, spinning around in the parking area and heading down the driveway. Lola lay on the seat next to Ellie. Her body trembled as she tried to lift a paw to cling to Ellie.

"It's okay," Ellie said, running her hand down Lola's back. "I'm here. It's okay. Just rest."

Mac glanced back at them in the rearview mirror. "How is she?"

"Scared," Ellie said. "She's shaking."

"Just hang on big Lol. We'll be there soon and Dr. Mike will take care of you."

Within minutes, Mac pulled up in front of a small brick building. He threw the shifter into park and leapt from the still rocking vehicle. He pulled the door open for Ellie.

As she climbed out, Mac said, "I'll get her."

Ellie stood aside as Mac wrapped Lola in the towel and hefted her from the back seat. Ellie hurried ahead of him and pushed open the door.

A brunette in blue scrubs stood from behind the desk. "Do you have an app—" she began, before hurrying around the counter. "Emergency?"

"Yes," Ellie said with a nod. "She was missing. We just

found her. She's got blood on her mouth and she keeps licking at something inside, I can't see what. And her paw is extremely swollen."

"Okay, I'll take her straight back for Doc to look at."

"Ellie!" Lola whined as Mac handed her off.

"Can I go with her? She's scared."

"Sure. You both can come back and stay with her."

They followed the nurse down a hall. Ellie shivered as she recalled her nightmare earlier.

Mac looped his arm around her shoulders. "She'll be okay, Ellie. Doc'll patch her up."

The nurse glanced over her shoulder and offered a smile before she ducked into an exam room. She carefully laid Lola on the exam table. Lola yelped as her foot hit the cold metal. "Doc'll be right in." She offered a warm smile before she pulled the door closed.

Ellie stood at the table, stroking Lola's head. "It's okay."

Lola sucked in a ragged breath and shuddered. "My foot." Her tongue poked out of her mouth a few times again as a whine escaped her.

Moments later, a scrubs-clad man pushed through the door. He studied the dog, then glanced between Mac and Ellie.

"Hi, Doc," Mac said. "Lola got herself into a bit of trouble. Ran after a prowler last night and disappeared. We just found her. Something's wrong with her paw. And she's got blood on her mouth, too. Oh, uh, before I forget, this is Ellie Byrne. Susie's niece. She's Lola's new owner."

The vet shook Ellie's hand before running his fingers through his dark hair and approaching Lola. "Let's see what we've got going on here, Lola."

He examined the golfball-sized paw. A gentle touch from his fingertips elicited a yelp from the dog. "Okay, okay. Easy."

He studied her mouth as her tongue flicked in and out again. He lifted her muzzle and peered inside.

Ellie stood with her arms wrapped around her waist. As he straightened, she said, "How does it look?"

"She should be okay, but we've got to figure out if she's got something stuck in her mouth and we've got to tend to whatever is causing this swelling in her paw. But she won't let me get too close, so we'll sedate her and check everything out. She'll likely be on antibiotics and pain meds when we send her home."

"Okay. Sure. Do whatever you need to do."

He nodded. "Okay. If you'd like to step out into the waiting room, we'll get her ready."

"Ellie," Lola said, her eyes bulging.

"Can we stay until she's asleep?" Ellie asked.

"Sure. I'll get the tech in to give her a shot."

"Thanks."

The man left the room and the nurse appeared moments later. "Just a little pinch, honey." Lola's wide eyes bulged more as she injected her with the sedative. Within moments, Lola's eyelids slid shut and she lay on her belly, gently snoring.

Ellie rested her forehead against the sleeping dog's head as the vet tech popped back in the door. She kissed the dog's nose. "Take good care of her."

"We will. If you'd like to wait in the lobby, we'll call you back when she's all finished."

Ellie nodded and she and Mac left the exam room and wandered back to the waiting room. "I'll text Mia and she can fill everyone in."

They spent the next two hours waiting in the uncomfortable plastic chairs on the perimeter of the waiting room. Ellie's leg bobbed up at down as her mind sought to come up with conversation topics to pass the time.

"Don't worry about it, Ellie," Mac said. "You must be exhausted. We don't need to talk."

Ellie smiled at him and leaned her head back against the textured wall. She closed her eyes for a moment then snapped them open, afraid she'd drift off to sleep. Instead, she pulled her cell phone from her pocket and scrolled through social media sites after returning Mia's text.

After what felt like an eternity, the vet tech strolled into the room and motioned for them to follow her. "You can come on back now."

"How is she?" Ellie inquired as she stood.

"She's doing okay. She's still pretty sleepy from both the sedative and the pain meds. She'll be pretty out of it for the rest of the night. But you can take her home as soon as you've spoken with the doctor and we get your scripts ready."

"Oh, good. I'm so glad. Thank you!"

"You're welcome!" the girl answered as she pushed through the door into the exam room.

Lola rested on the table, her eyelids heavy. Thick layers of gauze mummified her front paw. "Ellie," she murmured sleepily as her eyes fought to stay open.

"Hey, you," Ellie said. "How you feeling?"

"Sleepy," Lola admitted.

"You rest, pretty girl. We'll be home soon."

Ellie rested her hand against the dog's side as the doctor peeled off his gloves and approached the table. The dog offered a deep sigh, allowing her eyes to close.

"She did well. She had some debris that had cut into her foot. We got it cleaned up. It'll be tender for a few days and she'll probably favor it. If that continues longer than that, give us a call. We'll be sending you home with an antibiotic to prevent infection as well as some painkillers. Keep the bandage on for a day or so. If you can. She may pull it off. If she does, it's okay, just try to keep an eye on it."

"Okay, what am I watching it for?"

"Bleeding, redness, discharge, that sort of thing."

"Okay," Ellie said with a nod.

"You'll also want to keep an eye on her mouth." He spun back toward the counter and grabbed a plastic bag with a silver object inside. "We found this wedged in her mouth. It cut her gum and the roof of her mouth. She may drool over the next few days. And it's totally normal if it's a little tinged with blood, but if she's refusing to eat or crying whenever she moves her mouth, give us a call."

"What is that?" Ellie asked. "May I?"

"Sure," the doctor answered, handing the bag over to her.

Ellie studied the small jagged object. It looked familiar, but she couldn't place it. "Do you mind if I keep this?"

"Not at all," the doctor said.

Ellie shoved it in her pocket as he flipped through paperwork. He spun the papers for her to view and went over the instructions for Lola's medication and at-home care. After another hour, they were on their way.

Mac loaded the sleepy dog into his backseat and Ellie climbed in next to her. They arrived at the manor a few minutes later.

Mia and Jake hurried from the house to greet them.

"Hey, how is she?" Mia inquired as Ellie popped the door open.

"Asleep for the most part. She's pretty drugged up."

"Aww, poor pup."

Jake carried the dog into the house and up to Ellie's bedroom, laying the lazy animal on the bed. Ellie covered her with her paw print blanket as Cleo climbed from under the bed.

"Lola!" she shouted, leaping onto the bed. She sniffed at

the dog's bandage and the area where she'd gotten the injection. Her nose wrinkled. "Ew, she stinks! Smells like Dr. Mike's."

"Dr. Mike patched her up."

"Lola! Lola!" Cleo tapped at the dog's ear.

"She's asleep. He gave her a sedative and some pain meds. Just leave her be."

"Is she going to live?"

"She's going to be okay. Can you stay with her while I go tell everyone else the good news?"

Cleo had already curled next to sleeping Lola. Purring filled the air as the cat laid her head against the sleeping dog's rib cage. She squeezed her eyes closed as the dog's rhythmic breathing rocked her head back and forth.

Ellie glanced back at the scene and smiled before she pulled the door slightly closed and headed downstairs. She filled the others in on Lola's condition and positive prognosis.

"She'll be running around that yard again in a few days," Mac said.

"And barking at everything," Ellie said.

Mac chuckled. "Yep, that too."

Ellie's gaze fell on Jake. "Thank you so much for your help today in finding her. And please thank Scarlett, too."

Jake nodded and smiled. "I will. Still think she's the murderer?"

Ellie shook her head. "I don't know what to think." She sighed, then added, "But I doubt it."

"She was really upset when I told her Lola was missing."

"I'll have to have her over for Pookie to visit with Lola once she's up and around. Anyway, tell her thanks." She turned to Mac. "And Val, too. For the food and the help."

"I'll text her and tell her. And if it's all the same to you, I'm going to stay here tonight."

"You don't have to do that," Ellie insisted.

"The heck I don't. Last night someone tried to break in here with a gun. I'm not taking any chances!"

A knock stopped any response from Ellie. "Hold that thought," she said, raising a finger in the air. She backtracked to the foyer and pulled the door open.

Rick stood on the porch. "Heard you found her."

"Come on in," Ellie said, pushing the screen door open. "We did."

Rick followed her to the living room. "Glad you found her. She okay?"

"More or less. She's got a bum foot and had something stuck in her mouth but she'll be okay."

"That's good." He nodded at the others in the room in greeting. "Glad to hear that. I just wanted to stop by and check on everyone. And let you know I'm sending Nathan over for the night in a squad car."

"Good," Mia said.

"I won't say no," Ellie admitted. She flicked her gaze to Mac. "See, you're off the hook."

"No, I'm not. I'll stay, too. Between Nathan and me, you should be safe."

Ellie shrugged. "I'll get a room ready for you. And thanks, I appreciate both you and Nathan being here."

"Sounds like you're in good hands," Jake said. "I'm going to get out of your hair."

"No need to rush off, but I'm sure you're tired," Ellie said. "Thanks a lot, Jake. I really appreciate all your help today."

"You're welcome," he answered as he slung his bag over his head. "Hope Lola feels better soon. Can I stop by tomorrow to see her?"

"Yeah," Ellie said, walking with him to the front door. "You don't have to ask. You can stop by anytime."

"I'll bring you the paper with a copy of the article I write."

"Can't wait to read it. At least it has a happy ending!"

Jake smiled and nodded as he stepped onto the porch. "I'm really glad about that. See you tomorrow."

Ellie waved as he skipped down the steps and headed for his car. She pushed the door shut and blew out a long breath. Exhaustion coursed through every fiber of her body. She slogged into the living room.

"Whew, the day is really catching up with me."

"Well, I'll get out of your hair, too," Rick said. "I just wanted to let you know Nathan'll be out in about an hour or so."

"Thanks," Ellie said. "I really appreciate that. Mac, I'm just going to run up and make up a room for you and then I think I'm heading to bed."

"No problem. I can get it myself, Ellie," Mac answered.

"Nah, I've got it. Just give me a second."

"Okay, if you're sure, I'll run home and grab a few things. Will you ladies be okay for about thirty minutes?"

"I'll wait in the car 'til you're back, Mac," Rick said.

"You can wait inside if you'd like," Ellie offered.

"I've got paperwork to do. I'll just hang out in the cruiser."

"All right. Well, thanks, again, Rick."

The two men ducked out the door as Mia and Ellie climbed the stairs to make up a room for Mac. Within thirty minutes, Ellie had the work finished. Mac returned with an overnight bag in hand. After making sure he had everything he needed, she shut herself inside her bedroom. Lola rested on the bed, still fast asleep. Cleo remained curled next to her, her paw outstretched to cross over Lola's good paw.

Ellie smiled at the scene and snapped a picture on her phone before she slipped into her pajamas. Her bare feet shuffled across the room and she climbed onto the bed next to the two animals.

Cleo's eyes popped open a slit. Ellie stroked her sleek fur as she nestled under the covers.

With one arm wrapped around Lola and the other hand resting on Cleo's side, Ellie stared at them in the waning light. Her lips pulled up at the corners, reflecting her happiness over the dog's return. But one question still burned in her mind. Who was doing this?

CHAPTER 26

*B*right sunshine streamed through the window the next morning when Ellie awoke. She'd slept like a log for hours and well past the alarm she'd forgotten to set. She stretched and sat up, surveying the bed next to her.

"Oh, Lola!" she lamented, her shoulders sagging as she spotted the dog.

The once-neatly wrapped gauze lay torn to shreds. Lola licked at her foot. Cleo sat next to her, grooming her face.

"You were asleep. I couldn't do anything about it," Cleo said.

"You were supposed to keep that on!"

"Why? It's itchy. I don't like it."

"Because," Ellie said as she studied her still-swollen paw, "it could get infected. Stop licking at it."

"But it itches and feels weird."

"Because it's swollen. We'll put some ice on it for the swelling. But stop licking at it! Other than itchy, how do you feel? Pain?"

"A little," Lola admitted. "My mouth is sore. And my foot. It keeps going thump-thump-thump."

"Okay, I'll get you a pain pill with your breakfast and you have to take an antibiotic, too."

"Can I have two pill pouches then?"

"Pill pouches?" Ellie asked, swinging her legs over the bed and shoving her feet into slippers.

"Yeah, the little brown things. Susie stuck pills in them and gave them to me. Then the pills taste good."

Ellie pulled her robe on and flicked her hair over the collar. "Okay, yes, you can have pill pouches."

"Not to be a pain," Cleo said as she leapt from the bed and stretched, "but I also need to be fed. I am starving."

"Me too. And I'm tired," Lola said.

"You'll probably be more tired after the pills. But we need to talk about what you saw when you ran out after the prowler. Also, never do that again." Ellie put her hands on her hips and shook her head. "You had the whole town upset when you disappeared."

"And me!" Cleo admonished. "I couldn't eat. I could barely sleep. I was worried I would never see your ugly mug again."

"Aww, that's nice, Cleo," Lola said as she tried to stand. She faltered, pulling her front foot up and shaking it. "Ouch!"

"Careful," Ellie warned. "Wait. I'll help you."

Ellie wrapped her arms around the dog's legs and lifted her from the bed. She set her down gingerly on the floor. Lola took a few tentative steps, limping on the foot. "Ow!" she shouted.

"Okay, easy," Ellie said. "I'll carry you down. Do you think you can hobble around outside?"

"I'll try."

"It'll feel better after your pill," Ellie said as she hefted the dog into her arms.

Ellie stepped into the hallway and glanced at the two other doors. Both remained closed. She assumed both parties were enjoying a late morning after the upset of the previous day. Cleo darted down the steps in front of Ellie, who lumbered as she carried Lola, her shoulder pressed against the wall to steady herself.

She grasped the door handle clumsily and tugged the door open. A police cruiser sat in the middle of the driveway. Ellie lugged the dog outside and set her on the ground before waving to Nathan.

He offered a wave in return, climbing from the car and approaching her as she waited for Lola to hobble around and do any business.

"Good morning," Ellie called as he closed the distance between them. "Everything okay last night?"

"Yeah. Nothing to report."

"That's good."

"It is. I'm glad it was quiet. Did you get any rest?"

"Oh, yeah," Ellie said with a deep nod. "Slept like a log. I was exhausted."

"I'll bet. Well, I'm glad the night was quiet. I can stay if you'd like for another hour or so."

"No. I'm up and I'm sure Mac and Mia will be up soon, too. We'll be fine. You can head out."

"Are you sure?"

"Yep. We're all good."

"Okay. I'll let the Sheriff know it was all quiet, though I'm sure we'll be back tonight, just in case."

"Tell him I really appreciate it."

"Will do. You have a great rest of your morning, Ellie."

"Thanks, you too."

Ellie waved as he retreated to the car. "All done?" she asked Lola.

The dog held her paw in the air. "Yeah."

"Okay," Ellie said, scooping her up and climbing the steps to the porch. "Let's get you a pain pill so you feel better."

She carried her into the kitchen where Cleo already sat on the counter. "About time. I'm starving."

Ellie popped the top of a can of cat food and emptied it into Cleo's dish before rooting around in the pantry for the pill pouches. She found the red bag of treats and filled two with the medication before feeding them to Lola.

She filled her bowl with kibble and set it down. Loud crunching filled the air. Cleo ceased eating and glanced down at Lola. "Ah, music to my ears."

Ellie leaned against the counter, crossing her arms. "Now, we need to have a discussion. Firstly, you shouldn't have run after that prowler. Lola, you could have been hurt."

"I thought I could help."

"It's not worth risking your life. That person had a gun! They could have killed you!"

Lola sat down, licking her chops as she finished the kibble. "They shot it in the air."

Ellie's eyebrows shot up.

"I got scared after that and I ran away."

"What happened out there anyway? Do you know who it was?"

"No," Lola answered. "I don't know who it was. They smelled familiar like I met them before. But I'm not sure."

"Man or woman?"

"Ummm," Lola murmured.

"Okay, never mind. You can't identify them. Did they say anything to you?"

"No."

"What happened when you ran after them?"

"I bit them."

"You did?"

"Yeah. I bit their sleeve. And I tried to pull them back to the house, but they fought me. And then they fired that gun and it was so loud. I got scared and ran away. While I was running, something hurt my foot."

"You bit them?"

"Yeah."

"Did they cry out or anything?"

"Umm, they made a grunting sound."

"Like a male grunting sound or a female grunting sound."

"Ummm," Lola murmured again.

"She doesn't know. Dum—" Cleo's eyes went wide and she glanced at Ellie then at Lola. "It's good to have you back, friend."

Ellie crossed her arms over her chest. "You're lucky they fired it in the air. Promise me you'll never do anything like that again."

"Okay," Lola said.

"She doesn't mean it," Cleo added.

"That's not helpful."

"Well, she doesn't. First sign of someone at the door, she'll be barking her head off and running at 'em."

"Maybe your hurt foot will remind you not to do that."

Lola yawned. "I'm tired."

"It's the meds," Ellie said as she gathered the two pet dishes to be cleaned.

"I'm going to take a nap in the sunroom."

"Me too," Cleo said, leaping from the counter and stalking into the other room with Lola.

"Okay," Ellie called as she washed their dishes.

"Okay, what?" Mia asked.

Ellie twisted to face her. "I was talking to the animals."

"Oh. Giving Lola what for after she disappeared?"

"Something like that, yeah. I told her to never do it again," Ellie said, drying her hands with a dish towel.

"I wonder if she'll listen."

"She'd better."

"How is she today?" Mia asked, adding a few scoops of coffee to the coffee maker along with some fresh water.

"Still in pain. She's limping around on the foot and won't put much weight on it."

"Awww. Hopefully, in a few days, she'll be back to normal."

Ellie nodded. "You want some breakfast? I'll make eggs."

"I won't turn you down."

Ellie retrieved her cooking utensils and a carton of eggs while Mia loaded the toaster with bread. "I didn't hear a thing last night, did you?"

"No. Nathan said it was quiet. I'm glad. We all got some much-needed sleep."

"But no new evidence."

"I'm not complaining."

"Who's left on our list to check out?" Mia asked.

"Rick, though again, questionable. Would he post an officer outside our door if he was him?"

"Yes. Because no one came last night. And who knew Nathan would be here? Rick."

Ellie cracked an egg into the skillet. It sizzled as it hit the bacon grease she'd melted over medium heat. "That's a stretch. What is he going to do? Wait until he stops sending Nathan?"

"Yes!" Mia answered with an emphatic nod. "That's exactly what he'll do."

"Okay, so we still need to check his handwriting, but by your own admission, the handwriting looks more like a woman's."

"Maybe he has feminine handwriting."

Ellie chuckled as she cracked a second egg into the hot grease. "Bill is on the list but not really a suspect. That leaves Andy and Delilah. Oh, and Hazel."

"Can't forget her. She'd also know about the officer being here."

"Yeah," Ellie answered.

Mac wandered in as she shimmied the pan over the heat. "Morning, ladies. Everyone sleep okay?"

"Like the dead," Ellie answered. "You?"

"Can't complain. I got up a few times and checked around. Everything seemed quiet."

"Nathan said he didn't see or hear anything."

"Maybe Lola scared them off and that'll be the end of it," Mac suggested.

"I doubt it," Mia said. Mac shot her a glance. "This person was willing to kill Susie. Do you think they'll stop because the dog ran them off?"

"Good point. And how is big Lol this morning?"

"Still hobbling, but in good spirits."

"Good, good. I hope she's back to normal soon."

Ellie plated the eggs and handed them off to Mia before breaking two more into the pan.

Mia eased into the chair with a mug of coffee, eggs, and toast. "We were just talking about who may be the guilty party. We still need a few writing samples. Any chance you could help with that?"

"I'll help in any way I can," Mac said. "Who do you need?"

"Andy and Delilah," Ellie answered. "Among a few others but they're the next two at the top of the list."

Mac guffawed. "Oh, it couldn't be either of them."

"Why not?"

"They just wouldn't do something like that."

"I've never met Delilah, but Andy seemed like a firecracker."

"Seemed like is the key part of that phrase. He can't be guilty," Mac argued.

Mia sipped at her coffee. "Let's prove it."

Mac held his hands up. "All right. Well, I happen to know Andy handwrites the employees' weekly schedule. He posts it on a bulletin board outside the restrooms at the store. I could swing by and get a picture of it."

"That'll work," Ellie said as she handed him a plate of eggs and started cooking two more for herself.

"Now, just a plan to get Delilah's," Mia said.

"What are you going to do if none of them match?" Mac asked.

Ellie shuffled over with her plate and sat down at the table with a shrug of her shoulders. "I don't know. Widen the net. But we're running out of credible suspects."

"As far as I'm concerned, the list you have isn't too credible."

"I know you don't think any of them could have done it, but someone did, Mac," Ellie said. "Someone killed Susie, someone threw a brick through my window, stuck a knife in my door and someone fired a gun last night after Lola ran after them. This isn't a ghost. Someone did this."

"You're right," Mac answered as he polished off his eggs. He took another long sip of his coffee and wiped his mouth with a napkin. "I hate to eat and run but I have an appointment. I'll stop by the Salem Store after and get a picture of Andy's handwriting."

"Thanks, Mac."

The big man tipped an imaginary hat to her as he strode from the kitchen.

Mia sighed and shook her head as the front door slammed shut. "He really doesn't believe anyone is guilty."

"I guess he prefers not to suspect any of the people he probably has spent most of his life around."

Mia stood and collected the plates from the table. She waved Ellie back down into her chair. "Just sit down. I've got these." She dumped the plates off in the sink and poured Ellie another steaming cup of coffee.

"Thanks."

"Like you said," Mia called over her shoulder from the sink as sudsy water filled it, "someone did this."

"I didn't want to mention we suspected Rick or Hazel."

"I don't blame you. He'd probably blow a gasket. Hey, I think I may get that website deal with Val, by the way."

"Oh, really?"

"She asked me a few questions yesterday while we were searching for Lola. She seems interested and she said she'd give me a call soon."

"That's great," Ellie said as Mia rinsed the last plate. She dried her hands and refilled her coffee cup. "Let's take these into the sunroom."

Ellie squinted as she entered the brightly lit room and sank into one of the rockers, setting it in motion. Lola lounged against the outside wall. Cleo stretched out next to her, her paw slung over Lola's shoulder.

"Aww, how cute," Mia said.

"You should see the picture I had of them last night after we brought Lola home. That cat really loves her."

Mia chuckled at the misfit pair as she sipped her coffee.

"So, what's up with your web design services, anyway?" Ellie asked. "I didn't realize you were freelancing in that. I can't believe you have the time."

Mia shrugged. "It seems like a good idea to expand. Offer more beyond my day job."

"Everything going okay there? You mentioned something a while back about some shake-ups coming down the pike there?"

"Oh, yeah, everything's fine." Mia took another sip of her coffee.

Ellie nodded and stared out over the sun-drenched trees.

"I'm just surprised they approved this last-minute vacation for you. I know you said you could barely get away an hour early that Friday we had the show tickets."

"Yeah, they are much more laid back now. Must have worked through everything."

"That's good," Ellie answered. She drained the last of the dark liquid from her mug. "Well, I'm going to head up and get dressed."

"Me too," Mia said, leaping from the chair and darting into the kitchen.

Ellie shuffled across the room and ran a hand down Lola's back. The dog's eyes slid open and glanced sideways at Ellie. "You okay?"

A deep sigh and closing eyes answered her question. Ellie straightened and strode across the room. As she stepped one foot into the kitchen, a chime sounded. Ellie leaned back, spotting the source.

Mia's cell phone lay on the rocker she'd occupied. "Must have fallen out of her pocket," Ellie mumbled as she swiped the phone from the cushion.

About to shove it into her pocket, she glanced at the screen. A message from Joe showed on the lock screen. Ellie's eyebrows squashed together at the message.

You can't avoid this or me forever. We need to figure out what we're going to do now.

CHAPTER 27

"*W*hat?" Ellie questioned aloud. She shook her head at the message and shoved the phone into her robe's pocket before continuing into the kitchen.

After washing her mug, she climbed the stairs and dressed for the day. As she tied the laces on her tennis shoes, the doorbell rang. A bark resounded.

"Cleo was right," Ellie muttered as she tugged the laces tight. She hurried down the stairs, finding Lola hobbling around at the bottom. "Haven't learned your lesson yet, huh?"

Lola's tail wagged. "Someone's at the door."

"Yeah, the doorbell gave that away."

Lola's tail wagged more and she flashed her lower teeth before her mouth formed an "o," readying for another bark.

"Don't bark!" Ellie said as she pulled the door open.

Jake, Scarlett, and another man stood on the porch. Pookie wriggled in Scarlett's arms, sniffing the air.

"Jake!" Lola exclaimed.

"Good morning!" Ellie said, her eyes widening at the expanded group.

Jake smiled at her and flashed a newspaper. "Morning. Brought the paper like I promised."

"And," Scarlett chimed in, "we are here to get some shots of the brave pup that ran off the robber."

"I'm not certain the person was a robber," Ellie said as she pushed the screen door open and welcomed them in.

Scarlett swept into the foyer, her eyes scanning the area. "Hmm," she murmured, narrowing her eyes at the living room before she craned her neck to glance toward the kitchen, her eyebrow arching.

"Hiya, big Lol," Jake said as the dog danced on her hind legs to greet him. "How are you feeling?"

"She's still limping, but as you can see, it hasn't dampened her spirits."

Lola rested her good paw against Jake's leg as he rubbed her ears. She blew out a long breath and a rumble escaped from her throat as he scratched her.

"Ohhhh, that's the spot," Lola said.

"Maybe in the sunroom. I'm sure it's got great light right now," Scarlett said to the other man.

Judging by the massive camera bag dangling at his side, he was the paper's photographer.

"I'm sorry, the sunroom for what?" Ellie asked, glancing between Scarlett and the other man.

"Photos!" Scarlett said. "Oh, how rude of me. My mind is just whirling with the shots we need to get. Ellie, this is Bryan Wilcox, our photographer. Bryan, Ellie Byrne."

They exchanged pleasantries before Scarlett strode toward the kitchen. A black cat slinked along the floor and up the stairs in her wake.

Ellie followed Scarlett, along with Jake and a limping Lola.

"Oh, this is perfect!" Scarlett said. "We'll get a few shots of the proud pup, lit by the morning sun. And then a few shots of the reuniting of rescuer and rescuee." Scarlett bounced Pookie up and down.

Bryan nodded and began to unpack his bag.

"Now, where is our hero?" Scarlett glanced around until her eyes locked on Lola. "There you are. Come over here, Lola. Over here, come on."

She snapped her fingers and waved toward a spot near the window.

"Go on, Lola. They're going to take your picture," Ellie said.

Lola glanced at Ellie then Scarlett. "Take my picture?"

"Go on. Go to Scarlett and take a nice picture," Ellie encouraged.

Lola limped over to the spot. Scarlett encouraged her to sit down as Bryan lined up the shot.

"Sorry," Jake said under his breath to Ellie. "She was insistent."

Ellie waved the comment away as, across the room, Scarlett did her best to pose Pookie and Lola together in a heartfelt reunion photo. "It's fine. And she really did help. She deserves it."

"Still think she could have done it?"

Ellie sighed. "No," Ellie said. "I don't. But we're running out of suspects."

They remained silent for a moment. Across the room, Scarlett cooed at the two dogs, trying to coax another picture from them.

Ellie twisted to face Jake. "What do you know about Hazel?"

Jake's forehead pinched at the question.

Before he could answer, Mia appeared. "What's going on?"

"Oh, they're doing a photo shoot with Lola and her rescue dog for the story."

"Hmm," Mia grunted in response.

Scarlett clapped her hands and scooped the smaller dog into her arms. "I think we've got what we need!" She tousled Lola's ears. "We're so glad you're safe, Lola."

"Thanks," Lola said.

Scarlett sauntered toward them. "Let's go, Jake! We've got an article to write!"

Lola hobbled over. Jake squatted down and gave her another pat on the head. "Hope you feel better soon, Lol."

"Thanks, Jake," Lola answered.

He straightened and faced Ellie. "I'll get you a copy of that article with Lola's picture as soon as it's ready."

"Thanks. And thank you for stopping by to see her. She really likes you," Ellie said as she walked them to the door.

"No problem. Take care." As the other two descended the stairs in front of him, he spun and lowered his voice. "And let me know if you need anything else on the investigation front."

"Will do. We're getting a few more samples today. If anything looks like a match, I'll text you."

He nodded, offering her a furtive grin before he bounced down the stairs, answering something Scarlett said to him as they climbed into the car.

"Well, that was interesting," Ellie said to Mia as she pushed the door closed.

"I'll say. Scarlett is a real character."

"Yeah. I can't wait to work with her."

"Work with her?"

"Apparently, I own the majority stake in the paper." Mia's eyebrows raised. "And no, I still don't think she did it to get control of the paper."

Ellie waved her hands in the air before reaching into her pocket. "Oh, I almost forgot. You left your phone in the sunroom."

"Oh, thanks. I have been looking for it! I thought I left it in the living room last night." Mia scrolled through the notifications before she snapped off the phone. "Nothing interesting anyway. No one talks to me."

"I do," Ellie said. She narrowed her eyes at Mia, the message she'd accidentally spied earlier darting through her mind. "Everything okay?"

"Yeah, why wouldn't it be?"

Ellie shrugged as she made her way to the sunroom, restoring some of the furniture Scarlett had shoved out of the way for the impromptu photo shoot. "Eh, you said no one talks to you. Just wondering where that's coming from."

Mia sank into the rocker she'd sat in earlier. "I'm just kidding. Just me being dramatic, that's all. So, did Jake have any insight on who may have done this?"

"I was about to ask him about Hazel when you appeared and then Scarlett decided she had enough pictures and they left."

"Sorry," Mia answered with a pout.

"It's okay. He's pretty into the investigation, so I think he'll be back as soon as we have more evidence to parse through. I can ask him then."

"We need to—" Mia began when the doorbell chimed.

Ellie leapt from the chair she'd just dropped into with a sigh. "Who is that at—" she glanced at the clock ticking the time away in the kitchen "—eleven in the morning?"

"Maybe they need more pictures."

"Or maybe Jake found something."

"Or Mac."

Ellie hurried to the door and pulled it open. She found a woman about ten or more years her senior on the opposite side. Gray streaked her blonde hair and a few wrinkles suggested she'd spent a lot of time smiling in her life. She held a small basket in her hands, covered in blue gingham fabric.

Ellie plastered on a smile. "Can I help you?"

"Hi," the woman said with a smile, deepening the wrinkles around her mouth and eyes. "Sorry to turn up like this, I probably should have tried the house phone first. I'm Delilah Johnson. I own the pet store in town."

"Oh, yes. Right Meow."

"Yes," Delilah said with a slow nod, her soothing voice plodding along at a slow pace. "That's right. I heard about what happened to Lola. I just wanted to stop by and give her a little something to cheer her up."

She waved the basket in the air, ruffling the sweater tied around her shoulders and slung over her back.

"Oh, how nice of you." Ellie pushed the screen door open and motioned for her to enter. "Won't you come in? I've got coffee on or I can make tea."

Delilah stepped into the foyer. "Oh, I'd hate to interrupt your morning."

"No interruption at all. My friend, Mia, and I were just enjoying the sunroom. Come on back."

Delilah nodded and followed Ellie into the kitchen. "Tea or coffee?"

"Oh, tea, please, dear," the woman answered as she set the basket on the table and settled into a chair.

Mia popped her head in. Water splashed into the tea kettle as Ellie filled it at the sink. "Oh, Mia, please meet Delilah from the pet store. She stopped by to bring Lola something. Isn't that nice?" Ellie shot a wide-eyed glance at Mia.

Mia's expression turned into a Cheshire Cat grin as she eyed the woman like a cheetah eyes a gazelle. "Yes, it is." She sauntered over to the table and eased into a chair.

Lola hobbled in from the sunroom, eyes glazed from the pain pill.

"Aww, poor thing," Delilah said as she hobbled toward the woman, her tail wagging slowly.

"Hi, Delilah," Lola said before she yawned. "I'm so sleepy."

"She's on pain medication. I think they're hitting her hard."

"Of course they are. Look at that paw." Delilah stared down at the swollen appendage, now larger than it had been this morning. "Poor thing. I brought you something, Lola."

Cleo sauntered in, rubbing against the doorway as she yawned. "Did you bring me anything?"

"And you, too, Cleo!" Delilah called to the cat.

"Smart woman," Cleo said as she stalked across the room for a petting.

"If you'd like to open it," Delilah said, pushing the basket toward Ellie. "It's nothing much, just something to say I'm thinking of them after that terrible ordeal."

"Well, it's much appreciated," Ellie said, approaching the table. "And very kind of you." She pulled the fabric from the rubber band attaching it to the basket. Inside, fluffy tissue paper in a colorful paw print lined the bottom. On top sat a card, a bag of cat treats, dog treats, and a large bone.

"Ohhh, Lola, you'll like this!" Ellie said as she snatched the card from the basket and pulled it open.

"What is it?" Lola inquired.

"Look at the nice card Delilah sent." Ellie shot a glance at Mia whose lips curled into a devilish grin.

"Who cares about the card, where are the treats?" Cleo asked, perching on the edge of the counter.

Ellie pulled open the card. "It says, 'Dear Lola, I hope you are feeling better soon. Here's a nice bone for you to chew on while you recover. And a few treats for both you and Cleo."

"That's the good part," Cleo said. "The treats. Where are the treats?"

"Thank you, Delilah," Lola said as Ellie handed the card off to Mia.

"How sweet," Mia said, pretending the study the illustrated animals on the front before she flipped open the card to study the handwriting. "What a darling card."

"Yes," Ellie said as she pulled the goodies from within the basket. "We have Greenies for Cleo."

"Ohhhhh, my favorite! What flavor?"

"Salmon flavor."

"Oh, yes, that's my favorite flavor. Give me some."

Ellie pulled the other bag out. "And for Lola, we have Pupcorn!"

"Oh, I love those!" Lola said. "Can I have one now?"

Ellie pulled out the final item. The massive bone "And a giant bone!"

"Ooooohhhh, dinosaur bone! Dinosaur bone!"

"Let's save this for later and give you both some of the treats now."

Ellie pulled the bags open and gave each a few of the snacks before she darted across the room and poured water from the whistling tea kettle, filling three mugs before she waddled to the table with them.

After setting out sugar and a few cookies from the pantry, she settled into a chair between Mia and Delilah. Delilah offered her a warm smile. The ticking clock provided the only noise in the room.

"Ah, so, Delilah," Ellie began as silence filled the air, "how are things at Right Meow? I have been meaning to stop by but haven't had the chance yet."

"Oh," Delilah murmured, her voice faltering as she drew out the word. She stared down at her teacup, tracing the outline of the handle with her index finger. She lifted a shoulder and raised her eyes to Ellie's. "Not great, I'm afraid."

"I'm sorry to hear that."

Delilah pressed her lips together and returned her gaze to the brown liquid in her mug. She shook her head and sighed. "I'm afraid the last conversation I had with your aunt was rather dire. I regret it very much. The last words we spoke were not pleasant ones."

"I'm sure she understood," Ellie said with a consoling smile.

A tear rolled onto Delilah's cheek and she flicked it away. "I asked her for money, you see. We argued over it, really. I'm so ashamed."

The woman's chin sank to her chest. Ellie shot Mia a glance, cringing. She sucked in a breath and reached for the older woman's hand, wrapping her fingers around the woman's cold skin.

With a crinkled forehead and squashed lips, Delilah squeezed Ellie's hand and offered her a weak smile. "Thank you."

"I'm sure Aunt Susie understood you were under stress and didn't blame you for anything that was said."

"I hope so. I never imagined it would be the last time I saw her."

Delilah blew out a long breath. "This is why you should never speak in anger and never leave things unresolved."

"Sometimes it can't be helped," Ellie said.

"Yes," Mia agreed. "I'm sure Ellie's aunt realized you were struggling and didn't hold it against you."

The woman nodded and drew in a deep breath. "Well, at least things have improved since I spoke with Susie last. I just wish it hadn't gone the way it had."

"Well, that sounds promising at least."

Delilah wiggled her eyebrows. "Yes. Things were looking

very grim for the pet store when I spoke with Susie. But the situation is beginning to resolve."

"Oh, good," Ellie said.

"Yes," Delilah agreed, then chuckled. "At least I won't have to ask you for money now."

Ellie offered a forced chuckle, side-eying Mia.

"I'd really hate for us to argue on our first meeting and then you end up dead!" Delilah continued to laugh and slapped her hand against the table.

Ellie offered her horrified glance that she tried to mask with an amused expression. Not quite sure if she pulled it off, she cleared her throat and tried to guide the conversation elsewhere while calculating how long it may take the woman to finish her tea.

"That would be a shame," she said with a fake laugh. "Anyway, really nice of you to stop by with the treats for Lola and Cleo."

The grandfather clock in the foyer chimed the noon hour, twelve long thuds of the bell tolling.

"Oh, my, has it gotten that late already?" Delilah asked, shoving her mostly full teacup away from her. "I really should let you go." She started to stand.

"Oh, no problem. Are you sure you don't want to finish your tea?"

Delilah flicked her gaze between Mia and Ellie before she slowly lowered herself back into the seat. "Well, I suppose I could stay a few more minutes."

* * *

Ellie's gaze focused on the clock ticking away in the kitchen. Delilah's "few more minutes" had turned into forty-eight minutes, to be exact. Another cup of tea and a grilled cheese sandwich later, the woman finally sighed and suggested she should be going.

Ellie breathed a sigh of relief as she leapt from her seat and began to clear the table. "Well, it was a lovely visit and great to meet you."

"Oh, I'm so glad you think so. I hope I haven't worn out my welcome."

"Not at all."

The woman rose and adjusted the beige sweater tied over her colorful plaid shirt. "Thank you so much for the lunch."

"You're welcome and thank you for the treat basket."

"You're very welcome. And please do stop in at the pet store soon. We're animal friendly, so bring Lola and Cleo with you!"

"I will," Ellie promised, ushering her down the hall and out the door. She waved as the woman slowly made her way down the steps, shielding her eyes in the bright sun.

She paused and Ellie's heart leapt, wondering if she'd turn around and come back in. She twisted to face Ellie as she dug into the purse dangling at her side. "Have to find my sunglasses. It's so bright!"

Ellie laughed. "Don't want to forget those."

"No," Delilah agreed. "I may not be able to see while driving and run right off the road. That'd be the end of me! Ah, here they are." She slid a dark pair of wraparound sunglasses onto her thin face. "Saved!"

"Good thing!"

The woman continued down the steps and meandered to her car, climbing in and fiddling around for a few minutes before the engine rumbled to life. She tooted the horn twice and waved through the windshield before she swung the car around and headed down the driveway.

Ellie's shoulders slumped as she pushed the door shut.

"Wow," Mia called from the kitchen.

"Tell me about it," Ellie said, shuffling into the room and grabbing a dish towel to dry the plates as Mia washed them. "I didn't think she was going to leave."

"Well, she almost did until you asked her if she wanted to finish her tea."

"I didn't think she'd say yes!" Ellie exclaimed, flinging the wet plate in the air as she gestured.

"I don't think she knows how to take a hint," Mia answered.

"No, I don't either. She seems nice enough, though."

"And," Mia said, a triumphant expression on her face, "we got her handwriting sample."

"Yes, we did! I can't wait to compare it."

CHAPTER 28

*E*llie dried the last dish and slid it into the cupboard. Mia rushed across the room and grabbed the card while Ellie retrieved the copy of the threatening notes she'd shoved behind a canister of sugar on the counter.

They converged at the table, holding the two together. Ellie grimaced. "Not a match. Not even close."

"Nope, unless—"

"She changed her handwriting, I know."

"She could be a killer! She seems fairly emotional. Maybe it's because she killed your aunt!"

"Or maybe she's just an emotional lady. She seemed kind of strange."

"Strange like killer strange or…"

"No, strange like small town strange. Not like killer strange. Poor lady could barely dig her sunglasses out of her purse."

"Doesn't take much strength to poison someone."

"Duly noted, but Susie didn't eat anything when Delilah was here and the handwriting doesn't match."

Mia sighed. "Fine, fine. We'll cross her off the list, too. Though we're running out of suspects."

"I know!" Ellie exclaimed, flinging her hands in the air in frustration. She plopped her chin into her palm and sighed.

"What are you going to do if we cross everyone off the list?"

Ellie ran her fingers through her hair as she slouched further down in her chair, considering the question. A chime from her phone interrupted her response.

She grabbed it and swiped at the screen. "It's from Mac." She scanned the message, then tossed the phone on the table with a groan.

"What is it?"

"He went to the grocery store and there is no schedule posted. So, he couldn't get a picture of Andy's handwriting."

Mia's jaw dropped. "Well, that's interesting. And suspicious. Why would the schedule be missing?"

Ellie shrugged before grabbing her phone and typing a message.

"What did you send?" Mia asked.

"I asked him if that was normal. It's what, Wednesday? Maybe he takes the schedule down on Wednesdays and posts a new one on Thursdays or something."

A chime indicated the answer to her question. Ellie frowned at the phone. "He says no. New schedules are posted on Fridays and stay up throughout the week."

"So, why is it missing?"

"The million-dollar question. I wonder if—"

The doorbell's chime interrupted her musing aloud. "Another visitor," Mia announced. "Want me to get it?"

"No," Ellie said with a sigh as she dragged herself to standing. "I've got it. At least Lola isn't barking at every turn. Maybe her night out cured her."

The doorbell sounded again and a sharp bark sounded from the sunroom. "Never mind," Ellie called over her shoulder as she shambled out of the room with her hands shoved in her back pockets.

Mia chuckled as Ellie continued toward the front door. "Now what?" she asked no one as her fingers clasped the brass knob. She twisted and pulled the door open.

A curly-haired blonde stood on the porch with two boxes stacked on top of one another in her hands. Despite the warm afternoon air, she wore a long-sleeve cardigan over her summer top.

"Oh, hi, Ellie!" Hazel said as Ellie pulled the door open. Ellie marveled at the surprise in the woman's voice. Perhaps she hadn't expected Ellie to be at home.

"Hi, Hazel. How are you?"

"I'm good. I brought you some things!" She lifted the boxes.

Ellie opened the screen door and ushered her inside. "Come on in. I'll take those."

"Oh, thanks," her bubbly voice answered as she handed them off.

"Would you like some tea or coffee?"

"Sure!" Hazel said, following Ellie to the kitchen.

Ellie delivered the two boxes to the counter and spun to face Mia. "Look who stopped by. It's Hazel!"

Hazel waved at Mia as she stood in the opening to the hall. "Hi! I'm Hazel. I work for the Sheriff. Oh, maybe Ellie told you that." She tilted her head to face Ellie. "Did you tell her?"

"I have, yes," Ellie said. "Tea or coffee?"

"Oh, uh, tea," Hazel said.

"Why don't you take a seat?" Mia said, motioning to the chair across from her.

"Okay!"

Mia crinkled her brow before plastering a smile on her face. Ellie filled the tea kettle for the second time and set it on the stove, gathering three mugs again.

"May I ask what's in these?" Ellie questioned, poking a finger at the two boxes.

"Oh, one is a variety of cookies from the Salem Sweets bakery. And the other has a bone-shaped peanut butter cake and a fish-shaped salmon cookie."

Ellie smiled as she cut the string off one box.

"Oh," Hazel added, "the cookies are for humans. The peanut butter cake is for the dog and the salmon cookie is for the cat."

"That makes sense," Ellie said with a smile. She popped the top on each box. "Mmm, these cookies look delicious!"

She unloaded them onto a plate and set them on the table before pouring steaming water into each mug.

Mia grabbed a lady lock and bit into it as Ellie delivered the tea to the table. "Mmm, fabulous," she said with her mouth full.

"Thanks," Hazel said. "Oh, I mean, I didn't bake them. I don't work at the bakery. I work for the Sheriff."

"So you said," Mia answered. "How long have you worked for him?"

"For Sheriff Rick or the sheriff's office?" Hazel asked, her brow furrowing. "Because those are two different questions."

"So, you've worked for the sheriff's office longer than Rick's been sheriff?" Ellie questioned.

"Wow!" Hazel said, her face lighting with surprise. "It's like you're psychic!"

Ellie stared at her blankly, unable to formulate a response to the statement. As she pondered if the woman was making a joke or not, Hazel continued. "I've worked at the sheriff's office since I was twenty-two. That was twelve years ago! Sheriff Rick came six years ago."

Ellie processed the statement. After twelve years, she still couldn't transfer a call. Maybe the phone systems were new.

"Hmm," Mia murmured. "And did it take a while to get used to Rick?"

"A little," Hazel said as she selected a few cookies from the plate. "But he's nice. The old sheriff was nice, too."

"Why did he leave?"

"Oh, he retired. He was really old."

Hazel nibbled on the corner of a peanut butter cookie. She set the treat down on her napkin, wincing. With a slight groan, she slid her left arm under the table and cleared her throat.

"So, how is Lola? Sheriff Rick told me. That's how I knew."

"She's doing well. She's in the sunroom napping. I'm sure she'll enjoy the peanut butter cake later."

"Poor Lola. You must have been so upset when she ran out of the house after that prowler."

Ellie opened her mouth to respond but paused. She narrowed her eyes as Hazel rubbed at her left arm and grimaced again. "Yeah, I really was. Everything okay, Hazel?"

"Huh?"

"Your arm. You seem to be in some pain. Is everything okay?"

"Oh, yeah," Hazel said. "I just have an itch. My sweater is itchy." She offered an awkward chuckle.

Mia shot Ellie a pointed glance. "Maybe slip it off. We could turn the AC off if you're cold," Mia said.

"No, don't worry about it. I prefer to keep it on."

"You sure? If it's bothering you, I'd hate to see you suffer," Ellie said. "I can turn off the air."

She rose from her chair and wandered to the thermostat,

kicking it up a few degrees. She returned to the kitchen. Hazel offered her a polite smile but her sweater remained on.

The temperature quickly rose in the room as the air conditioner ceased to run and they sipped at the hot tea. Sweat beaded on Ellie's forehead and dripped down her back. She shoved the hot tea away.

Mia fanned herself with a napkin. Hazel still wore the sweater. They chatted for a few more moments before Hazel rubbed at her arm again, then suggested she should head back to the sheriff's office.

"Oh, are you sure? You barely touched your tea," Ellie said.

Hazel stood and grabbed her purse, wriggling her arm in the sweater again. "Oh, yeah. Sheriff Rick'll be wondering where I am."

"Before you go," Ellie said, leaping from her chair and grabbing a pencil and notepad, "could I get your number?"

Hazel cocked her head at the statement. "I'd like to keep in touch. You were so kind bringing the cookies over."

Hazel eyed the pencil and paper then flicked her gaze to Ellie's phone on the table. "Is this your phone?"

"Yes," Ellie said with a confused expression.

Hazel grabbed it from the table. "I'll just put it in here!"

"Oh, but—" Ellie began as Hazel tapped around on the screen. "I wanted to get your full name, too."

"I put it in here. Hazel Duncan." She spun the phone around to show Ellie.

"Oh," Ellie said, her voice deflating as she dropped the pencil and paper at her side, "yeah. I see. Well, thanks."

"You're welcome!"

Ellie shot Mia a glance. The expression on her face suggested she could come up with no reason to get a sample of Hazel's writing. "I'll walk you out," Ellie said.

She delivered the woman to the door. Hazel stepped

into the afternoon heat and strolled to her car, tossing her purse into the passenger seat before sliding in behind the wheel. The engine fired. Her curls blew wildly as the air conditioner blew cool air against her. Ellie waved as she pulled away, sweater still on despite climbing into a hot car.

"Well, well, well," Mia said as Ellie pushed the door shut. "Wasn't that interesting."

"Wasn't it though," Ellie said. "I hope those cookies weren't poisoned."

Mia's face blanched. "Are you serious?"

"Aunt Susie was poisoned. I stopped eating once I saw her fiddling with her left arm."

"And then she refused to take her sweater off."

Ellie headed to the kitchen and cleaned up from the afternoon snack. "Covering up a dog bite maybe?"

"Wouldn't be surprised."

"And then she wouldn't write her name and number down. She insisted on putting it in my phone. Which, by the way, is also suspect."

"What do you mean?"

"She's terrible with technology. She's been working at the Sheriff's office for twelve years and she still has trouble transferring calls. She also forgets to let her finger off the button on the walkie when using it. But she knows how to add her contact info to my smartphone?"

"You think she's faking?"

Ellie nodded as she dumped the cookies back into their pink pastry box. "Yeah. I think she's playing dumb. I think she's the one who threatened Susie. And I think she hides behind that dumb-girl facade."

"What's her motive?"

Ellie pressed her lips together in thought. "I'm not sure, but she said something odd to me when we first met. Mac mentioned me reopening the B&B and Rick said people would be happy to hear it. She said not everyone would be."

"As in not her?"

Ellie raised a shoulder at the question. "Maybe."

"Why?"

"I don't know but it was an odd statement to make and it stuck with me."

Silence filled the air as they both pondered their current suspect.

Ellie stared down at the cookies and the treats for Lola and Cleo and frowned. "I think I may ditch these. Just in case."

"You don't think she'd poison the dog and cat, do you?"

"I don't know but I don't want to take any chances." She pushed the boxes to the back of the counter. "I'll grab a bag and toss them out later."

She sauntered to the kitchen table and sat down. "You know," she said after a moment, "if it's Hazel, she would obviously know we're searching for a handwriting match because she'd probably see the new evidence at the Sheriff's Office."

"She'd also know about Nathan being posted here last night to watch the house."

"Yep. She'd have the inside track."

Mia nodded and they fell silent again. Ellie chewed her lip as she considered the evidence mounting against Hazel. All circumstantial, but still the largest body of evidence they'd found to date in their amateur investigation. They needed a sample of her handwriting.

Mia narrowed her eyes as she stared in the air. "You know if it's Hazel…" She paused, her voice trailing off as she continued to parse through her thoughts silently. "Rick knows. Right?"

Ellie cocked her head and stared at her friend. "He does?"

"Well, think about it. He has the notes. Surely, he's seen her handwriting. The man has worked with her for six years. He'd probably recognize it. So, once you gave him the notes, he had to have known it was Hazel."

Ellie considered it, her eyes widening at the prospect. "So, he's covering it up for her?"

Mia shrugged. "It seems that way."

"Wait, wait. Maybe we got this all wrong. Because that's crazy. The local police are covering up a murder because their secretary did it?"

"Come on. It all points to her. She was here the day your aunt died. She said people wouldn't be happy about the reopening of the B&B and your aunt was planning to reopen it. She works for the police, so she can track the investigation. No one came to the house last night when the police were sitting right outside."

"That could be because they got scared off the night before. Especially after Lola bit them."

"Which leads me to my final point. She kept fussing with her arm and refused to take her sweater off. It was roasting in here. I thought I was going to pass out from the heat and she just sat there with that sweater on. Why? Because she was hiding a wound, maybe? Like a dog bite?"

Ellie pulled one corner of her mouth back as she added up their theory. She shook her head. "So, if that's the case, what do we do? We can't report her to the police. We can't even mention our theory to them. They're probably all in on it!"

"State police? Feds?" Mia suggested.

"What? Call the FBI?"

"Why not? You've got a major bust here. Small town cops covering up murder. So, yes! Call the FBI!"

Ellie nodded slowly and sucked in a deep breath. "Okay, but before we do that, we need more than just conjecture."

"We've got a good case."

"But no proof. Law enforcement sticks together. I'm not accusing an entire sheriff's office of covering up a murder with absolutely no proof."

"How can we prove it?"

Ellie bit her thumbnail. "We need her handwriting. If we can at least tie her to the notes Aunt Susie received, we may have something."

They settled back into silence for a few moments before Mia slapped her hand against the table, startling Ellie. "We need proof. And I'm going to get it." She leapt from her seat and strode toward the hall.

Ellie climbed to her feet and hurried behind her. "Hey, where are you going? How are you going to get proof?"

"I'm going to the Sheriff's office. And I'm going to ask her to write down a few local attractions for me to visit while I'm here."

"Seriously?"

"I'm so stupid. I should have thought of it before."

"Mia, I don't think this is a good idea."

"We need proof. And she's not going to kill me at the Sheriff's office."

"You wanna bet? According to you, Rick is in on this. You don't think he'll just help her hide your body?"

"No. Because that would be really obvious."

Ellie grabbed her purse. "Maybe I should go with you."

"No, you stay here. Take care of the animals. I'll be back with our proof. Wish me luck."

Ellie let the purse drop onto the foyer's table. "Good luck. If I don't hear from you in an hour, I'm calling the FBI."

Mia smiled at her, tossing her blonde hair over her shoulders and giving Ellie a wink before she disappeared through the door.

Ellie gnawed at her lower lip as the sound of Mia's car

disappeared. She crossed her arms across her chest, butter-
flies filling her stomach at what Mia was about to do. She
picked up her purse and put it back twice.

She'd have to walk to town if she followed her. By the
time she arrived at the police station, Mia could be on her
way back. Or dead. Ellie shook the idea from her head. The
police wouldn't kill Mia in broad daylight. Probably. She
picked up her purse again.

The soft tink-tink-tink of a three-legged dog's nails
limping across the hardwood reached her ears.

"Ellie?" Lola said, her voice wavering. "Are you leaving?"

Ellie dumped her purse on the table and spun to face her.
"No. What's—" Her voice trailed off as she spotted fresh
blood on Lola's swollen paw.

"My foot hurts."

"I'll bet! It's bleeding again. You need your pain medicine
and we need to get that cleaned up."

Ellie strode past the dog into the kitchen. Lola limped
behind her. Ellie led her into the laundry room, soaking a
washcloth in warm water and wiping the blood from her
foot.

"Oww!" Lola shouted.

"Sorry. But I have to get this clean and wrapped."

"No, not the wrap again," Lola protested. "I hate it."

"You'll be getting a pain pill. You'll probably fall asleep.
We'll take it off when you wake up."

"Promise?"

"I promise." Ellie rummaged through the first aid supplies
in the cupboard and found supplies. After ten minutes of
wrangling with Lola, she got it wrapped. Lola sniffed at the
white wrap and tried to bite it.

"Stop biting it. Leave it be."

"I don't like it," Lola answered as she hobbled into the

kitchen with Ellie. Cleo sat on the counter, already awaiting her meal.

"Hurry up. I'm hungry," Cleo said.

"Okay, okay, I'm going as fast as I can," she answered as she jiggled the contents of a can of cat food into Cleo's bowl.

After giving Lola her pill, she set a bowl of kibble on the floor. The dog made short work of the food, settling onto her haunches as she licked her chops.

"Okay? Feel better now?" Ellie asked them.

Cleo yawned. "Yeah. Time for a nap."

"Me too," Lola agreed. "I'm so sleepy."

"You should have a good nap now with that pain pill."

"I'm heading up to the bedroom," Cleo said as she stretched. "Bed is nice and comfy."

"That sounds nice," Lola agreed.

"Come on, I'll go up with you. I can clean out a few more of Susie's drawers."

With trash bags in hand, Ellie mounted the first step. Cleo danced up the stairs in front of her, disappearing into the bedroom. Lola struggled to balance as she tried to hobble up the stairs.

"Wait, I'll get you." Ellie scooped the dog into her arms and carried her up, settling her on the bed next to Cleo. With a big sigh, the dog settled into a nap.

Ellie smiled at the pair of sleeping animals as she set the trash bags on the dresser. Across the room, her clothes from the day before were heaped in a pile on the armless chair. Ellie wrinkled her nose at them before deciding to put them away before beginning anything else.

She grabbed the pants and folded them, tossing them into her suitcase. She really needed to finish cleaning out the closet and drawer space so she could move her own things into them, she thought as she folded the shirt.

A small object toppled out of the pocket as she jockeyed

the shirt around. She finished folding it and placed it on top of her pants before she bent down to swipe whatever had fallen.

The plastic bag marked with the vet's logo lay on the area rug. Ellie held it up to her face, studying the contents. She'd forgotten she'd shoved it into her pocket at the vet's office. What had Lola bitten that became stuck in her mouth?

Ellie snapped open the ziplock on the bag and shook the metal object from inside. She studied it, turning it over in her hand. Something about it seemed familiar. With one edge jagged, the other appeared to form the letter "g." The tail of the letter snaked into a "ds" below it.

Ellie furrowed her brow at the shiny silver object. Her mind ran through possibilities. Where had she seen these distinctive bubbly letters before?

She flicked her gaze into the air as realization dawned on her. She closed her fingers around the metal and raced from the room, hurrying down the stairs and around the railing. She hustled into the kitchen, skidding to a stop in front of the refrigerator. She scanned the various items plastered to it with magnets, finding the one she sought on the left door, near the top corner.

She snatched it from under the colorful seashell magnet that read "Bahamas," and held the object up to it.

She eyed the business card's logo compared to the shiny letters. They matched. Ellie read the paper rectangle. For an at-home nurse assistant service called Helping Hands, the card detailed contact information for Evelyn Lewis. She recalled the note from the woman about being her aunt's nurse.

Why would this be stuck in Lola's mouth? A hot tingling shot through her body as realization dawned on her. Her eyes widened. She tossed the business card on the counter and yanked open the skinny cabinet next to the refrigerator.

Pill bottles lined the lower shelf. Across from them, post-it notes with reminders about medication. Ellie snatched one of them, her eyes scanning the handwriting. The note fluttered as a gust of air blew past her, giving her the chills.

Her heart beat hard in her chest as she hurried across the room and grabbed the copy of the notes she'd given to the police. She held the sticky note next to the paper. The handwriting matched.

CHAPTER 29

*H*er stomach somersaulted. They'd been dead wrong about who did it. They'd never even considered her. How stupid they had been. But why had she done it?

It didn't matter. She needed to alert the authorities. And Mia. Before she said something stupid and embarrassed herself.

Ellie grabbed her phone from the kitchen table and toggled it on, accessing her contacts and dialing the number for the police station. She pressed the phone to her ear.

A click sounded. Ellie froze. She recognized the sound of a gun being cocked.

"Put the phone down, Ms. Byrne," a female voice said.

Ellie lowered it from her ear and turned slowly, raising her hands in the air as she stared down the pistol clutched in Evelyn's hands.

"End the call and toss the phone away."

Ellie swallowed hard as she tapped the round, red button to end the phone call. She lowered and placed the phone on the floor, kicking it toward the gun-wielding woman.

"So," Ellie said, finding her voice, "you killed my Aunt Susan?"

Evelyn's eyebrows raised and she gave a slight nod. "The old broad just wouldn't listen to reason."

"Why? You were her nurse."

Evelyn threw her head back with laughter, a shrill cackling noise that sent shivers through Ellie.

"I'm not really a nurse. I just used that to get into the house."

"You don't work for Helping Hands?"

"Oh, I work for them. Got the job just for the occasion. But I'm not a nurse." The woman's lips curled into a cruel smile. "I may have fibbed a little on my application."

Ellie frowned at the statement.

"Truth is, they're so hard up for home health care, they didn't even check my references!"

"But—"

Evelyn waved the gun in the air, motioning toward the back door. "Let's take this conversation outside." Her gaze darted around. "Before that blasted dog bites me again."

She brandished the red marks in the shape of Lola's jaw on her left arm.

"I'm not going anywhere with you!" Ellie said.

Evelyn narrowed her eyes and leveled the gun at Ellie. "You don't have much of a choice."

Ellie lifted her hands again and inched around the woman toward the back door, doing her best to keep her distance from her.

"S-so, what are you going to do? Shoot me?" Ellie asked as she stepped into the bright sunshine.

"That'd be rather obvious," Evelyn said as she marched Ellie toward the stream in the back. "I thought drowning seemed fitting. Like aunt, like niece."

"They realize Aunt Susie was murdered, you know. No one will ever believe I drowned myself."

"Maybe not," Evelyn said with a shrug. "But the knock on your head won't be traceable, unlike a bullet."

Ellie puffed out her cheeks.

"But if you want to do things the easy way," Evelyn said, with another wobble of the gun, "I'm game."

"Wait, wait, wait," Ellie said, her breathing turning ragged. "Before you kill me, I'd like to know why. Why did you kill my aunt? Why are you killing me?"

"Ha!" the woman barked. "You're kidding? Do you really think I'm going to stand here and explain it? To indulge your desperate attempt to prolong your life?"

Ellie shrugged, her hands still raised in the air. "There has to be a reason. I'd just like to know why. Why someone posed as a nurse to kill an old woman. And then went through what you did to… what? Kill me? Drive me away? Are you just crazy? Or…"

"I'm not crazy!" Evelyn shot back.

"So, what is it then? Because that's the only thing I can figure out. What are you getting out of this?"

"I thought the manor," Evelyn said.

"You thought my aunt would give it to you?"

Evelyn shrugged a shoulder. "I thought she'd give it to her long-lost daughter."

"Daughter? You're Aunt Susie's daughter?"

"Not really. But I thought I could pull it off. She had a baby once, you know? I found the information in the registry. Figured I could show up, get to know her a little, snoop around the house, then give her the convincing story that I was her long-lost kid.

"Only the old lady was too wise for that. Said the kid died. That's not what the records said. Denied I could be hers. She threatened to turn me in to the cops."

"So, you killed her."

"I told her she'd better get her head on straight and give me what I wanted or I'd tell everyone about her indiscretion. Whether I was her kid or not. Apparently, upstanding Susie never told the good folks of Salem Falls that she'd had a baby way back when. And she didn't want anyone to find out either.

"Once I threatened to tell, well, she didn't take kindly to that. I figured I could work a different angle. Get what I wanted in a different way than I'd anticipated, but still, I'd get what I wanted."

"You did all this to get the manor?"

"Yeah. And the money didn't hurt either. She was a pretty rich lady. Well, you should know. You're inheriting everything."

Ellie shook her head with disgust on her face. "You're disgusting."

"Call it what you want. Maybe now I can get my hands on this place. Well, once you're out of the way."

"How do you figure that?"

"I doubt you have a will. At least not for all this yet." She waved her gun around to encompass the property. "I'll swoop in with my long-lost daughter routine and take over in the absence of other family."

"You'll never get away with it."

Evelyn shrugged and raised her eyebrows. "Looks like I already have."

Ellie glanced over the woman's shoulder. "I don't think so."

Confusion crossed the woman's face for a brief second before she started to twist to glance behind her. Her eyes widened as Rick's arm swung down. Evelyn's arm swung wildly as he chopped at it. She stumbled back a step as Ellie ducked.

The gun fired in the air. Rick tackled her to the ground, pinning her weapon-wielding arm to the ground.

He knocked it repeatedly into the dirt in an attempt to force her to drop the gun. After multiple thumps on the ground, the weapon toppled from her fingers. She swung at Rick with her other arm, striking a blow against his chin.

With him momentarily stunned, she wriggled free. Ellie raced toward them, scooping up the gun from the ground.

Gasping for breath, she raised the weapon and pointed it at Evelyn. "I don't think so," she growled.

Rick recovered and leapt to his feet. He wrangled Evelyn's hands behind her back and handcuffed her.

Mia raced around the side of the house and ground to a halt, staring at the scene. Ellie gulped in a breath and lowered the gun, dropping it on the ground as a tear rolled down her cheek.

"Ellie!" Mia shouted as she sprinted toward her.

"Mia!" Ellie said as the woman's arms wrapped around her in a tight embrace.

"Thank God you're okay!"

Rick read Evelyn her rights, placing her under arrest for a variety of crimes including the murder of Susan Byrne. He marched her away, shoving her into the back of his police cruiser. Nathan arrived moments later, retrieving the weapon and bagging it.

Ellie, still shaking from the experience, clung to Mia for another moment. "Oh, I'm so glad you're okay," Mia said.

"Me too," Ellie admitted.

"So, is she the one who killed your aunt? The one who sent the messages?"

"Yeah," Ellie said, wiping the tear from her cheek. She shook her head. "I realized it when the metal thing the vet pulled from Lola's mouth fell out of my pocket while I was cleaning up the bedroom. I recognized it as the Helping

Hands logo. Once I realized where that came from, I checked the medication notes inside the cupboard. The handwriting, Evelyn's handwriting, matched the notes. I was about to call the police when she showed up."

"Rick got your call. We were in the middle of arguing about Hazel being the guilty party when you called. The call cut off and he came out right away."

Mia wrapped her arm around Ellie. "Let's get you inside. We can talk there."

"You accused Hazel?" Ellie questioned as they strolled toward the house.

"I did," Mia said with a laugh. "It didn't go over well."

"I can imagine, especially since she was innocent."

"A fact which she insisted upon over and over."

Ellie stepped into the kitchen and slumped into a kitchen chair. "At least it's all over now."

"Why did she do it?" Mia asked, setting a kettle of water on the stove to make tea.

"I'd like to hear what she said to you myself," Rick said as he strode into the kitchen.

"She was basically scamming Aunt Susie. She used her position with Helping Hands to get into the house and gather some basic details. She then claimed she was her long-lost daughter. She was hoping for a handout, a place in her will."

Rick screwed up his face. "Long-lost daughter?"

Ellie shrugged. "Apparently, there's a record of Aunt Susie having a baby a long time ago. I've never heard about it."

"Why did she kill her?" Mia questioned.

"Aunt Susie said her baby died. She realized the woman was lying."

"So, she killed her so Susie couldn't out her?" Rick asked.

"No. Evelyn then blackmailed Aunt Susie. Apparently, Aunt Susie didn't want word to get out about her indiscretion. Evelyn used that to her advantage and tried to blackmail her. When Aunt Susie wouldn't budge, she killed her, figuring she could use the long-lost daughter trick to stake her claim. When I showed up, she tried to scare me off, then when I didn't leave, she figured she'd try the same thing. Kill me and show up to claim the property as the closest living relative."

"Wow," Mia muttered. "What a piece of work."

"Yeah. She nearly got away with it, too. If you hadn't shown up when you did, Rick, I'd be toast."

Rick nodded at her. "My pleasure."

"What I can't understand is how she poisoned Aunt Susie. She didn't bring her any food that day."

"The meds," Rick said. "Helping Hands nurses often deliver meds. Do you happen to have the medications Susie took?"

"Yes," Ellie said with a nod. She climbed from her seat and opened the cupboard to showcase the vials inside.

"I'm going to need to take these in as evidence. Have them tested."

"Of course."

Rick grabbed one of the post-its inside. "Here's the matching handwriting."

"Yep," Ellie said. "That's how I pieced it together, too."

Rick shot a glance to Mia and snorted a laugh. "And you thought it was Hazel."

"Don't blame Mia. We both did," Ellie said.

"And we had a pretty good circumstantial case," Mia said in her defense.

"She's right. Hazel would know everything the police were doing about this case. She also had visited with Aunt Susie on the day she died and brought her food."

"But they didn't argue," Rick countered.

"No, but she said people wouldn't be happy if Aunt Susie

reopened the B&B. So, maybe she had some kind of grudge against her."

"People wouldn't be happy," Rick repeated. "Not Hazel. She thought it was a great idea. But she wanted you to know a few people would give you some issues. Not her."

Ellie shrugged. "Well, we didn't know that. And when she showed up and kept fiddling with her left arm and refused to take her sweater off, we thought—"

"What? That Lola bit her?"

"Well, yeah," Ellie admitted.

"Yeah, explain that. It's odd behavior. Even you have to admit that."

Rick flicked his gaze between the two women, his jaw clenching. "Don't say anything about this but Hazel has eczema. She's really embarrassed about it. She wears the sweater to cover her arm where she has it."

Ellie shut her eyes for a moment and planted her palm against her forehead. "Oh boy. What idiots we were."

Mia offered a sheepish glance at Rick, then a wince. "Sorry."

They stood in silence for a moment until Mia said, "Okay, what about the whole refusing to write down her number thing? That's suspicious, right?"

Rick squeezed his lips together and shook his head. "Hazel's terrible with technology. Nathan and I have been encouraging her to practice with it to improve. She was trying to be proactive and use more technology."

Ellie licked her lips and rubbed the back of her neck. "Please tell Hazel how sorry we are."

"I will pass that along," Rick answered. "Don't worry. She won't hold it against you. She's a really nice person."

"Apparently way nicer than the two of us," Ellie admitted.

Rick offered her an amused grin. "You're not that bad. I

guess under the right circumstances, everyone looks like a suspect."

Ellie wiggled her eyebrows. "Thanks."

He motioned to the pills inside the cupboard. "I'll send Nathan in to bag these as evidence. We'll test 'em and see if one of these was poisoned."

"She'll go to jail for a long, long time, right?" Mia asked.

"Yeah. I think so. If one of these is poisoned, we'll have a real solid case."

"And if not?" Ellie asked.

"We've just got enough to prosecute her on the other charges. She won't be bothering you for a long time."

"Good," Ellie said with a nod. She blew out a long breath. "Now I can focus on moving. I'm so glad this is over."

CHAPTER 30

*E*llie lugged a box out of her rental and lumbered up the porch stairs.

"I'll get that," Jake said, lifting it from her arms and toting it inside and up the stairs.

Ellie wiped her arm across her brow as Mia joined her on the porch. "How many more?" she asked, tossing her blonde braid over her shoulder.

"One," Ellie said with a sigh.

"Let Jake get it."

"That kid's got way too much energy," Ellie answered as she sank into a wooden rocker on the porch.

Lola lifted her head from the wooden floorboards. "I'm glad you're almost done moving, Ellie."

"Me, too," Cleo said, perched on the wooden railing, her tail swishing in the air. "And I'm glad the fake nurse didn't kill you."

Ellie smiled at the two animals. "Cause who else would feed us," Cleo said.

Ellie resisted the urge to roll her eyes at the cat. "I will be glad when that last box is in the house."

"Yeah, but then we have to unpack them all," Mia reminded her.

"I know. But it'll be better than lugging them around. My back is killing me."

Mia took a long sip from her water bottle. "You and me both."

"That reminds me," Ellie said, "thanks for your help. I am so sorry to have burned another week of your vacation."

Mia waved the statement away. "It's fine."

"It's not. That company is so stingy with vacation time and you've wasted it all on helping me."

"Helping you find a killer? Totally worth it."

"I still can't believe they let you take two weeks like that," Ellie said as she stared out at the trees, their leaves rustling in the gentle breeze.

Mia licked her lips. "About that…"

Ellie flicked her gaze toward her friend. "Yeah?"

Mia bit her lower lip and sighed. "I don't work for Your Web Design anymore."

"What?" Ellie asked, flabbergasted.

Mia fidgeted in her seat and shot Ellie a guilty glance. "I got fired a month ago."

"What!" Ellie exclaimed. "Why didn't you say something?"

Mia lifted a shoulder and wrinkled her nose. "You were going through so much with Toby and the divorce. And then your aunt died. Then suddenly you were moving. And then you were having all the trouble with being threatened and the murder. I just didn't want to pile on."

"Pile on? Are you kidding me? Mia! You're my *best* friend! You should have told me."

"I'm not great at dealing with these things."

Silence fell between them for a moment. Ellie sucked in a breath and restarted the conversation. "Since we're confessing things, I wondered if something was going on with you. The day Evelyn nearly offed me, I found your phone in the sunroom."

"I remember."

"I saw a message from Joe. About not being able to avoid 'this' and him forever. I was so wrapped up in myself I never followed up."

"I wouldn't have told you anyway. I'm only telling you now because I couldn't keep hiding it."

"I don't understand how you have been out of work for a month. You were going to work when I left."

"I was leaving the house and pretending to go to work. I did that for a week before I told Joe."

"Oh, Mia."

"And now after all that, Joe and I are barely speaking. He says he can't trust me and that I do crazy things."

"Sometimes you do," Ellie said. "That's part of your charm."

"Joe used to think so. He doesn't find it so charming anymore."

"He's upset. He'll get over it."

Mia stared out at the woods. "I'm not so sure. We've been growing apart. Not sure we'll pull out of this one."

"Well, he's an idiot, then."

Mia chuckled.

Ellie reached out and grabbed her hand and squeezed. "We're a real pair, aren't we? Jobless, middle-aged soon-to-be divorcees."

"At least one of us is getting her life together."

"You will, too. Look, you're already making websites for half the town. You'll rally."

"I will rally. Even if I'm living out of a suitcase in a motel."

"Or a B&B."

Mia glanced at her.

"You'll stay here until you're on your feet."

"I couldn't—"

"You won't be. You'll be working for me. Not only my website, but I need help pulling my business plan together and getting this place into shape. You'll be my project manager. Free room and board is the going rate." Ellie grinned at her.

"I'll take it," Mia answered.

They sat for a few more moments before Ellie climbed to her feet with a groan. "I guess we better get at it. Especially since it sounds like we'll be unpacking two of us."

Jake popped onto the porch through the front door. "Good news, Jake," Mia said. "You may be hauling more boxes soon. I think I'm moving up here, too."

"Sounds good to me!" He bounded down the stairs in search of the last box in Ellie's car.

"At least we picked a nice town to move to," Ellie said as she stepped into the foyer.

"Yes," Mia agreed. "Nice and quiet."

"You know what they say. Nothing much ever happens in Salem Falls. And I am looking forward to that nice, quiet life."

The End
To be continued…

Want to Read More About Ellie?
Click here!

Join Ellie in a thrilling quest for a hidden treasure and the truth behind a murder in book two of this enchanting paranormal women's fiction cozy mystery series. As Ellie reopens her aunt's bed and breakfast for a murder mystery weekend, she uncovers the legend of a cursed treasure that has claimed the lives of former owners.

With threats looming and secrets lurking, can Ellie solve the mystery and track down a murderer before she becomes the curse's next victim?

Find out what happens in *Business is Murder* available on Amazon now! Click HERE to get your copy now!

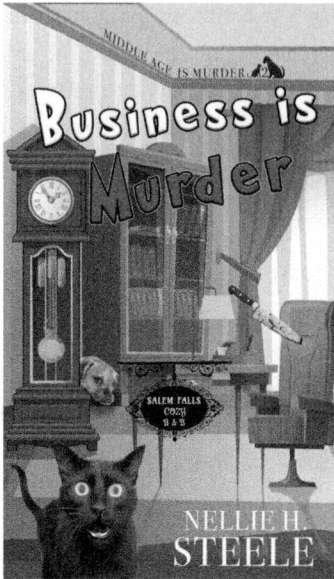

Click HERE to get your copy of Business is Murder!

Let's keep in touch! Join my newsletter and receive five free books!

ABOUT THE AUTHOR

Award-winning author Nellie H. Steele writes in as many genres as she reads, ranging from mystery to fantasy and allowing readers to escape reality and enter enchanting worlds filled with unique, lovable characters.

Addicted to books since she could read, Nellie escaped to fictional worlds like the ones created by Carolyn Keene or Victoria Holt long before she decided to put pen to paper and create her own realities.

When she's not spinning a cozy mystery tale, building a new realm in a contemporary fantasy, or writing another action-adventure car chase, you can find her shuffling through her Noah's Ark of rescue animals or enjoying a hot cuppa (that's tea for most Americans.)

Join her Facebook Readers' Group here!

OTHER SERIES BY NELLIE H. STEELE

Cozy Mystery Series

Cate Kensie Mysteries
Lily & Cassie by the Sea Mysteries
Pearl Party Mysteries
Middle Age is Murder Cozy Mysteries

Supernatural Suspense/Urban Fantasy

Shadow Slayers Stories
Duchess of Blackmoore Mysteries
Shelving Magic

Adventure

Maggie Edwards Adventures
Clif & Ri on the Sea

Printed in Dunstable, United Kingdom